REBECCA TOPE lives on a smallholding in Herefordshire, with a full complement of livestock, but manages to travel the world and enjoy civilisation from time to time as well. Most of her varied experiences and activities find their way into her books, sooner or later. Her own cocker spaniel, Beulah, is the model for Hepzibah, but is unfortunately ageing much more rapidly.

www.rebeccatope.com

Deception in the Cotswolds

REBECCA TOPE

Allison & Busby Limited
12 Fitzroy Mews
London W1T 6DW
www.allisonandbusby.com

First published in Great Britain by Allison & Busby in 2011.
This paperback edition published by Allison & Busby in 2012.

A CIP catalogue record for this book is available from
the British Library.

10 9 8 7 6

ISBN 978-0-7490-1062-1

Typeset in 10.5/14.2 pt Sabon by
Allison & Busby Ltd.

The paper used for this Allison & Busby publication
has been produced from trees that have been legally sourced
from well-managed and credibly certified forests.

Printed and bound by
CPI Group (UK) Ltd, Croydon, CR0 4YY

In fondest memory of
Martha Grutchfield

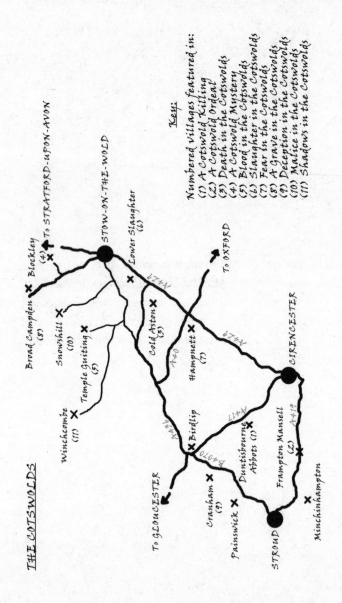

THE COTSWOLDS

To GLOUCESTER

To STRATFORD-UPON-AVON

To OXFORD

Blockley (4)

Broad Campden (8)

STOW-ON-THE-WOLD

Snowshill (10)

Lower Slaughter (6)

Temple Guiting (5)

Winchcombe (11)

Cold Aston (3)

Hampnett (7)

CIRENCESTER

Birdlip

Cranham (9)

Duntisbourne Abbots (1)

Frampton Mansell (2)

Painswick

STROUD

Minchinhampton

A429

A40

B4077

A424

A417

B4070

A419

Key:

Numbered villages featured in:
(1) A Cotswold Killing
(2) A Cotswold Ordeal
(3) Death in the Cotswolds
(4) A Cotswold Mystery
(5) Blood in the Cotswolds
(6) Slaughter in the Cotswolds
(7) Fear in the Cotswolds
(8) A Grave in the Cotswolds
(9) Deception in the Cotswolds
(10) Malice in the Cotswolds
(11) Shadows in the Cotswolds

AUTHOR'S NOTE

As in other titles in this series, the story is set in a real Cotswold village. Cranham is much as described, including the pub, and the 'mushroom yews' in the churchyard. However, the Manor and other individual houses, as well as the people, are all products of my imagination.

CHAPTER ONE

Light was streaming into the entrance hall as Thea walked in. Her spaniel's claws clicked on the polished wooden flooring, and the scent of beeswax brought with it associations of affluence and solid English stability. Hollywell Manor, in the village of Cranham, was to be their home for the next two weeks, and the weather seemed set fair. Cranham was – she hoped – an undiscovered gem of the western Cotswolds, and the house-sitting responsibilities a lot less onerous than usual. Despite a lurking sense of caution, Thea felt optimistic and light-hearted.

The month of June was about to begin, with all the usual mixed feelings that accompanied the start of an English summer. A cold wet June was a loss that could never quite be compensated for by July and August, however lovely they might turn out to be. A flaming heatwave in June, however, could bring with it a surge of Continental well-being, a pretence that real summers could happen, even here on the north-western corner of Europe where the Atlantic troughs habitually held sway through much of the year. Weather, thought Thea, became increasingly important the older you got. Or perhaps it was just her – spending so much time outdoors, often involved with livestock and at the mercy of the elements.

The Manor was approached up a steepish drive, the entrance to which had been difficult to locate in the confusing lanes. 'There's a Lodge,' Harriet had told her, when she had made her preliminary visit a month earlier. 'You can't miss it.' It wasn't the property itself she missed, but the entire section of the village in which it sat. Twice she had failed to take the required turning, dismissing it as too insignificant to be the one she wanted.

But she got there eventually, to be welcomed by Harriet and given a comprehensive tour of the house and a list of her duties. The Manor, it turned out, was something of a fraud. Built of the ubiquitous honey-and-cream Cotswold stone, which had faded to an unpretentious pale yellow-grey, it had never actually been the manor house in the parish. Harriet Young, the owner, had manifested some irritation at Thea's questions as to its history. 'Oh, I think it was built around 1860,' she had said, with a challenging look that added, *Isn't that old enough for you?* Harriet was American. To her, 1860 was pretty much as old as anything got. When Thea hurriedly expressed her profound and genuine admiration for the proportions, furnishings and situation, Harriet had been mollified. 'It's completely unchanged,' she insisted. 'No additions or alterations since the day it was built.' She indicated the oak panelling, the boxed-in staircase, the first-floor gallery, all of which Thea thought wonderful. Outside, Harriet pointed out the impressive pair of wrought-iron gates at the foot of the long drive. 'They were done by hand,' she said proudly. 'The letters from the owner to the blacksmith still exist.'

Thea had not, on that initial exploratory visit, properly calculated the size of the house, but it clearly had space for a large family with numerous servants. The fact that Harriet Young lived there alone was so outrageous that Thea found it almost funny.

But Harriet was not entirely alone. There was a capacious cellar, which was home to dozens of creatures, living in tanks full of greenery and difficult to discover amongst the leaves and stems. 'They're geckoes,' Harriet had explained. 'I breed them for pets. You'd be surprised how many people keep them.' She had fished out an example, and let it walk onto Thea's hand. It clung with bulbous fingers, pressing coolly into her flesh, rolling prominent eyes at her. The light-brown skin was matt and rather beautiful.

'Breed?' she queried. 'How?'

'They lay eggs, which I take away and incubate for them. It's an extremely precise science. Everything has to be just right. And of course, this climate's completely wrong.'

Thea took a step back. 'Whoa!' she protested. 'I'm not qualified for anything like that.'

Blithely, Harriet had assured her that it was easy, and there would be no recriminations if things went wrong. 'But why,' asked Thea, 'don't you get somebody who knows what they're doing?'

Something in the woman's face hinted at the answer. Her eyelids lowered, and she avoided Thea's gaze. 'Well, I'm not entirely *orthodox*,' she admitted. 'It's still a bit of an experiment, you see. If I got involved in it professionally, I'd be in for a whole host of regulations and restrictions. As far as you're concerned, they're just a few pets living in the basement – OK?'

Thea had no qualms about regulations, but she still worried about letting the wretched creatures fall ill or die under her care. 'Well . . .' she had prevaricated, already knowing that the village, the house and the time of year would suffice to persuade her to take the commission '. . . so long as I won't be liable for any disasters.'

'You're insured, are you?'

'Absolutely not,' laughed Thea. 'I agree with you that the less paperwork the better, in all areas of life. Why – you don't think I should be, do you?'

'Not if you don't. I'll trust you if you'll trust me. Nobody sues, whatever happens. Right?' Harriet heaved a long sigh. 'That's one of the main reasons I left the States, you know. Everything you do runs the risk of some sort of litigation.'

'It's getting as bad here,' Thea told her. 'You'll have to move to somewhere like Greece or Mongolia next.'

'At least that'd suit the geckoes,' Harriet had smiled. 'Oh, and there's Donny to consider as well,' she'd plunged on. 'You'll need to understand about Donny.'

She had understood only too well – or thought she did. Donny was seventy-nine, and suffering from a distressing collection of ailments which prevented him from driving or walking very far. He lived in the former Lodge of Harriet's large house, under the official care of his daughter, Jemima. 'And he has a lady friend, Edwina,' Harriet had added. 'But she's away at the moment. They're very close friends, but she doesn't live with him.'

Donny, it seemed, had developed the habit of

visiting the Manor most afternoons as part of an exercise regime his womenfolk had ordained for him. It would be incumbent on Thea to make him a drink and let him talk for half an hour before launching him down the drive on his tottering journey home. 'It is a bit restricting, I'm afraid,' said Harriet.

Thea had found the balance of pros and cons rather more even after that particular disclosure. 'Anything else?' she had asked warily. 'You don't mind me bringing my dog, do you?'

'Your dog is adorable,' Harriet gushed. 'It'll all be fine, trust me. And I promise you the weather's going to stay perfect the whole time you're here.'

The well-designed house compensated for everything. Cleverly positioned on a south-west-facing slope, with views across one part of the village, including the square church tower and beyond to the sprawling beech woodland, it was exactly right in all particulars. Thick walls, with window seats in the main rooms as a result; old flagstones on the kitchen floor; good-quality carpets upstairs – she recognised that it had been built by an Arts and Crafts aficionado along medieval lines as far as the basic structure went. The overlaid Victorian elements gave it the best of both worlds, despite the concerns that purists might have as to its hybrid character. How on earth did Harriet afford it, Thea wondered, without having presumed to ask the question aloud. The American appeared to be in her fifties and without visible means of support, if she was at home every afternoon to receive Donny. Even if the Manor was a fake, it was still a property of very considerable value. And it was fabulously comfortable. The hot water worked effortlessly, which even in June was a high priority, and the sitting room was a joy to relax in. Hepzibah, the cocker spaniel, found a favoured corner on the two-seater sofa, moulting gently as she turned round to get herself more comfortable. 'I can brush the hairs off on my last day,' Thea told herself, ever mindful of the inevitable mess her dog caused in other people's houses.

Harriet had gone to Lindisfarne for two weeks' retreat. There was no conceivable reason to contact her, she insisted. In fact, she would like to place a total veto on doing so. 'That's another reason for hiring you,' she said, obscurely. 'If I'd gone through some stupid agency, they'd have forced me to leave a number.'

Thea closed her eyes in a silent prayer, and wondered again about such extraordinary levels of trustfulness.

The first afternoon was spent in assessing food supplies, examining a large-scale map of the area and pondering the possibilities of Cranham's single pub. Routines were minimal where house-sitting was concerned, but this, her ninth commission, could hardly fail to fall into something like a familiar pattern. None of her friends or relations had undertaken to visit her, but she supposed she might tempt one or other to come over for an evening or weekend. She had been disappointed to realise that she had just missed the famous Coopers Hill cheese-rolling race, which had been a local tradition for centuries. Even though the authorities had tried to cancel it in recent years, because of the dangerously large crowds, some hundreds of determined stalwarts kept it going. It had taken place the previous Monday and sounded like a highly entertaining day out, watching people of all ages launch themselves down a near-vertical grass slope.

But there were plenty of other attractions: Painswick was close by, an obvious destination for a long country walk. Slad, made famous by Laurie Lee, was further on, in the same direction but in another valley.

The dog itself forced certain absolutes into place. She had to be walked, preferably along pathways free from traffic and sensitive farmers. Woodland was ideal – something Cranham possessed in abundance. The settlement was in a deep natural bowl, far from busy thoroughfares, its little approach road continuing aimlessly on to join another road scarcely larger. The landscape altered rapidly to the north, where it swept upwards in a dramatic lift. Any sense of direction became unreliable in the village itself, where points of reference disappeared amongst high hedges and wooded hollows.

The evening was as long and golden as anyone could wish for. Harriet Young's garden was disappointing by Cotswold standards, but it managed to provide a patch of healthy lawn, and a magnolia which had just dropped the last of its blooms. For herself, Thea would have planted a lot more shrubs and small trees to fill some of the oddly naked areas that made the house seem unduly exposed. A closer inspection revealed that substantial trees had been cut down in recent times, their stumps still visible. Inwardly tutting at the vandalism, she arranged herself comfortably along a hardwood bench, and let the slowly descending sun illuminate the book she was reading. Hepzie left the cosy sofa indoors and flopped contentedly onto the patch of shade beneath the bench cast by her mistress.

'This is the life,' said Thea.

Next morning, her first glimpse of the sky from her bed brought sharp disappointment. It was altogether the wrong colour: dove-grey when she had expected forget-me-not blue. A thick blanket of cloud spread from east to west without interruption. A sense of outraged betrayal gripped her, as she realised it wasn't just cloudy, but actually raining in a fine drizzle that more closely suited February than June.

The geckoes in the cellar were invisible, as before. Thea checked the temperature gauge and humidity monitor, then she peered at the dozen or so eggs in the incubator. Harriet had said that there was a slight chance that one or two would hatch, but it was very unlikely. 'Just leave them, if that happens,' she instructed. 'I don't think they'll want to go anywhere for a few days.'

The walls had been painted brilliant white, with a large mirror to catch all available light from the small window high in the south wall. It was the antithesis of a classic cellar with the expected cobwebs and shadowy corners, but it still carried the aura of isolation and strangeness that came with underground rooms. It was low-ceilinged, approached by a flight of stairs from the kitchen, and the floor was rough stone. A faint smell of drains was discernible. In the early years of the house's history it would have been used to store wine, perhaps, and cheese. At first Thea had assumed it might also have housed the coal used to heat the many rooms, but she had found a more obvious coal-hole on the other side of the building during her initial explorations.

Breeding geckoes seemed a very peculiar activity, when she thought about it. The poor things had a dull existence in their restricted tanks. Harriet had manifested little affection for them – she had not given them little treats or cooed sweet nothings at them. If all the eggs hatched, surely they would earn far less than had been spent on refurbishing the cellar. How many hundreds would have to be sold in order to realise enough for even a modest income? Of course, people did pursue strange hobbies of this sort. Thea had encountered a number of weird pets since she began the house-sitting. One of the main reasons for employing her had almost always been to take care of livestock, indoors and out. A parrot, donkey, ponies, cats, dogs, rabbits – she had managed them all with varying degrees of success.

It was mid morning, and the drizzle persisted. The sun-filled bowl that had been Cranham the previous day was now a dark and unappealing trap. What would it be like in winter, wondered Thea. If the roads were icy, it would be hard to escape up the steep hills. If it snowed heavily, the whole place might disappear completely. Torrential rain must surely fill the main street with running water that would threaten many of the houses.

To make matters worse, it was a Sunday – a day when one might justifiably plan long rambles or lazy days in a sunny garden. Irritably, Thea made herself an early lunch and considered activating her laptop for some time-killing games of Scrabble with strangers from foreign lands. It was something she had been doing on and off for the past two years and more, and which maintained its sporadic appeal when life turned dull and aimless as it had that day. An hour or two passed with the help of the radio and the computer, but the sky showed no sign of lightening.

She saw the old man approaching some minutes before he reached the front door. His head, with its covering of floppy white hair, was unprotected from the rain, and he wore no jacket or raincoat. It was as if the weather made no impression on him at all.

'You must be Donny,' she greeted him, when he finally arrived. 'I'm Thea Osborne and this is Hepzibah.'

'Yes,' he agreed with a nod. His shoulders were narrow and slumped, his legs spindly inside the cotton trousers. A constant tremor kept his whole body moving as if he were shivering in a cold wind. His eyes were a faded brown, peering through lids that seemed to lack the energy to open properly. Stubble covered much of the lower half of his face, suggesting four or five days without a shave. But there was a vitality to him that Thea recognised instantly. This was a man who made things happen, and didn't wait for life to come to him. Wasn't he here on a drizzly Sunday, ready to meet somebody new and take his chances with her, rather than huddling in his little house watching inanities on the television?

'Cup of tea?' she suggested.

'Coffee,' he corrected, with a hint of reproach, as if she should have known his preference. 'Black, no sugar.'

He followed her into the kitchen and sat at the table watching as she hunted for a mug and teaspoon. 'The blue one's mine,' he said, in his light piping voice.

She gave him a look. 'Is instant all right?'

'Perfectly, thank you.'

The kitchen had fewer modern gadgets than many Thea had experienced. Harriet Young was pleasantly normal in that respect, it seemed. A faintly grubby microwave sat on one counter, near a large wooden bread bin. The fridge-freezer was stuffed with anonymous bags and trays of assorted meat, bread, ice cream and vegetables. The top of it, too high for Thea to reach, was piled with dusty-looking cookery books and a fat half-used candle. Fruit for the geckoes was in a special plastic box, with some dried insects that looked like raisins.

'Managing, then, are you?' Donny asked.

'So far. It's not very difficult, really, although I'd banked on decent weather. I'm trying not to worry about the geckoes.'

'Silly things,' he smiled, his head quivering in the perpetual tremor. 'Don't know what she was thinking of.'

'Oh well. They're quite sweet, I suppose.'

He waved the topic away, and cautiously sipped the coffee, holding the mug tightly in both hands. It was a tense business, and Thea realised she should have made sure it wasn't filled too close to the brim.

'Never get old, not if you can help it,' he said, having managed a swallow of the hot drink. 'It's a miserable business.'

'Not much choice, is there?' She sat down opposite him and tried to concentrate. Would she really get old one day, like this man? Like everybody, more or less. 'I suppose it's better than dying young.'

He shrugged. 'My daughter died last year. She was forty-one.'

'Oh gosh! I am sorry. My husband died three years ago. He was forty-two.'

He closed his eyes. 'Forty-two,' he murmured, as if it hurt. 'That's another one dying too young. Was he ill?'

'No. Car accident. Was your daughter? Ill, I mean.'

'Oh yes. Had a bad heart all her life. They did a transplant and she died.'

They did a transplant and she died. Thea heard a whole anguished story in that little sentence. 'Right away?' she asked, too horrified to mince her words.

'Eighteen months after the operation,' he said. 'You should have seen her.' Again he closed his eyes. 'It should never have been allowed. They think they're so clever, but there are things they never even stop to consider.'

How did we get into this so quickly? Thea wondered. It was as if Donny needed to unburden himself of this enormous trauma before they could settle into a normal discussion of the weather or the next general election.

'Such as?' she prompted.

His eyes opened fractionally wider, to reveal a rage undimmed by his own physical failings. 'Such as, how is a person supposed to live with somebody else's heart inside them? They just laughed it off as fanciful when she said she didn't feel as if she was herself any more. She would hold herself . . .' he clasped his own mottled hands over his chest '. . . and say she could feel the person's life thumping away, trying to escape.'

'Sounds a bit . . . well, oversensitive,' Thea suggested with a smile. 'Although I can see it must feel terribly strange, especially at first.'

'That was her nature, taking everything hard. She'd always been like that.'

'And I suppose she would have died young, without the new heart?'

'So they told us.'

'You didn't believe them?'

'She'd never have managed a baby, or climbed Mount Everest, or run a marathon. But if she looked after herself, and kept herself quiet, she'd have lived more than the time she did. And she'd have been easy in her mind. They break the ribs, you know, to get at the heart. For a woman . . .' his eyes lost focus, filmed with tears '. . . well, she was dreadfully scarred. Like cutting up a piece of meat.'

Too much information, Thea thought, with a wince. But it was all true, as far as she understood the procedure, and it chimed with the occasional fleeting notions she had entertained on the subject. Could she ever be so utterly desperate to live that she would permit such drastic medical interference for herself? Did everybody cling to the hope of continuing life so passionately that they were willing to pay such a price when it came to the crunch?

'I've made a living will,' he said, conversationally. 'So I won't fall into their clutches.'

'Oh?' She had heard the phrase before without being entirely sure what it meant. 'How does that work?'

'They're to leave me to die,' he said fiercely. 'That's what it means.'

'Oh,' said Thea again, a jumble of conflicting thoughts all clashing together in her head. 'But . . . I mean, are they *allowed* to do that?'

His bravado evaporated. 'It depends,' he said.

'They mean well, you know,' she said feebly. 'Palliative care and all that. Lots of people say it's really nice in a hospice, if you can get a place in one. Everybody being so honest and open, and making every minute count.' She smiled tentatively. 'That sort of thing.'

'I'd never get a hospice bed. They give them all to people with cancer. That's about the only thing I haven't got. I'm just supposed to slowly crumble away, until I can't control any of my bodily functions.'

He breathed heavily for a few seconds, and then drained the coffee with difficulty. Thea had no choice but to hear and understand what he was telling her. No platitudes would help him, nothing she could say would change the reality. Pity flooded through her, and a surging desire to help. She reached for his quivering hand. 'Don't think about it,' she advised, earnestly. 'I know it sounds pathetic, but you're here now, chatting to me, and it's OK this moment, isn't it? That's all that matters. You don't know what's going to happen. We can't plan our own deaths, you know.

You could drop down dead now, with a stroke or something, and all this worrying will have been for nothing.' She smiled into his eyes. 'And you look to me like a man who enjoys life.'

Again, the film of tears sluiced his eyes. 'I knew you were a good 'un, soon as I saw you,' he said faintly. 'It's a rare thing, for a woman to talk so frankly as you just have. I just wish Mimm would listen to me sometimes. She's always in such a tizz, she can't stop long enough to hear what I'm trying to say.' He was mumbling, forcing the words through a wash of emotion.

'Mimm?'

'Jemima. My daughter,' he elaborated, rubbing his midriff. 'It's not such a good day, today, to tell you the truth. Too many aches and pains.' He fingered his stubbly chin. 'And I ought to get myself a shave as soon as Weena comes back.'

Thea refrained from questioning this second odd name. Edwina! she remembered. His lady friend. 'Doesn't your daughter do it?' she asked.

He snorted. 'I won't let her. Far too ham-fisted, she is. I'd lose half my skin.'

Thea winced in sympathy, hoping there was no requirement for her to volunteer to do it. Donny went on, 'I miss Weena when she goes off. She's always very good to me, even if we do have our disagreements. She means well, nobody can deny that.'

Hepzie, noticing her mistress's solicitude, decided to join in. She approached the old man and pawed gently at his leg. He looked down and smiled at the large liquid eyes and floppy black ears. Automatically he reached down and fondled the soft head. 'It might be different if I had a dog,' he murmured. 'Something to live for, that would be. You can't let them down, can you?'

'Have you ever had one?'

'Once. We had a little Westie when we were first married. He got run over and my wife said she couldn't bear another one, knowing it would die one day. Silly, really. Same with Mimm. She's like her mother, though she won't hear of it if I say so.'

Thea recognised a feeling of mutual understanding that went beyond the brief verbal exchanges on this first encounter. Rightly or wrongly, she thought she understood this old man, his wishes and fears, priorities and prejudices. She could hear a lot of his thoughts between the words, and even thought she grasped some of the essence of his daughter as well.

He sat quietly for a few minutes, mastering his emotions, then he gathered himself and got to his feet. 'Thank you, my dear. I'll be going now.'

He straightened slowly, and turned for the door. A final thought detained him. 'But you're not right altogether, for all that,' he said, without meeting her eye. 'One thing's sure – I will end up dead. And I need to get the funeral sorted out. Mimm has some plan for putting me and Janet together in the churchyard, but I'm not sure that's what I want. She won't let me talk about it, you see.' He gave her a searching look. 'Have you any suggestions as to how I might go about fixing that?'

'As a matter of fact, I have,' she said. 'I know the very man to help you.' And she detained him on the threshold for another ten minutes while she explained all about her friend Drew Slocombe and his alternative burial ground.

CHAPTER TWO

She phoned Drew soon after Donny had left, and explained the situation. 'I've no idea how much time he's got, or what he can afford. I only just met him this afternoon. But I thought you could maybe send a leaflet or something, and he could contact you,' she said carefully.

'But . . . will he want to be brought down here, away from where he lives?'

It had been over two months since she had heard his voice, but it was as if they'd been speaking every day. Dimly she noted that she had established an almost instant friendship with Drew, much as she had with Donny. It made her feel slightly complacent, the way she could simply take up the threads again, despite not having seen or spoken to Drew for so long. Preliminaries had been minimal – she could hear everything she needed to know in his easy response to her initial words.

'What about the Broad Campden field? Is that going ahead?'

He sighed loudly. 'Extremely slowly. Your man would have to live the best part of another year at this rate to stand any chance of a grave there. But at least it's still under discussion, and I've completed a large mountain of paperwork for the planning committee.'

'Oh. Well, I should think he might manage that. He's still walking, and feeding himself. I don't know what his prognosis is. I don't even know what the matter is, except it looks like Parkinson's.'

'Poor chap. And you've only just met him, did you say?'

She gave a self-deprecating snort. 'I know. Seems crazy, doesn't it? But we just seemed to hit it off from the first moment. He had no intention of settling for small talk. Just plunged in with the serious stuff.'

'He's lucky.'

'What do you mean?'

'Well, to find you. Nobody but you would have let him talk about his own grave after five minutes' acquaintance.'

'Rubbish. You would. And your Maggs person.'

'That's different. It's our job.'

'He wanted to talk about it. He asked if I could give him some help with his funeral, a minute before he left, and I told him what you did, in a fairly general sort of way. So where do we go from here?'

'As it happens, I'm coming up on Tuesday, to see the legal people. I might be able to drop in and talk it over with him. Where are you?'

'Cranham. It's on the western edge of the Cotswolds, down a maze of little roads. Have you got a map? But let me check with him first and call you back. It'll be this time tomorrow, I expect. He comes every afternoon, so we could easily fix something up for Tuesday.'

'OK. I can probably find it. If this is to be the first customer in the new cemetery, it's worth getting a bit lost.'

'Good,' she said vaguely, thinking it would be nice to see him again.

'Thanks, Thea,' he said warmly. 'I appreciate you thinking of me.'

'Don't mention it,' she said.

She took Hepzie around the village at five, when the drizzle finally gave up and a late sun emerged to brighten the evening. It shone warmly on the damp hedgerows and verges, creating a steamy humidity that felt quite foreign. She had no real feel for Cranham yet. The only resident she had met was poor old Donny. She passed quiet stone houses with flower-filled gardens and no signs of life. It was no different from many other Cotswold villages she had experienced in that respect. A few cars passed by, containing the first of the trickle of people coming home from a day out – some probably even worked on a Sunday. Once back, they seemed to disappear out of sight, regardless of the weather. Long summer evenings were no more effective at tempting them onto their front lawns than a November downpour would have been. Occasional voices floated from back gardens, where privacy was guaranteed by walls and fences and hedges.

But there were a few people in the woods when Thea and Hepzie turned off the road and passed the unusual community playground which the locals had evidently established for their children. This, she remembered, was the last weekend of the half-term holiday. School would begin again the next day, with whatever small snatches of freedom modern children enjoyed curtailed for another six or seven weeks. There were two girls sitting on top of a sturdy climbing frame, talking intensely, heads close together. A man with a large grey poodle approached her. He wore a blue Breton cap with a wide brim over his face, and a lilac-coloured shirt. He had shapely, fleshy lips, reminiscent of the figures in many a Pre-Raphaelite painting. *The only gay in the village*, flashed through Thea's mind, and she gave him a warm smile, prompted largely by inner amusement at the inevitable reference. He smiled back, and stopped walking.

'Nice little spaniel,' he observed. The poodle was ignoring Hepzie completely, its sharp nose averted.

'Thanks.'

They watched the dogs in silence for a moment, pausing before the inevitably continued conversation. The balance had been tipped the moment the man halted and spoke. And yet there remained the traditional British reluctance to engage with a stranger.

'Haven't seen you around before,' he said.

'No. I'm house-sitting for Harriet Young, at Hollywell.' She waved towards the Manor.

'Are you indeed? Well done you. Fabulous house, of course. Full of good things. I like good things. And hasn't she got some kind of reptile in the cellar?'

Thea smiled again at the image of a massive iguana lurking in the shadows that the words evoked. 'A few, yes. Only little ones.'

'And you'll have to suffer the miserable Donny Davis as well, I imagine?'

'He drops in. I don't find him at all miserable.

I rather like him.' She sounded stiff, even to her own ears.

'People do, at first. He'll soon drive you crazy with his self-pity.' He raised his eyes to the sky. 'Please let me die,' he quoted, in Donny's quavering tones. He looked hard at Thea then. 'Why doesn't he just find the guts to put an end to his misery, and do us all a favour, if he's so adamant that he won't let a doctor look at him?'

Thea was shocked. 'He enjoys life too much, I suppose. It's not so easy to just kill yourself because it might be convenient to your family. And I imagine he's within his rights to stay away from doctors and hospitals after the dreadful time he had with his daughter.'

'If you ask me, it's a sign of dementia. And you're wrong about dying – it's as easy as pie. It's staying alive that's difficult.' He gave her a straight look. 'I should know.'

The man was in his late thirties, she estimated. Probably quite affluent and apparently in good health. He obviously had no idea what he was talking about, despite his claim. Her mouth felt full of arguments, jumbled assertions about fear of death, and essential human ambivalence, and a burning need to leave some sort of trace behind.

'Oh,' she challenged. 'Why's that, then?'

'As it happens, I'm a doctor myself. Cardiovascular surgery, to be exact.'

Thea gulped back her astonishment. 'Fancy that,' she managed. 'I would never have guessed. But I stick to my point. I still don't think you understand about Donny. You probably have to be old and ill to have any hope of getting inside his head.'

He held her gaze. 'But you're neither, and you seem to be claiming some special insight.'

She quailed for a moment at his refusal to give way. 'At least I've been *listening* to him,' she blustered.

The man shrugged elaborately. 'Well, I don't mind telling you I head for the hills if I see him coming my way. Jasper and I know a few nooks and crannies in these woods, if we need to make an escape.'

'I wouldn't worry,' she flashed, determined not to be intimidated by him. 'Donny's not very fast on his feet, after all. I wouldn't think there's much risk of him catching you.'

'Ooh—' even before he finished his remark, she had found herself registering this outrageous parody of Kenneth Williams '—listen to you! Here for five minutes and already knows all about it, am I right? Well, Madam House-sitter, you'll learn. Come back to me in a week and tell me I was right. You will, you know. My name's Philippe, by the way. What's yours?'

She told him, but neglected to introduce her

35

dog, as she normally would. This *Philippe* was quite frivolous enough for both of them, and if that made her seem stiff by comparison, then so be it.

'Have fun, then, Thea Osborne,' he said, and continued on his way.

She released the spaniel from the lead and wandered slowly along the woodland paths, one eye on the plumy white tail that bobbed amongst the holly and brambles beneath the big beech trees. Cranham was still quite unknown to her after a busy twenty-four hours. Part of her hoped to keep it that way, staying quietly at Hollywell Manor, making coffee for Donny and catching whatever sunshine there might be on offer. A year earlier she had been at Temple Guiting in a blazing hot spell, with Detective Superintendent Phil Hollis. Now a new Philip – she would have been happy to bet that was his original name before he Frenchified it – had crossed her path, albeit highly unlikely to find himself in anything like the same kind of relationship to her as Hollis had been. Now firmly in the past, she preferred not to think about him and the perverse way she had treated him. Since then, men had been in short supply in her life.

Except for Drew Slocombe, of course. And Drew didn't really count.

The evening wound down slowly, still light at half past nine, albeit cloudy. The gecko eggs slumbered peacefully, their heedless parents marginally more active when Thea went to inspect them. She caught the quick movement of one, at the top of its tank, just before it froze halfway behind a large palmate leaf, the clever camouflage unsuccessful once she had seen it move. Where did geckoes come from, she wondered. How long did they live? She had blurry memories of reading about them sitting above windows inside houses in hot climes, waiting for flies to come their way. A sort of tropical version of Dickens' cricket on the hearth; something people regarded as benign, even rather auspicious. But quite how it evolved from there to a British craze for owning them as pets was obscure. As far as she could see, they were singularly unrewarding.

She thought about Donny, bracketing him with the geckoes as another element of her responsibilities. Would he appreciate her introducing him to Drew, forcing him to confront the reality of his own grave? She acknowledged that the poodle-owning Philippe had already sown a few seeds of doubt, despite her indignation at his attitude. But she clung to the idea that arranging a meeting between Drew and Donny would be an interesting experiment for both men – even possibly therapeutic for Donny if Drew could manage to be as sensitive and understanding as she believed him to be. If the old man backed off, muttering that he really wasn't quite ready for anything so concrete, then he might relax into enjoying the summer and forgetting about his bleak future.

Except he had already seemed pretty relaxed. Thea's first impression of him as a man who relished life felt rock solid. She would never have charged him with self-pity, despite the terrible story about his daughter, and his own limitations, and Philippe's unfeeling accusations. With difficulty she recalled what Harriet had told her. There was a lady friend called Edwina. Why hadn't she, or the daughter, not helped to settle the matter of his funeral already? Did they refuse to discuss anything to do with death and dying, as many people did? Were they relentlessly, mindlessly, jolly when all the poor man wanted was to clarify the arrangements for something that was sure to happen eventually? Did they laugh it all away and change the subject? What did they think about the living will and its implication that Donny would wish to die at home, with their full cooperation? Had he perhaps gone so far as to appeal to them for assistance in committing suicide, when he felt the time had come, only to meet with frozen faces and a determined change of subject?

The questions came and went, the answers all pending further contact with the man himself. Thea found them absorbing, in a way she had not felt absorbed for some time past. Death had touched her many times in the last three years, until it seemed it was following her around, stalking her like a persistent admirer. Repeatedly she had promised herself that it would not happen again, only to be foiled. And now, here it was again in a different guise, intriguing in a new way. A man who both did and did not want to die, who did and did not want to *live*. It felt like being shown a window onto something rare and vital, where she might be able to contribute, thanks to her ability to face up to more reality than most people could.

She went to bed, eagerly looking forward to her next encounter with the sick old man.

CHAPTER THREE

Next morning, she was awake at eight, after a solid nine hours' sleep. Hepzie stirred lazily when her mistress threw back the light duvet and went to look out of the window. Her room was next to the main bedroom, both of them overlooking the front garden. The Manor boasted no fewer than five bedrooms, as well as an attic where servants had once slept.

Outside, a middle-aged woman was blithely cutting roses from the bushes which grew along the inside of the hedge. She carried an old-fashioned trug on her arm, and wore a long cotton skirt. 'Good God, it's a ghost,' Thea muttered. The fact that the spaniel had given no hint of the invasion only fortified this idea. Boldly, she threw the window wide open.

'Hey!' she called. 'What are you doing?'

The woman turned, too far away to see her face properly. She put up a hand to shield her eyes from the morning sun and squinted up at the window. 'Hello,' she said. 'Sorry – I didn't want to disturb you. It is rather early, I know.'

'Does Harriet let you take her flowers?'

'Of course. You didn't think I was stealing them, did you?'

Not a ghost, Thea concluded, with a stab of disappointment. And apparently not a thief either. 'Are they for the church?' she asked, trying to inject some logic into the situation.

'What? Oh no, of course not. Don't be daft.'

'Wait there,' Thea ordered. 'I'm coming down.'

She had not brought a dressing gown with her, but Harriet had thoughtfully provided one, which hung on the back of the door. It was pale blue and far too big, but she donned it anyway. Almost tripping on its trailing belt and the skittering spaniel, she got downstairs unscathed and flung open the front door. It was already warm, she noted, with satisfaction, all the clouds of the previous day quite dispelled.

'So, who are you?' she asked, trying to sound friendly.

'Jemima Hobson. Daughter of Donny Davis. I gather he came to see you yesterday. Rather a cheek, if you ask me, but he seemed to think you didn't mind.'

41

'Oh! Pleased to meet you.' She did not offer a hand to shake. There were roses and dressing gowns and a dog in the way. 'No, I didn't mind a bit. Do you live in Cranham?'

'Actually, no. We've got a market garden place four or five miles away.'

'But it's so *early*,' Thea groaned, brushing tangled hair out of her eyes.

'Come on. It's after eight. The sun's been up since about five. I can't bear to waste it this time of year. It all flies by so fast and you never know when we might be in for a month of rain.' There was a restless, worried air to her, which echoed Donny's remark about Jemima always being in a tizz.

'True,' said Thea, recognising her own thoughts of the past few days. She also remembered the people she had found herself amongst the previous June, and their similar habit of rising uncomfortably early. 'I still think eight's quite soon enough to get up.'

'It may be for you – I have to fit so much in, I can't lie around in bed. Dad sent me for the roses. Harriet won't mind, I promise you.'

'Is he up as well, then?'

'Not yet, no. I generally go in about half past, to get his breakfast and help him get going. It's not so bad this time of year, but in the winter he can take half an hour just to dress himself.'

'Doesn't he have somebody official – like a home help or something?'

Jemima Hobson gave her a look. 'No, he doesn't. He won't consider it.' She sighed impatiently, and then seemed to inwardly reproach herself. 'You can see his point, I suppose. They'd send a different girl every time, who'd only want to get it all done as fast as possible and on to the next place. Even the cheerful ones are a pain in the backside. We had all that with my sister. I don't think either of us could bear it all over again.'

'He told me about your sister. I'm so sorry. It sounded awful.'

'Yes, it was beastly. We miss her much more than we ever expected to, which probably sounds silly. I mean – you don't think about it beforehand, do you? You can't imagine what missing someone will be like.'

'Right,' said Thea, thinking about her dead husband and what a feeble phrase 'missing him' was when applied to the reality of the pain his loss caused. 'I know exactly what you mean.'

'Cecilia was seven years younger than me, and I adored her,' said Jemima matter-of-factly. 'From the first day she was born, I behaved as if she was mine. My mother had breast cancer in her early forties and was always tired and depressed, so I took the baby on. I hated going to school and leaving her. She was the centre of my life. And her

43

bad heart just made it more important that I look after her properly.'

Thea had forgotten that she was standing outside in a voluminous blue dressing gown, talking to a woman she had never met before. She was hooked into the story of the Davis family, visualising how it must have been for them, wanting to know more. Here was the person who could answer some of the profound questions from the day before as well, if Thea could manage to phrase them tactfully.

'It's all so sad,' she said, sincerely. 'What happened to your mother?'

'Nothing, really,' Jemima grimaced. 'She never quite got over the trauma and embarrassment and physical damage the cancer involved. She survived it physically, against the odds, and she's still alive, but bit by bit she just got tireder and more depressed until it turned into senility, even though she's not seventy-five yet. She just gave up when Cecilia died. She's in a nursing home in Cirencester, more or less out of it. We don't seem to have much time for her any more.' She frowned. 'That sounds bad, I suppose, but it's the truth. Dad hardly even mentions her these days. She didn't know me last time I visited. I'm not sure I can face going through that again, quite frankly.'

The story had lurched from sad to seriously

lowering. Thea understood that Donny's wife's experience had been repeated in his younger daughter's, in that they had both been subjected to extreme medical interventions designed to save their lives. The whole family must for years and years have been immersed in hospitals and medication and fear for the future. It happened to thousands of people, of course: the visits to the specialist a regular dramatic event in their lives, the repeated rounds of tests and X-rays and trials of the latest drugs. It became their sole topic of conversation, obsessively discussing symptoms in hushed voices. To their friends and neighbours they became 'Sally with the bowel cancer' or 'Henry with the heart bypass'. Illness became a way of life, survival the sole goal, even if they did nothing more than sit in front of the telly all day.

She felt prompted to do something to lighten the mood before the whole day was spoilt.

'There were just you two girls, then, were there?'

'Oh, no. We've got a brother as well. He came between me and Cecilia. Silas, he's called. He's in Nigeria at the moment, doing something terribly noble with handicapped children.'

Thea grinned. She liked this busy restless woman. She liked the whole family, from what she'd learnt thus far – even the defeated mother and do-gooder brother. She liked their refusal to kowtow to the conventional norms of patienthood – especially where Donny was concerned. 'Well, your father has a good spirit,' she said unselfconsciously.

Jemima took a perfect yellow rose from the trug and sniffed it, her gaze on the Lodge two hundred yards away as if it was tugging at her. 'That's a nice way of putting it,' she said thickly. 'It takes a stranger to say something like that. To me he's rather a nuisance most of the time.'

'You've certainly got your hands full,' Thea sympathised.

'I'm not complaining. Families are prone to get complicated, after all. I'd rather have it like this than sit around all day with nothing to do. At least my own kids are behaving themselves, for the moment.'

'You make me feel awfully lazy,' Thea confessed. 'But I did do something for your dad,' she remembered. 'I hope it wasn't out of order, but I approached an alternative undertaker on his behalf. He said yesterday that he wanted to settle the details of his funeral, and did I know anybody, and as it happens—' Belatedly she noticed the expression on Jemima Hobson's face. 'What? What's the matter?'

'Out of order isn't even close,' the woman snarled. 'What in the world did you think you

46

were doing? He doesn't need to discuss his *funeral*, for God's sake.'

'Um . . .' flailed Thea helplessly. 'But he *did* say . . .' Rapidly thinking back, she understood that she had been dreadfully precipitate. Donny had done little more than express a polite interest when Thea had told him about Drew. With shamefully little encouragement, she had gone flying to the phone moments after he'd left. Now it began to look as if she'd made a big mistake.

Jemima groaned aloud. 'After all my efforts, you go and wreck everything on the first day you meet him. Didn't it occur to you that things might not be as they seem on the surface? I can't believe anybody could be so blunderingly insensitive as to do something like that. We all spend every waking moment trying to steer him away from anything morbid, for heaven's sake.'

'Wait a minute,' Thea protested. 'What's so terrible about it? Drew's utterly approachable and friendly. He's not going to force anything onto Donny. We can cancel the whole thing if necessary.' *Besides*, she wanted to add, *there will have to be a funeral at some point*.

'Listen,' Jemima said in a low hard voice. 'We're not happy with the way Dad's been thinking. He's started talking about assisted suicide and living wills. He's scared stiff of ending up in hospital, dying slowly after weeks of being

47

kept alive with tubes and machines and all that business. It's getting to be an obsession with him. If you introduce some touchy-feely undertaker, who'll tell him he can be reincarnated as a lovely cherry tree, he'll just get worse. Don't you see?'

Thea dug her heels in. 'Not really. His attitude seems quite logical to me. But I admit I have been interfering where I shouldn't. It never occurred to me it would cause trouble with his family.'

Jemima snorted. 'You've been swayed by all the media hype and emotional appeals for changes to the law on suicide. It's a million miles from the reality for actual individual people. If you ask me, it was better when suicide was illegal. People just had to put up with what fate dealt them in those days.'

'I suppose you're against divorce as well, for the same reasons?'

'That's a completely different issue, and you know it. I'm talking about all these idiots thinking they can have an easy painless death at the flick of a switch.'

'I agree with you, more or less,' Thea said, deflating much of the other woman's animosity. 'But I don't agree that it helps to avoid the subject. Your father can cope with hearing your views, from what I've seen of him.'

'*He* probably can. But *I* can't. Have you ever talked to your own father about how and when he'll die, and who's going to help him?'

'My father died last year. But no, we never had a conversation remotely like that.'

'It's as if an iron hand clutches your throat and stops the words coming out. You can *think* them, and practise saying them, but when it comes to the point, it just doesn't happen. And I've come to the conclusion that it's much better to keep everything superficial, take it a day at a time, and smell the flowers.' She put the rose to her nose again to illustrate the point.

'And that's the general consensus in the family, is it?'

'Not entirely. Edwina's a bit of a problem. Dad got her to make some impossible promises, but I think he understands that she can't hope to fulfil them.'

Until that moment Thea had forgotten the man in the woods – Philippe, the doctor who thought dying was easy. Had she stumbled into the midst of a whole community with passionate views about euthanasia? Was there some large factor in the argument that she had failed to grasp? Already she was losing sight of Donny himself and what she had believed he wanted.

'Look,' Jemima began again on a mellower note. 'I know how Dad can be when you first meet him. I've seen it happen before. He's always been a charmer, getting everybody onto his side, although I admit I've never known it to work quite so fast before. This undertaker bloke – can you head him off? I promise you it wouldn't be a good idea. He's not going to get any business out of us. If you must know, we've always assumed that both my parents will be buried in the churchyard here. It's been a foregone conclusion for years now. Dad really likes the church, even if he isn't remotely religious.'

'Is Cecilia there?'

'No, no. Sissy's husband insisted on a cremation. Her ashes were scattered on Lundy Island. Don't ask,' she added, seeing Thea's mouth start to open. 'It's a long and irrelevant story.'

Husband? had been the question Thea intended to ask. She had assumed from what she'd heard that Cecilia had been single, a cherished unmarried sister, far too poorly to venture into matrimony.

'Don't worry,' she said with a touch of bitterness, referring back to the earlier query. 'Drew won't barge in where he's not wanted. He's had enough of disagreements over graves as it is. There was a major row only a few months ago in Broad Campden—'

But Jemima wasn't interested in Drew Slocombe's problems, and Thea could hardly blame her, with all the family complexities she already had to deal with. 'That thing you said, about his spirit,' she began. 'It's all to do with that, do you see? He shouldn't be worrying about dying and becoming dependent. It wouldn't alter how we remember him and the brilliant father he was to us.'

It would, though, Thea thought to herself. They were never going to forget the final months or years of helplessness, if that's what it came to. Jemima herself had already called him a nuisance, and it was obvious that things were only going to get worse.

'It really isn't my business,' she said. 'I realise I overstepped the mark in calling Drew so quickly and I'm sorry. I think Harriet wants me to do as much as I can to take some of the weight off your shoulders. I'm more than happy to do that, if you'll let me. In fact, if I don't, then I wouldn't be earning my pay. The geckoes are hardly a full-time commitment.'

'I doubt if anything would prevent him from making his daily trek up here. We all think it's the main thing that keeps him going. He looks forward to it all morning, and thinks about it afterwards. Just don't go taking him too seriously – all right?'

She could easily phone Drew and tell him he would not be needed after all. Would he be disappointed or pleased to avoid the pressure? Probably he would not be very surprised. Thinking it through again, she winced at how stupidly headlong she had been. No wonder Jemima had been so angry with her – she'd have felt the same if the situation had been reversed. But then she thought of Donny himself. Surely he must have felt almost desperate to broach the subject as he did, with a complete stranger. Whatever gave him the idea that she could help, anyway? Unless he'd already heard that she was acquainted with Drew Slocombe – that might explain an approach that seemed more and more unlikely as she thought it over.

She assumed he would come again that afternoon, for his black coffee and intense conversation, and she could ask him what lay behind his request. At the same time, having met his daughter, Thea was very much less eager to see him than she had been. She was being drawn into something too important to be mishandled, forced to give it her whole attention and avoid saying the wrong thing. Jemima had warned her not to take it too seriously, as if understanding that this was exactly what Thea would do. But it was apparently what Donny wanted above all else. Perhaps, she concluded, it would be better to phone Drew *after* Donny's next visit. She would be clearer then about what would be the best thing to do.

For lunch she made herself a lavish salad full of all her favourite tastes – olives, beetroot, rocket, prawns and cherry tomatoes. It might not be orthodox, but she enjoyed it, along with a glass of cold white wine. It left the contents of the fridge rather depleted, which meant she would have to go off to find a shop the next morning. Painswick would be nearest, she supposed – a town she hardly knew at all, other than as the home of Phil Hollis's sister, Linda. They had met two or three times; enough to recognise each other easily in the street. 'I really hope I don't bump into her,' Thea muttered aloud. 'That could be a bit awkward.'

She had disappointed Phil in a number of ways, one of which being her failure to befriend the lonely Linda and shake her out of her reclusive ways. 'That's too big a task,' she had protested. 'Besides, she seems to like things as they are.'

Where many of the small Cotswold villages were tucked away in folds of the landscape, a scattering of sturdy yellow houses arranged around the home farm or the Manor or the church or the green, the towns were of a different appeal. Often on a river, like Naunton or Bourton, they were all entirely distinct from each other. Northleach, for example, was on rising ground, with the huge church standing guard over the main square as if it had been there since the world began. Naunton snaked cheerfully along the banks of the river, the beautiful buildings basking complacently in the knowledge that they had achieved a perfection that could never be surpassed. Stow had an air of importance, standing at a point where several roads intersected, offering bounteous quantities of free parking for visitors and little old shops from a bygone age. Broadway, which Thea had only glimpsed once, some years before, had its own claims on the tourist trade, which on that single visit she had failed to comprehend. She ought to give it another chance, she decided, but strongly suspected she would not like it any more a second time. Blockley, on the other hand, was full of fascinating contradictions and historical mysteries. And Painswick was different again, with a busy road running through its heart and yet another large church asserting its presence.

The sheer miracle by which a rich density of occupation combined with a sense of unchanging rural life was one of the main charms of the area. There were literally hundreds of settlements, ranging from the tiny hamlet of Hampnett to the major town of Cirencester, and yet there was always a feeling of sparse human presence. The tourists tended to converge on a few centres, leaving the undiscovered glories of the little Duntisbournes or this unheard-of Cranham in almost perfect peace.

The weather was teasingly uncertain throughout the day. A breeze was blowing from the east, far from cold, but enough to lower the temperature from Thea's optimum 25 degrees or so. White clouds with pale-grey centres were milling about overhead, pretty enough, but unwelcome just the same.

In the cellar the geckoes and their eggs were boringly inert. She sprayed a fine mist of ionised water onto the eggs as instructed, and left them to their slow incubation.

CHAPTER FOUR

Donny arrived early. It was just short of two-thirty when she heard his shuffling feet on the threshold of the open front door. 'Hello?' he called breathlessly. 'Can I come in?'

Hepzie trotted ahead to welcome him, but did not jump up at his unsteady legs. He nudged her gently with his walking stick and she backed away, long tail slowly wagging.

Thea smiled and extended an arm to usher him into the kitchen. She felt awkward and dumbstruck after their previous exchange and all she had learnt about him subsequently. He seemed to be feeling something similar, his smile uncertain and his eyes querulous. Foolishly, she was reminded of the morning after a one-night stand, where the sudden night-time intimacies are revealed as excessive and inappropriate in the cold light of day. Not that she had had many such experiences, she thought ruefully.

'I met your daughter this morning,' she said.

'So I gather. She seems to be rather cross with us both.'

'Mmm.' With difficulty she kept back the words that would have placed her firmly on his side – where he obviously wanted her to be.

He was quick to see how things stood. 'She's a very good girl,' he said. 'We've always got along pretty well, me and Mimm. Did well at school, married a decent man. Fine, healthy kids.' He sighed. 'Counts for very little now, though. All she does these days is fight me.'

'I like your children's names,' Thea offered, in the hope of keeping things light. 'I heard them all this morning.'

'Do you? Jemima was her mother's idea. Named her for some old maiden aunt I never even met. And Silas – that was nearly as bad. I made sure I got my choice for the last one. I always liked the name Cecilia. It sounds musical to me.'

'I like Silas,' said Thea. 'It's unusual.'

'It doesn't suit him.'

'My daughter's Jessica. Nice and safe. Not too ordinary and not too unusual. She seems quite happy with it.'

He nodded absently, tired of the small talk. He rubbed a hand absently across his abdomen, pressing hard at one spot. 'Have you got a pain?' she asked him.

'Blockage,' he said curtly. 'Not a subject for polite company.'

Where was the boldness of the day before? All courage had deserted her in the ineluctable fact of a disintegrating body. Her medical knowledge was scanty, especially where it concerned old people. 'Oh dear,' she said.

'Have you ever had an enema?'

'No.'

'Ghastly business. And nobody wants to do it.'

'It has to be a nurse, I assume?'

He scowled, sitting in his usual place at the kitchen table, thin legs tucked out of sight, but their constant movement intrigued the spaniel, which watched intently. 'I won't have a nurse,' he muttered.

Well, I'm not going to volunteer, thought Thea, suppressing a shudder. 'Have you any choice?' she asked, aware that the same question had arisen on the previous day.

Donny too noticed the repetition. 'That's a favourite word with you, isn't it?' he accused. 'One of those jargon words the politicians like to use. Of course I've got a choice. Take it or leave it. Hold out or give in. I make the same choice every day.'

'You've tried prunes and stewed apple, and all that, I suppose?'

'Syrup of figs and liquorice sticks,' he added. 'All hopeless.'

'I can see your problem,' she said, thinking she would have entirely the same reaction. One reason she stopped after one child had been her profound resistance to the indignity of the birth process, the sense of helpless victimhood in the hands of uncomprehending medical people. Donny's situation was so much worse, with no happy outcome to look forward to, no consoling new baby to salve the wounds to his self-esteem.

Perhaps it was the necessity for dignity that made her resolve not to exclude him from what had been said by Jemima – Mimm – that morning. She would not be party to conversations behind his back, and the feeling of betrayal that came with them. 'Your daughter doesn't like the idea of you talking about your own funeral,' she said.

'You're right there. She's furious about it. I told you.'

'Did she tell you I'd already contacted my friend Drew?'

'Not exactly. She said you'd been over-enthusiastic. Something like that.' He ducked his head, glancing at her from beneath his straggling grey eyebrows. 'It's a battle,' he summarised.

'He did say he could come and talk to you tomorrow, while he's in the area. He lives in Somerset, you see.'

'No harm in talking,' he remarked carelessly.

'No – we couldn't.' She was scandalised at the ease of the idea. Say nothing to Mimm and let Drew call in on a casual footing, as much to see her as to offer Donny his services.

'Just how friendly are you with this chap?' His eyes twinkled teasingly, and Thea felt herself flush.

'Only vaguely. I met him in March, and we had a bit of an adventure. But he's married to a very nice person. He's quite young for an undertaker, but very experienced.'

'Expensive, I shouldn't wonder. They all are, these people. Captive market, of course. Who's going to argue?'

'I've no idea about the money, but I would guess he keeps it all as low as he can.'

Donny said nothing, keeping his gaze on the coffee in his hands, but managing to kink an encouraging eyebrow to keep things going.

'So, if I were to ask him to call in for a cup of tea, about three tomorrow afternoon, it wouldn't be an official consultation, would it? Just a chance encounter,' she suggested. Again there was no reply, so Thea carried on, 'Except that your daughter already knows I've talked to him about you. She wouldn't be deceived for a second.'

Finally he spoke. 'Not if somebody told her about it, no. But she's never here of an afternoon.

She's busy with the strawberries just now. Has to watch out for the Pick Your Own people helping themselves.' He chuckled chestily. 'Should have been a sergeant major, that girl. I've said so to her face.'

'I liked her,' said Thea, uncomfortably. 'She has your best interests at heart.'

'She loves me too much,' he said flatly. 'And what's it to her what sort of funeral I want?'

Therein lay a whole new argument, which Thea had engaged in more than once in her life: was a funeral for the person who had died, or the people left to mourn? The obvious glib answer always came back, that it was the latter. She had never been quite so sure. It was something she looked forward to discussing with Drew one day.

There was some other matter nagging at the edge of her mind, going back to Harriet's quick summation of Donny. 'And what about your lady friend – Edwina? What's she going to think?'

His palsied head shook in a sideways motion. 'She's no lady,' he asserted. 'She's a force of nature.'

Unlike his wife, then, if Jemima's description could be believed, but not dissimilar to his daughter. 'So where is she?'

'Away. She goes off at half-term to stay with her daughter and the grandchildren. Five of them there are, all school age. She makes them do treasure hunts and read books about boarding schools and steam trains.'

'Like me with my sister's kids,' said Thea. 'They think I'm a bit mad, because I organise amateur dramatics and stuff they can't do on a computer.'

'Mischief, that's all it is. Weena's family must dread her coming, but it's traditional by this time, and they can't get out of it while she's alive. Twice a year, Whitsun and Christmas, she takes over. Don't know how she does it, with her hip the way it is, but she says it rejuvenates her.'

Thea was thinking. If Edwina *and* Harriet were both away at the same time, then no wonder a house-sitter had been enlisted as backup. It might even have been a deliberate plan hatched up between all the women together – Jemima included.

'A force of nature and a sergeant major is quite a combination,' she smiled. 'You're being very well looked after, compared to some.'

'And Harriet wouldn't let me go wanting, either,' he agreed. 'I tell them they're all just wasting their time. There's nothing in the bank for me to leave them.'

It gave her a jolt. Even if he was joking – and surely he was – it was a nasty thing to say. She eyed him considering. 'You don't really think that's their reason for looking after you, do you?'

He avoided her scrutiny. 'Why do people do what they do?' he shrugged. 'Habit, mainly. And some sort of moral duty that comes from what the neighbours think.'

Blimey, thought Thea, with a flash of anticipation. *Now we're onto moral philosophy.* 'Social pressure, you mean? Hasn't that all died out these days? What neighbour is going to even notice, let alone judge you?'

'Them, not me. Nobody judges *me*. I'm excused all that, at my age. But Mimm likes to keep in with people, do the right thing. Weena's pretty impervious, I grant you – but she's got a bad dose of *noblesse oblige*. Her father was an "Honourable" and she can't ever forget it.'

'And Harriet?'

'Harriet's American,' he said. 'She doesn't understand.'

'They say Americans are good at being neighbourly.'

'And it must be true. She bakes pies for me, and phones Mimm if she thinks there's cause for concern.'

'And still you don't count yourself lucky?'

His tremor increased and his thin lips tightened. 'I find such ideas are far too relative to be taken seriously,' he piped. Pomposity sat oddly on the quavering frame, but it was unmistakably present, for all that.

'Come off it,' she protested. 'Count your blessings, why don't you.'

His look intensified, causing her to flush. 'Sorry. I'm being crass,' she retracted.

Donny chuckled happily. 'And I'm wallowing in self-pity. I do it a lot.'

'It must be tempting to blame somebody,' she sympathised. 'When it's really just the way things are.'

'You got it exactly,' he applauded. 'Except I don't see why we all put up with it so spinelessly. We're not even allowed to mention it in polite company. Getting old is a taboo. Look at all the accolades you get if you can manage to look ten years less than your real age. It's just society's way of rewarding you for not being embarrassing.'

'People I know in their sixties say all that's going to change when they're old. They're not going to put up with it.'

'Good luck to them,' he grumbled. 'Not going to do me much good, is it?'

'More coffee?' she interrupted, unable to come up with any more attempts at reassurance. Friendship was in the air – a sense of mutual acceptance, comradeship, wanting things to go well for each other. Despite his stubble and tremor and slight air of grubbiness, she would have liked to hug him. But she did no such thing. Plenty of time for that, she thought, anticipating many more amicable afternoons.

He put up a quivering hand to decline the

offer of coffee. 'What about your friend, then?' he asked.

She screwed up her face as she tried to assess the risks. 'Well, it would be nice to see him. If he's free, I'll invite him over for this time tomorrow. The rest is up to you.'

'Thank you,' he said, graciously.

Another walk in the woods seemed in order when Donny had gone. Thea had belatedly discovered that the Cranham Woods were rather more famous and special than she had realised, when she consulted the Internet for local places of interest. Pictures of them abounded, as well as reports by cyclists as to their condition. They stretched almost to the neighbouring village of Sheepscombe, and were plainly much valued.

As if to endorse her researches, three bicycles sped past her before she had walked two hundred yards. All men, with heads down and legs well muscled, it was as well that Hepzie had not got entangled with them. What possible pleasure they could be gaining from such intent pedalling, with no attempt to admire the scenery or converse together, she could not fathom. A century ago, the bodies of the riders would be vertical, the pace sedate. There would be a picnic in the panniers and a sense of awestruck freedom to enhance the jaunt. Now cycling had changed out of all recognition, with its overtones of moral superiority combined with protective headgear and Lycra garments that made the Edwardian plus fours seem quite ordinary and sensible. It could hardly even be said to comprise an environmentally benign, low-cost means of transport, when the price of the machine itself could amount to as much as a second-hand car, and the hazard presented to walkers and their animals was so considerable.

The weather remained ambivalent, hazy cloud overhead and a cool breeze blowing. More spring than summer, with nothing approaching a firm promise of warm sunny days ahead. Thea wore a long-sleeved shirt and cotton trousers, reluctant to expose skin in the shady evening woodlands. No other walkers had come into view, the dog had gone sniffing off ahead of her, and thoughts of death never quite went away.

She was forty-four – her own death surely need not worry her for a long time yet. It was Donny's demise that preoccupied her, but by extension that of other people also intruded into her head. Her mother was in her mid-seventies, for example, her father gone for less than a year. People of her acquaintance had died suddenly, sometimes violently, leaving her to wrestle with the mystery of the whole business, time and again. She had seen dead bodies five or six times, both lying in their coffins and in the first hours after losing their lives, still untidy and undignified. There had generally been somebody very much to blame for the premature curtailment of a young life – in at least two instances far too young.

But it was June, and the final few bluebells were still visible in one or two places. The whole place throbbed with life, birds breeding rampantly overhead and new plants emerging on all sides. This was one of the most lovely parts of the country, timeless in its own special way. The very buildings were rooted like great immortal trees and the undulating land swept serenely in every direction. It was not a scene for morbid thoughts, despite her instinctive tendencies that way. She would see Drew again the next day, and enjoy the mild deception of introducing him to Donny against his daughter's wishes. The idea of mischief gave her a lift, despite some worry as to how Jemima might react. She could be irresponsible and get away with it, never needing to come to Cranham again if she made an enemy in the process. But she could not persuade herself that she was being especially feckless, given Donny's frame of mind. In any case, Drew would know what to do. He would understand the different motives and thread a careful path through the minefield of sensibilities, as he must have done many times before.

The woods were increasingly shadowy as she

carried on along the well-marked path, pounded by all the cycling and walking and even some horse riding. Her stomach suggested that it was close to seven o'clock and time for some food. 'Come on, then, Heps,' she chirped. 'Let's go home.'

The absence of any response did not at first alarm her. Although she had lost the dog once or twice in the past, she had always been found again. This time, a passing squirrel or rabbit must have distracted her. If she had got herself caught in a bramble or wire, she would have called out. *When did I last see her?* Thea asked herself. *Only a few minutes ago*, came the reply. The dog had come back to her from further along the track, nosing briefly at her legs before running off again. The ordinariness of it had been reassuring in itself, the usual routine on a country walk. There had been no more people since the cyclists – despite it being a dry summer evening, when locals might be expected to take the air.

'Hepzie!' she called. 'Come on, now. Hepzie!'

She stood quietly, listening for a rustle, watching for the white plumy tail to come wagging through the undergrowth. Walking quickly, she went along the track to where she thought she had last seen the dog. It made a bend to the right, big beech trees growing on both sides. There was a steep slope to the right, with ledges formed by tree roots, dropping abruptly down to a lower level. It would take an undignified scramble to get down there.

Still she was not alarmed. The woods carried no sense of threat or danger. Nobody was waiting behind a tree to shoot squirrels or crows or people or spaniels. No dog snatcher lurked with a net and chloroform. 'Hepzie!' she called, deliberately making her voice as sweet and encouraging as she could. No trace of anger or anxiety tinged it.

She was rewarded by a faint yap away to her right, down the steepest section of the slope. 'Hepzie – where are you?' she shouted.

The yap came again. As far as she could tell, it was not a cry of pain or distress. More, *I'm over here. Come and find me.*

With an inward groan, she left the path and started to step carefully down the untrodden terrain, with all its prickly and knobbly hazards. Tree roots were buried by dead leaves, straggly young holly trees grew almost horizontally in places and brambles snatched like cunning woodland sprites.

Another yap floated through the trees. Thea visualised the dog at the foot of a large beech, jumping at a tantalising squirrel safely out of reach. Something was occupying her attention enough to prevent her from obeying her mistress's orders. Not that she was overly obedient, it had to be said.

'Where are you?' she shouted. 'What the hell are you doing?' Now she was cross, as a bramble snagged her ankle on the single inch of vulnerable skin between trousers and shoe. She had to jump down a small vertical cliff almost three feet in height, landing on an invisible root and hurting her foot.

Suddenly, she could see the dog. It was sitting staring at a clump of vegetation growing next to a fallen tree which must have been left for the benefit of wildlife. A young holly tree and the drooping leaves of bluebells had been flattened to reveal an entrance to a cave-like hollow beneath the tree trunk. 'Is it a badger?' Thea asked the dog. 'Be careful, Heps, if it is. They're rather fierce if you annoy them.'

Hepzie squeaked anxiously, her gaze never shifting from the shadowy cavity. Thea moved forward for a better look. She met two brown eyes and a moist black nose. 'Oh! It's a dog!' she exclaimed. 'Hello, darling. What are you doing here?'

She assumed the animal had become snared or stuck in some way, hunkered down to die in the makeshift shelter. It growled as she approached. 'I won't hurt you,' she soothed. 'I want to see if you're all right.'

A peculiar sound merged with the growls. A musical squeal that was like nothing she had heard

70

before. 'What's that?' she said. Hepzie added her own worried cries to the chorus.

Gradually, the scene beneath the log came into focus, as Thea's eyes adjusted to the gloom. A black and white dog was curled up, squeezed into a small space. Something squirmed and heaved further into the cavity, and it was several seconds before Thea understood what she was seeing. Small bodies were in there, along with the dog. 'Puppies!' she finally realised. 'You've come out here to have your puppies! What a clever girl!'

It was a collie type. *Clever girl* seemed to be a familiar phrase, and the head came forward at this suggestion of friendly praise. But when Hepzie stepped forward to share in the new rapprochement, the mother dog snarled angrily and the spaniel retreated. Like several collies Thea had encountered, this one appeared to be more comfortable with human beings than with her own species. But something was wrong if she had to crawl away into the woods to produce her babies. If she was a working dog, then it was quite possible that her owner would drown all the pups at birth, as Thea knew from experience did happen from time to time. Perhaps it had already happened in the past to this one, and the intelligent animal had worked out a way of avoiding such a cruel loss again.

'Don't worry, I won't betray you,' Thea assured

her. 'But you're going to get terribly hungry out here, even if you can nab the odd rabbit. I'll try and bring you something tomorrow morning – OK?'

The dog grinned at her, but made no further move. The squealing pups had subsided into near silence. Curious to see them, Thea knew better than to stretch a hand into the burrow. Perhaps if everything went well for the next week or so, she would earn enough trust to be able to handle them.

With a careful check for anybody watching, Thea withdrew from the scene, dragging the spaniel after her. 'You'd better not come with me next time,' she said. 'You'll only give the whole game away.' Which was what Hepzie had done already, she realised. 'But it was quite bright of you to find them, I must say.' And if a visiting cocker spaniel could do it, so could other dogs, she thought. What chance did the poor outlaw have of bringing her offspring to any kind of independence? Feral dogs were certainly not going to be tolerated in the neat and tidy Cotswolds, even if they could manage to feed themselves, which she doubted.

She retraced her steps to the village, torn between excitement at the discovery and anticipated guilt if she was questioned about a missing collie. Had the owners not noticed that the bitch was in pup? Would they be searching far and wide, furious with the absconding animal? Or would they perhaps relent, in the face of her obvious need to keep her offspring, and at least spare one or two of them? Her vivid imagination showed her the struggling little dogs in the bucketful of icy water. In Duntisbourne Abbots something of the sort had taken place, and that quite recent memory made her shudder.

Whatever pangs her conscience might deal her, she had unswerving priorities. The lactating bitch would need fluids most of all. There were no visible watercourses in the woods, and the drizzle of the day before had been unlikely to create any useful puddles. She would also need meat. There was nothing suitable to hand in the Manor, despite the various packages stuffed haphazardly into the freezer. Besides, Harriet had seemed reluctant to give her free access to them. 'You do generally cater for yourself, I assume?' she had asked at their first encounter.

'It varies,' said Thea, frankly, thinking of some of the luxury foodstuffs she had been invited to consume at other house-sitting commissions.

It was half past seven. There had to be a supermarket still open somewhere, so she bundled the spaniel into the car, collected her handbag, and set out in search of provisions.

* * *

She had to go to Stroud to find what she wanted, throwing minced beef and pork belly into the trolley, along with a lot of milk and a large box of dog biscuits. Even as she did it, she had a sense that it was money wasted, that the desperate bitch would not accomplish her goal, long-term. There was too much against her, especially once Thea departed from Cranham – unless she could find a substitute dog-feeder, who would respect the secret and deal with the burden of a litter of homeless dogs at the end of it.

Back at Hollywell she phoned Drew. His wife answered, sounding tired and uninterested. 'Is it about a funeral?' she asked.

'Yes,' said Thea, feeling vaguely uncomfortable. 'At least—'

'I'll get him. Hang on a minute.'

It was almost a full minute before his voice came through. 'Sorry – I was reading a story to the children,' he said, before he knew who was calling. Thea was impressed that he would reveal such a personal side of his life to a probable stranger.

'It's me. Thea,' she said. 'Sorry to interrupt.'

'No problem. We'd just about finished anyway.'

'What was the story?'

'*Charlotte's Web* for about the tenth time. I keep suggesting they're too old for it now, but maybe they're not.'

'Have you seen the film?'

'Once. It's dreadful. Not a patch on the book.'

'Oh – I quite liked it. Anyway,' she gave herself a little shake, 'I've arranged for you to meet Donny here tomorrow afternoon, if you can manage it.'

'Right. What time exactly?'

'Just after three would be good.'

'Should be possible. Where are you?'

'It's a fair way from Broad Campden, I'm afraid.' And she carefully explained how to find Cranham and the Manor.

'Sounds very grand,' he said.

'Oh, it is. I'm sure you're going to like it.'

'And is everything nice and calm for a change?'

'So far,' she laughed, touching the wooden surface of the telephone shelf.

'Good,' he said; then, as if remembering something, he quickly curtailed the conversation with a brief, 'See you tomorrow, then.'

The dog situation raised a host of imponderable questions about the relationship between mankind and other species. 'Leaving it to nature' had very little meaning when it came to creatures that had long ago learnt to depend entirely on human beings for their survival. A cat in the woods would raise her kittens with little trouble; a dog had lost almost all its survival instincts. Which meant that any human coming across a struggling mother dog carried a responsibility to help. It was a debt due from one species to another, and it almost made Thea tearful to contemplate this stark truth. The burden was a heavy one, which a great many people dropped without proper thought. It was also not the first time Thea had been called upon to face it. Dogs, somehow, seemed to be her nemesis. Like it or not, she repeatedly found herself caring for them, one way or another.

There was still just enough light to enable her to return to the burrow when she got back to Cranham. Thoughts of the hungry and thirsty mother decided her to do it, so she shut Hepzie in the house and set out with the bulging carrier bag. She had planned to cook the meat before presenting it, but on consideration, she concluded that the dog would not be fussy.

She had made a careful note of the way, marking one or two distinctive trees as she had returned from her earlier walk. Even so, it was difficult in the twilight to recognise any landmarks.

She carried a supermarket bag containing a pound of raw mince and a litre-bottle of milk, with a plastic bowl to pour it into – which she'd have to take back with her, for fear of leaving telltale evidence. There was no sign of human life, but birds were singing overhead, acknowledging the end of the day. There would surely be badgers and foxes emerging from their lairs any time now.

It was quite a different world from the one most people knew, not so much hidden as completely ignored. She had heard mocking remarks about the way Australians clustered around the very edges of their terrifying country, facing steadfastly out to sea, their backs to the incomprehensible desert. But Europeans were not so different. They were uneasy with their wild places too.

Sliding down the steep bumpy slope, she finally located a tree she recognised, and turned right into undergrowth which seemed to have become taller and thicker than a few hours earlier. There were no sounds of cheeping pups or rustling night creatures until she had walked into an even darker patch of woodland, when she saw the fallen tree and heard a muffled whine.

The dog could smell the meat, she assumed. Quickly, she approached the burrow and took the food from the bag. The dog's sharp nose sniffed eagerly from a safe distance, and then darted forward and gobbled Thea's offering almost in one gulp. Belatedly, Thea remembered that farm dogs were almost invariably fed with dry complete food in convenient small shapes, raw meat a rare delicacy. Would it upset this poor animal's digestion, she wondered. Too late to worry about it now.

The milk also disappeared in seconds, the urgent lapping somewhat inefficiently scattering drops on all sides. When it was finished, she gave Thea a grateful smile and retreated into her hole, where the puppies were making their odd undoglike sounds.

'Bye, then,' said Thea, beginning to worry about getting lost in the deep dark woods, and glad she had left her own dog behind. Far from leading her home, Hepzie would be quite liable to get lost in the shadows and delay things further.

Her own clumsy footsteps sounded loud in her ears as she stumbled back to the main track. Dry sticks cracked beneath her feet, and young holly trees swished as she passed. Last year's dead leaves still lay thickly on the woodland floor, crunching when trodden on. She sounded like a small elephant blundering around. It should hardly have been a surprise when she met a person on the track, head pushed forward, listening to Thea's approach.

It gave her a nasty turn, all the same. The features were indistinct in the dying light, but they did not look very friendly.

'What in the world are you doing?' came a cut-glass voice.

'Oh! I got a bit lost, that's all. Sorry if I startled you.'

'Lost? Startled?' The voice rang out on a high indignant note. 'Don't be ridiculous.'

Something connected in Thea's mind, and she

thought she might be able to put a name to this person. 'I bet you're Edwina,' she said recklessly.

'And if I am, I fear you have the advantage of me.' It was like talking to somebody out of a P.G. Wodehouse story.

'I'm Thea Osborne, Harriet Young's house-sitter. Donny told me about you.'

'Well, you've jumped to quite the wrong conclusion, young woman. I am in fact not Edwina, but her sister. I dare say Donald neglected to mention me. He generally hopes to eradicate me from existence by the sheer force of his will. We enjoy what you might call a mutual antipathy.'

'Oh,' said Thea.

'My name is Thyrza Hastings. I live close by, in a house that has been in my family for three hundred years.'

Is that all? Thea thought impertinently, well aware that there were still families in England who could add several more centuries than that to their tenure. And who would take it over after Thyrza, she wondered inconsequentially. The details of inheritance was a pet interest, leading as it often did to people behaving badly.

'Pleased to meet you,' she said, offering her hand, whilst trying to hide the carrier bag containing the plastic bowl behind her back.

Thyrza Hastings took her hand fleetingly, as if impatient at the irrelevant gesture. Thea took a closer look at the woman's face, settling on the Cupid's bow mouth. 'Are you related to a man called Philippe?' she asked boldly. 'You look rather like him.'

'He's my son. How very observant of you. Very few people can detect a likeness. But then they only look at things like hair and height.' Her hair was thick and frizzy, forming a dark-grey halo around her head. Philippe's had been brown and floppy.

'Does he inherit the ancestral home, then?' she asked with a smile, hoping she didn't sound too rude. 'I suppose he lives with you?' The stereotype of the spoilt only son of a dominant mother seemed to fit the man with the poodle rather well.

Thyrza bridled, her neck stretching as she pulled her head back. 'I do not consider that any of your business,' she snapped. 'I can't imagine why it would matter to you.'

'You're quite right,' Thea conceded. 'I'm incorrigibly nosy, that's all. I like to get a sense of where everybody fits, in a small place like this.'

'Perhaps you ought to bear in mind that curiosity killed the cat,' the woman warned. 'Now I think we should both be getting home. It's nearly dark.'

'It's not half past nine yet, is it? I thought it would stay light a bit longer than this.'

'It's the trees,' said Thyrza. 'And it's cloudy tonight.'

80

'Of course.'

They walked along side by side, without speaking for a few minutes. Thea was glad of the company, and grateful for the absence of searching questions as to exactly why she was in the woods all alone on a darkening evening. Her companion appeared preoccupied with her own thoughts as she marched sturdily along the track. No hint of any sisterly echo of the bad hip that Donny had said afflicted Edwina. 'Do you and your sister live together?' she asked, as they finally left the woods and emerged onto the road down to the village. Then she added meekly, 'Sorry. I'm still not minding my own business, am I? I don't think I can help it – I find new people so interesting, you see.'

The woman had evidently thawed somewhat during the walk. She snorted, half laugh, half impatient protest. 'Heaven forbid!' she replied. 'She lives on the other side of the common from me. She and I are very different.' Thea thought she could detect a note of wistfulness in these words.

'And she's visiting her daughter,' Thea recalled. 'Donny said something about that.'

'Due back any time now. They'll be glad to be shot of her – might even persuade her to set off this evening. Her duties expire when half-term finishes, but she insists on staying one more day, to help get the house straight or some such nonsense.'

81

They were approaching the edge of the wood, where the road ran through the centre of Cranham. 'I go that way,' said Thyrza Hastings, tilting her chin to the right.

'And I'm straight over the road,' said Thea, sounding more certain than she really was. The light was fading fast and she had emerged onto a different point from the one she knew.

'You can see the Manor from the corner there,' said the woman, with a glimmer of humour. 'It's easy to lose your bearings around here.'

'Thank you. Maybe I'll see you again.'

'Maybe you will. Goodnight, then, Thea Osborne.'

'Goodnight,' said Thea, impressed that her name had been so accurately noted.

She passed Donny's Lodge as she turned into the driveway of Hollywell Manor. There was a light on downstairs, and the front window was open. She glimpsed, without taking any proper notice, the back of a car parked around the side of the house. In the twilight, she gained no clear impression of its colour or make. Voices floated from the open window, which she took to be the television at first. The absence of close neighbours made it unobjectionable to anybody, she supposed, although it was rather loud.

'No, I will not!' came a man's raised voice.

'I've told you a thousand times, damn it.'

'For heaven's sake,' a woman replied. 'Calm down, will you?'

'Don't patronise me!' he almost screamed. 'Don't be so bloody condescending all the time.'

Thea realised that it was Donny's shrill old-man tones she was hearing. Presumably Jemima had come to see him, and an argument had developed. Well, she thought – it's none of my business, and she hurried up to the Manor, where her eager dog welcomed her as if she'd been away for a month.

CHAPTER FIVE

She ended the day with a glass of wine that she felt had been well earned. The geckoes were stirring when she paid them a bedtime visit. 'I suppose this is the start of your day, not the end,' she murmured to them. A greeny-grey tail flicked at her from behind a large leaf. She activated the water spray over the somnolent eggs, imagining the tiny reptiles curled inside them. It was sweet to think of the new lives quietly incubating, unaware of their future existence in captivity, at the whim of feckless humans. 'Sleep tight,' she crooned softly to them.

Tuesday morning was another uncertain day, weather-wise. High white cloud almost covered the sky, but there were encouraging patches of blue here and there. Thea and her dog had woken early, slowly surfacing to greet the morning and learn more about the people of Cranham. Outside, all was quiet and still.

Drew, she remembered, was coming that afternoon. The fresh-faced undertaker, who looked younger than his thirty-eight years. Drew was witty and bright, the best possible fun to talk to. It would be a treat to see him again.

She pottered through breakfast before taking a circuit of the garden with Hepzie, her mind more or less empty as she savoured the new day. In a while, she would mash up some banana for the geckoes and do a bit of dusting in the big living room. She had bought everything she needed for the next day or two – bread, biscuits, milk, eggs and more meat for herself and the dog in the woods.

The dog! That was her most urgent consideration for the coming morning. She should take more food for it – a much more difficult task in broad daylight, with the risk of being seen by passing walkers or cyclists. And the necessity of leaving Hepzie behind meant that she should go for another walk with her own dog, in a different direction. Suddenly she felt much busier, having forgotten for the moment her new responsibility.

Most dogs only fed once a day, in her experience. Perhaps, then, the new mother could wait at least until the afternoon. That would leave

Thea with a pleasingly lazy morning, reading, emailing one or two people and not much else.

By nine-thirty she was activating her laptop and preparing to send short updates of her whereabouts to her daughter and mother. None of her family understood or approved of her career as a house-sitter. Jessica had joined her a few times, becoming involved in the adventures that so persistently befell Thea when she intruded into the complications that seemed to characterise small English communities. As a newly trained police officer, Jessica was often torn between roles and alarmed at her mother's cavalier approach. But the girl was currently distracted by a demanding relationship, with little attention to spare her mother. 'Besides,' Thea had assured her, 'I've demonstrated by now that I can look after myself, haven't I?'

The front door stood open, weak sunshine brightening the hallway, which Thea could see from the living room. She liked open doors and fresh air – something she was generally able to ensure in the Cotswold houses she looked after. Double glazing and complicated locks made her impatient, the way they created airtight boxes in which she felt suffocated. Whilst doing her best to follow specific instructions, she was quite relaxed about the matter of security in general. This infuriated Jessica, who reminded her mother that there had surely been enough incidents of violence and criminality around her for her to have learnt to keep herself safe. Thea just shrugged and said if somebody was intent on attacking her, a locked door probably wasn't going to stop them. She pointed out that hardly anybody had offered her direct aggression, and that she was simply in the way most of the time. The vacuum created when somebody left their house often gave rise to opportunistic felonies, it was true, but Thea's role to date had mainly been to bear witness and make sensible suggestions to the police.

Or so she chose to characterise her career thus far. She conveniently overlooked the times when she had been seriously frightened, when the animals in her care had come to harm and her suggestions proved to be much less sensible than she cared to recall.

Frowning at her computer screen, she composed a buoyant message for her daughter that would allay any lingering worries the girl might have. *Weather tantalising, work not a bit arduous, great walks and much to explore.* A bit telegrammatic, she decided, and added a few embellishments before sending it off.

'Are you there?' came a female voice from the hallway. 'Hey – I need somebody, quickly.'

'In here,' Thea called back. 'What's the matter?'

Jemima Hobson was standing in the doorway, breathing heavily. She must have run up the drive from the Lodge – a short but rather steep avenue. 'It's Dad. I can't rouse him.'

Thea did not react very quickly. She glanced at the large antique clock on the mantelpiece, thinking perhaps the old man had merely slept in. It was a few minutes after ten. 'What do you mean? Have you been into the house?'

Jemima shook her head. 'The door's locked. I banged and shouted, but there's no sign of him.'

'Haven't you got a key?'

'It's at home. I never normally need to use it – he leaves the back door on the latch.'

'Gosh! Isn't he worried about burglars?' She heard her own hypocrisy, in this question. Why should she assume that Donny was any more paranoid than she was herself?

Jemima shrugged impatiently. 'Not very, no. He hasn't got anything of value in the house. I imagine any marauders would make directly for the Manor, don't you?'

Which wasn't much more secure, Thea acknowledged silently. 'Could he have gone out?' she asked.

'He only really comes up here, these days, unless Edwina takes him somewhere.'

'Has he got a car?'

'Yes, but he doesn't drive any more.' Jemima

danced agitatedly. 'Please come with me. We'll have to break in.'

'I don't know how useful I can be,' Thea demurred. 'I'm not especially good at bashing doors in.'

'At least you can be a witness,' said the woman.

'We could phone him,' Thea suggested. 'That should wake him up, if he's overslept.'

'I tried that already. Honestly, I am very worried. This has never happened before. He seemed perfectly all right yesterday.'

'Well, I'd better shut the dog in, I suppose.' She followed Jemima outside, and closed the front door firmly. Only then did she remember the argument she had heard the previous evening. 'Were you here last night?' she asked.

'No. Why?'

'I heard him shouting, and a woman answering him.'

Jemima barely seemed to hear her. 'Oh, come on. We have to get back. Tell me as we go.' She began trotting down the drive towards the Lodge.

Thea persisted. 'It was about half past nine, I suppose. I was walking past and heard raised voices. He sounded quite cross. I thought it was you. I saw a car—'

'I was not here last night,' said Jemima, loudly. She slowed her pace and turned to meet Thea's eye. 'I was at home.'

'OK, I believe you,' said Thea. 'I don't suppose it matters, anyway.'

'Let's hope not. Now – I'm going to bang as loud as I can. If that doesn't work, we can go round the back and break the glass in the door.'

'Did you say he doesn't usually lock the door?'

'Right. Not the back, anyway. The front's got a Yale lock, which he mostly clicks down before bed. But the back just has a bolt, and he never puts it across. I couldn't believe it when I couldn't get in.'

A lot of Thea's energy was going into resisting all the insistent thoughts that were crowding into her mind. She had been here before – an old man lying on the floor, killed by an unknown attacker. She did not want to find the same thing again. She liked Donny and had looked forward to talking to him every day of her stay. 'I hope he's all right,' she said.

'So do I. He's been threatening to take things into his own hands, but I never thought he'd really do it.'

'What – you think he's killed himself?' The idea had not occurred to Thea. 'Surely not! He was in such a good mood yesterday.'

'The doors are locked,' Jemima repeated. 'That's what worries me most.'

She banged, as promised, and called 'Dad!' at a deafening volume. Then she fell quiet, and they both listened intently. Not a sound could be heard.

'That's it, then. Come on.' Jemima led the way around the back. Thea noticed fleetingly that the car she had seen the previous evening was still there.

The back door had a glass pane in its upper half, and without ceremony, Jemima took a brick to it. Then she reached in carefully and pulled back the bolt that secured the door. The women moved silently through the kitchen, and out into a narrow hallway that led to a living room and then a bedroom at the back of the single-storey house.

'Dad!' Jemima yelled again.

There was no option but to proceed along to the bedroom, after a cursory glance into the front room. Thea followed Jemima's lead, her mind almost blank as she awaited the outcome of their search.

'This is his room,' Jemima announced, unnecessarily. She pushed the door, which was half closed, and peered in. 'Oh God!' she cried. 'This is just what I was afraid of.'

It sounded odd to Thea – a stilted remark which did not match the situation at all. She pushed Jemima aside and looked for herself. Donny lay tidily on the bed, dressed in striped pyjamas, uncovered by sheet or blanket, arms by his sides, and a plastic bag over his head, fastened tightly around his neck with wide, brown, sticky parcel tape. A purple-hued face was inside the all-too-transparent bag, looking nothing like a human being. The bag was tightly welded to the skin around the nose and mouth, and Thea could see smooth cheeks and chin. *At least somebody shaved him*, she thought.

A lot of clashing thoughts occurred to her at once. Donny had killed himself, as he had reportedly threatened to do over the past months or years. The person he had argued with the previous evening had somehow driven him to do it. He must have drugged himself before putting the bag over his head, because nobody could take suffocation so quietly as he appeared to have done. And his daughter Mimm was acting strangely. And she heard a voice in her head saying: *Why doesn't he just put an end to his misery, and do us all a favour?* Philippe, son of Thyrza, would be satisfied, at least. As would Thyrza herself, if her own report of 'animosity' could be taken seriously.

'We shouldn't move him,' said Thea.

'No. He really is dead, you think?'

Thea silently pointed to a dark patch at Donny's crotch. The relaxation of all bodily muscles meant that bladder and bowel had released their contents just after death. Beyond that, the unnerving stillness in the room gave Mimm her answer.

'Yes, he's dead,' she said. 'Poor old Dad. I honestly didn't think he would ever do it. Not alone, anyway.'

More flickering thoughts crossed Thea's mind along with a range of feelings. Helpless sadness was the primary one, and a violent regret that she had somehow permitted this to happen. You were supposed to stop people from killing themselves, striving to convince them that there was still hope, still pleasure to be had from life. All the media controversy about assisted suicide, which came and went through the years, altering emphasis and demanding a variety of major changes to the law, came back to her. In her teens, there had been a lot of discussion about the best methods of killing yourself – a topic that adolescents found deeply fascinating – with pills and plastic bags a favourite. People who helped their terminally ill relatives to die were advised to take this route. More recently, and quite bizarrely, the more affluent would-be suicides went to an expensive killing clinic in Switzerland to drink a toxic mix they could surely have acquired in the UK if they made the effort. But the main point always seemed to be that there ought to be another person involved, even when the central figure was entirely capable of mixing a drink and swallowing it, or pulling a bag over their own heads – as poor Donny had evidently done at some point during the night. It was a taboo subject surrounded by myths and emotions that carried very little rationality. It was assumed that nobody wanted to die alone, and yet the majority of people in hospitals and nursing homes hung on until the last visitor had left, before allowing themselves to sink into oblivion. Conversely, it was assumed that there were a lot of fates worse than death, and it should be made easier for people to curtail the process and cut to the final stage more quickly than nature intended. In Thea's experience, this was a false assumption. As far as she could see, people clung to life ferociously when it came to the crunch.

The arguments flashed through her mind, fragmented and contradictory, and all accomplished in a few seconds, like a dream that feels as if it lasted all night.

'I don't believe he wanted to die,' she said softly.

So why had Donny not clawed at the bag, ripping it from his face? Had he wound the tape so tightly because he knew he might change his mind? She tried to imagine the sequence of events, only to find several difficulties. If he had possessed the strength and clarity of mind to pull the bag down over his face, and fasten it so securely, this strength must have quickly deserted him when, after four of five breaths, there was no more air in the bag for him to breathe.

'*Was* he alone, I wonder?' she muttered aloud.

Jemima made a kind of croak. 'What do you mean? Of *course* he was.'

'I'm sure you're right,' said Thea quickly. 'We'll have to call the police. They'll bring their own doctor.'

'There won't be a post-mortem, will there? He had a horror of post-mortems. It was all part of his general loathing of medical procedures.'

Thea remembered Donny's anguished description of his daughter's body after the heart transplant. Something about being cut about like a piece of meat. 'I'm afraid there will,' she said. 'If ever there was a case for one, then this is it.' And wouldn't Donny have known that, she wondered. Wouldn't that have been one of the main reasons for avoiding this sort of death for himself?

Jemima was making no move to call the authorities. She was rooted to a spot about a foot from her father's body, her hands clenching spasmodically. 'Can we take that bag off his face?' she asked.

'Better not.'

'Why? It isn't the scene of a crime, is it? There won't be detectives and SOCOs and all that stuff.'

'There'll be an inquest,' said Thea. 'They'll want an exact description of how he was found.'

'It's so awful,' said Jemima flatly. 'Just utterly awful. I can't take it in.'

'You said it was what you were afraid of,' Thea reminded her. 'As if you weren't surprised.'

'He *talked* so much about killing himself. He was morbid about it, discussing all the different ways of doing it. He gave me nightmares.'

'Suicides hardly ever think about what it's like for the people finding them.'

'No. He didn't think about that at all.'

'But it looks as if he went ahead and did it. All on his own.'

'Yes.'

The women exchanged uncomfortable glances, nodding at each other's words, glancing back at the dead Donny, breathing quick shallow breaths. Jemima's hands were shaking, and Thea felt surging waves of anxiety in her guts. The death of a nice old man such as Donny was quite enough to account for such distress – of course it was.

Somehow hours passed, and although it was not the first time Thea had been closely involved in a sudden death, she could not remember ever being in such a state of paralysis since her husband Carl had been killed in a car crash. She could not decide what to think; her emotions were so tangled they seemed to cancel each other out. Donny had said he wanted to die, and yet he had seemed so completely alive that nobody had quite believed him. What he had really wanted, surely, had been the same as everyone wanted – an easy, painless death, while still functioning mentally. A chance to say last words to those one loves, and set at least a few affairs in order. Not to dwindle by inches in a nursing home lounge, staring at the television and the same blank faces for months on end.

The police had taken everything at face value: an old man with a debilitating illness, who had frequently spoken of his wish to die, had taken a well-worn route to oblivion. 'Did he leave a note?' asked the uniformed sergeant who attended the scene.

'I haven't found one,' said Jemima with a frown. 'That's a good point, actually. I would have expected us all to have a letter from him. It's the sort of thing he would do.'

The police doctor made his tests before declaring life extinct and calling for the undertaker's men to remove the body to the mortuary in Gloucester. Jemima used the Lodge phone to call Edwina, who was difficult to persuade to stay away. 'No, you shouldn't come,' she said three times. 'I don't want you to.' Then she called her husband on the farm to explain her prolonged absence.

'And Toby,' she sighed to herself. 'I suppose I'll have to tell Toby.'

Thea's raised eyebrows were enough to elicit clarification. 'My sister's husband. He was quite fond of Dad, even though they argued all the time. He's kept in touch, of course, since Cecilia died.'

Thea had hung around, thinking Jemima would appreciate the company. The atmosphere in the Lodge was cold with the fact of death in general and the sadness of Donny's departure in particular. She missed him already, despite their brief acquaintance.

Jemima performed a hurried search for a possible suicide note, finding nothing. Thea wrestled with the dilemma as to whether or not to report to the police the argument she had heard the previous evening. It was surely relevant, even crucially important, but the more she rewound it in her mind, the less sure she was of what she had actually heard. It could even have been the television, she told herself, while knowing it had not been anything of the sort. Jemima had reacted as if being accused of something when Thea had told her about it again. The car she had assumed belonged to the visiting woman was actually Donny's. Nothing was clear, and she badly wanted to avoid making things worse. The police had gone, as had Donny, with the undertaker's men. Thea's rumbling stomach alerted her to the passage of time.

'Gosh – it's nearly two o'clock!' she noticed with a shock. 'That's incredible.'

'Don't hang about on my account,' said Jemima. 'I'll have to be going, anyway. But the house isn't secure, now I've broken that window.'

'I thought you said Donny never locked it, anyway. It isn't likely to be burgled now.'

'It might, when the news gets out that he's gone. They watch out for that sort of thing, the bastards.'

'They watch for the day and time of the funeral, but I think they'd expect too much coming and going over the next few days for it to be a good prospect.' She entertained an image of lurking shadowy criminals, watching for a chance to steal the mahogany davenport and antique clock that seemed to be the only things Donny possessed of any value. 'And to be honest, I doubt whether they'd think it worth the trouble, seeing how little there is to nick.'

'That davenport was valued at fifteen hundred quid, twelve years ago,' said Jemima, eyeing the thing speculatively. 'Not that it's ever been very useful.'

'I have a feeling they're out of fashion at the moment. There hasn't been one on *Antiques Roadshow* for ages.'

Jemima laughed, before clamping her mouth shut and widening her eyes. She moaned an inarticulate self-reproach, which Thea recognised. It would not be until after the funeral that Donny's relatives felt they could smile or laugh normally again. Even in a culture almost devoid of ritual, there were powerful protocols surrounding the whole business of death.

'I'll have to eat something,' Thea announced. 'I'm starving. Do you want to come up to the Manor and have a sandwich? And a cup of tea.'

'That'd be nice. I'm not hungry, but my throat's parched.'

'Should we try to find a number for Harriet and tell her what's happened, do you think?' This was far from the first time that Thea had been obliged to ask such a question. 'She did say, loud and clear, that she was not to be contacted.'

'No, I don't think so. There's nothing she can do, and she might well be back before the funeral, anyway. I imagine it'll take a couple of weeks to get everything sorted.'

'She's sure to want to be at the funeral.'

Jemima shifted irritably. 'I can't worry about Harriet now,' she snapped. 'I've got my own family to see to.'

'Right,' Thea nodded understandingly. 'And my dog's going to be wanting a walk. Half the day's gone already.'

It was only then that she remembered the dog in the woods, by association with her own spaniel. The stab of guilt at her desertion, however irrational, was the strongest emotion she had felt all day. Quickly she persuaded herself that the animal would be perfectly all right after its meal the day before, but the guilt would not go away. 'I'll have to do it soon,' she said to Jemima, worriedly.

'What on earth for? She can relieve herself in the garden here, can't she? How can it be that important?'

Thea could not disclose the secret of the collie in the woods, especially to Jemima, who might know the owner and betray the trusting animal. Neither could she quell her own sense of responsibility. It had something to do with the new lives, even more significant now that somebody had died. In a jumbled kind of way, she felt there was a balance in operation – that it might make Donny's death less dreadful if the puppies survived. At the same time, she knew this was an outrageous attitude – she did not question that a human being outweighed a dog by a million to one. More – it was not a comparison that could be made with any numbers. And yet, somewhere deep inside her, it was a real compulsion. If it lay within her power, she was going to ensure that those dogs survived.

Fortunately, Jemima was increasingly aware of pressure on her own time. She drained a large mug of tea, and accepted another, before trotting off to the car she had been forced to move to halfway up the drive, to make way for the official vehicles that had arrived through the morning.

'I am really sorry about your father,' said Thea, on the doorstep. 'He was a lovely man.'

'Don't!' pleaded Jemima. 'Don't start me off now, for God's sake.'

And she was gone.

CHAPTER SIX

Thea treacherously shut Hepzie in the house again, having collected more mince and milk and biscuits. Feeling furtive, she hurried across the road and into the woods, meeting nobody on the way. Children back at school, fathers and mothers off up the motorway to an office in a large town or city somewhere, the whole place abandoned for the day – the chances of seeing anyone were reassuringly small.

The dog must have heard her coming, and was whining with the familiar mixture of worry and welcome. The black nose came forward and the eyes gleamed like those of a wild animal. But this was a sheepdog, bred for millennia to obey human beings, and defer to them in every way. The deception practised on her master was extreme, and the source of considerable guilt. The conflicting duties of motherhood and work were afflicting her severely.

'Poor old girl,' Thea sympathised, understanding much of this. 'What's to become of you? I don't expect I'm doing you any favours, in the long run.'

As if to reward her for the compassion, the dog backed into her hole, twisting her head behind her, and reappeared with a wriggling pup in her gentle mouth.

'Oh!' Thea accepted the offering with due reverence. The puppy was blind, with a vivid pink nose and large splayed paws. The coat was black and slightly ridged, as if promising to grow long and fluffy in the future. 'Who's your daddy, then, I wonder?'

She handed the baby back, and extracted from her bag the provisions she had brought. The mother dog took it delicately, plainly less ravenous than the day before, although thirsty enough to make short work of the milk.

Thea lingered a while, reluctant to abandon the little family to their fate, whatever that might be. The death of Donny Davis had shaken her badly, and made her wonder about her own situation. It was possible that Harriet might decide to return prematurely, if the funeral was scheduled for a date before she was due home. She had persuaded herself that it was not her place to try to get in touch with Harriet, however.

Funeral! The word hovered in her mind, and only then did she remember the appointment with Drew. She looked at her watch, to find it was three-fifteen. 'Bloody hell!' she muttered, and scrambled heedlessly away, hoping that Drew would not have given up and gone away before she reached him. Somehow she must have missed the barely visible track she had made for herself on her trips to and fro, through the undergrowth to the established path. It should take no more than five minutes, but instead she found herself still negotiating bumpy terrain strewn with sharp brambles and debris from the trees after ten. The walking wasn't difficult, but it certainly wasn't the way that everybody else used to navigate through the woods.

Ridiculous, she told herself, to get lost in an English wood in the middle of summer and feel that determined swirl of panic in your guts as a result. The urgency of having to find Drew made it much worse. She ought to give herself time to think, to locate the sun, which would indicate a westerly direction and use all her senses to identify a familiar landmark. But all the big beech trees looked the same, and the sun was nowhere to be found. Even if she'd had Hepzie with her, she doubted things would be easier. The spaniel had no concept of being lost, assuming her mistress to be omniscient, so strange behaviour like walking in circles ten yards from the usual path must have a human logic that she was not expected to question.

Then a dog trotted up to her, like the materialisation of a dream, and sniffed her legs in a polite and friendly manner. It was the grey poodle she had met two days before. It turned and walked sedately along in front of her, clearly intending her to follow.

'Heavens! You're an intelligent creature, aren't you?' Thea congratulated it, as she emerged onto a track that she guessed led directly to the village. 'Where's your master, then?'

'Hiya!' called a voice from some distance behind her. 'Has Jasper been doing his rescuing act again? He always thinks people must be lost if he finds them in these woods.'

'He was right,' she shouted back. 'I had no idea where I was going.'

'That'll make his day.' Philippe was hurrying towards her, smiling broadly. 'Make sure you show him how grateful you are.'

Thea bent and fondled the topknot on the dog's head, wondering fleetingly what poodles looked like without the attentions of a beauty parlour. Was it a law that you had to keep them trimmed and primped if you owned one? 'Clever boy,' she praised him. 'I might have been there for ages. It never occurred to me to come this way.'

'It's easy to lose your bearings,' said Philippe tolerantly.

'Now I have to rush, I'm afraid,' Thea apologised. 'I should have been back half an hour ago, or more. I completely forgot I had somebody coming.'

'Sad about poor old Donny,' he said, almost casually, stopping her in her tracks. 'Didn't think he'd do it so soon, not with Harriet away.'

'Perhaps he thought it would save her the distress.'

He gave her a probing look from beneath the brim of his silly hat. 'Perhaps he did,' he said, obviously not believing it for a moment.

'I met your mother. It must have been yesterday.'

'So I gather. Apparently you think I look like her, perish the thought. Now go. Your guest won't wait for ever.'

Drew was sitting in his car, reading a magazine and showing no sign of annoyance or impatience.

'Did something happen?' he asked mildly, as she panted up the drive to him. 'Or did I get the time wrong?'

She looked at him, unconsciously comparing the face she last saw two and a half months ago with the reality before her. Not a lot had changed. 'I am terribly sorry,' she puffed. 'I forgot about you.'

'I see. And where's my potential new customer?'

She let her breathing settle down before replying. Drew got out of his car and waited. 'He died in the night, I'm afraid,' she said.

He didn't laugh, or curse his bad luck, or gasp in amazement. He merely raised one eyebrow, and held her gaze for a full fifteen seconds. 'Oh?' he said.

'It looks like suicide. It *was* suicide. A plastic bag over his head. He must have decided he couldn't leave it any longer.'

'Poor man. And poor you. You don't have much luck with this house-sitting stuff, do you?'

'I'm not really involved in this,' she said with a jerky motion of one hand, not wanting to hear such a sentiment uttered out loud. 'He just came up here for coffee once or twice.'

'Hm,' said Drew sceptically. 'So what now? Shall I just go away again?'

'Of course not. Stay as long as you can. I've hardly eaten anything today, so I'm planning to cook a big supper and have it early. When do you have to go?'

'I should be home by dark, if I can. That would mean leaving here by eight or so, I suppose.'

'You found it all right, then?' she asked belatedly. 'It's nice, isn't it?'

'I took one or two wrong turns, but it wasn't too bad. And yes, it's lovely. A proper traditional manor house. What's it like inside?'

'Come and see. It's actually a bit of a fake. A Victorian copy of a manor house. Some local magnate built it, probably with the advice and even help of William Morris, in a much older style. The windows are wrong, look – too big for a genuine medieval house.'

She led him into the house, pushing away the effusive spaniel, who was even more excited than usual thanks to the scent of puppy on Thea's hands. Drew gave his full attention to the features of the house, while admitting he knew all too little about architecture. 'Wood panelling,' he observed. 'Is it handmade?'

'Hand-carved, yes,' said Thea, pointing to the intricate designs. 'There's no machine that could manage that.'

'It feels expensive. Who's the owner?'

'She's called Harriet Young. American. I don't know where her money came from. She's really nice.'

The tour of the downstairs rooms was a diversion from the distressing details of Donny's death. Thea could sense a simmering sympathy in Drew, wanting her to share with him the trauma of the morning. She resisted because she did not want to be left holding all the miserable feelings she only could intensify by talking about them, once he'd gone back to his family. Also because she did not really know him, and had no right to drag him into a story that was nothing to do with him.

He read her thoughts. 'He was almost my client,' he said. 'I get the feeling I'd have liked him. And I'm upset because he probably won't get the funeral he wanted now.'

She frowned. 'I hadn't thought of that,' she admitted. 'I could be a witness to the fact that he definitely would have been interested in using you for his burial. But his family will probably fight it,' she added defeatedly. 'They don't like the idea. They want him to be buried in the churchyard here. Jemima was very cross with me for contacting you without asking her first. And that was *before* he died. Goodness knows what she would say now.'

'I don't think she'll have changed her mind,' he said easily.

'We didn't tell her about you coming today. It was a secret assignation.'

Drew tutted under his breath. 'Bad idea,' he reproached her. 'It's important to have everybody on the same side.'

'Maybe Donny realised that. Maybe that's why he gave up.'

Too late she realised her defences had collapsed, and there was no stopping the wave of sadness and shock that had been building since the discovery of Donny's body. 'Oh, Drew! That poor old man!' she burst out. 'He still had such a zest for life – everyone could see it. He had a twinkle in his eye, and it was easy to make him laugh. What must have happened to send him over the edge like that? Could it have been *my* fault in some way?'

Drew's eyebrows went up. 'Doesn't sound like any suicide I've come across,' he said. 'Is it absolutely certain that it was self-inflicted?'

'I don't know. It looks like it, yes. And I suppose it always comes as a huge surprise when anybody actually does it.'

'It doesn't, oddly enough,' he contradicted gently. 'Usually there's been a long slow build-up that's quite obvious to all concerned. They deny it to themselves beforehand, but afterwards, they admit they could see it coming.'

'Well, it's not like that with Donny. Although Mimm did say it was what she was afraid of, when she first found him.'

Thea's frown deepened. The story had layers of confusion, contradiction and puzzlement to it. 'I really did not get the impression that he was at all ready to die, despite what he said.'

He held her gaze. 'So what are you saying?'

'Nothing. Honestly, nothing. Except . . .'

'What?'

'I passed his house quite late last night, and

heard him shouting at somebody. A woman. Mimm says it wasn't her. I saw a car and thought he had a visitor, but the car's his, I think. It's still there today. He was protesting at being bullied – bossed about – something like that. I remember now – it was "patronising". He said, "Don't be so bloody patronising." Not a very dreadful thing to say, I suppose.'

'Did you tell the police? They always ask who was last to see the person alive.'

She shook her head. 'They weren't interested in me. His daughter dealt with all that.'

'But it's surely important.'

'I don't know. He's got a lady friend, Edwina, and she's got a sister, Thyrza, and *she*'s got a son, Philippe. I could go on, but they're the main players. They all appear to know him well and at least Edwina cares about him and visits him a lot. The other two don't seem to have been so enamoured of him. I haven't met Edwina. She's a force of nature, according to Donny.'

He listened and nodded, but asked no more questions. It felt to Thea as if he was being careful with her, and perhaps with himself as well. 'Are you all right?' she asked suddenly. 'What's been happening in Broad Campden?'

He sighed. 'Oh, it's just a typical British legal mess. Everybody can see what has to be done, but some perverse spirit always gets in the way. I'm not sure it'll ever get operational. I'm not even sure I want it to.'

Drew's alternative burial service was based in Somerset, where he lived with his wife, children and business partner, Maggs. He had recently been given the opportunity to expand into a new branch in the Cotswolds, which he could hardly refuse, despite the complicated implications for the whole family.

'Why not?'

'Karen isn't well. The children are quite happy at their local school. Maggs says there's no way she's going to move to a village even more remote and quiet than where she lives now, even though she's excited about the business prospects at Broad Campden.'

'Did you ask her to? Move, I mean.'

He snorted. 'Not at all. She could run North Staverton, and I could set up the new place. She doesn't see it that way, for some reason.'

'You could double your income, if it worked out.'

'In theory, after a few years, maybe. But there are still things I haven't thought about properly. It takes ages to establish a reputation and earn the trust of all the people who matter. Nursing homes, for a start. They're very slow to absorb a new idea or transfer their loyalties to a new business. To be honest, I'm almost at the point of deciding to let it all go.'

Thea's sigh was even deeper than his had been. 'What a shame,' she sympathised. 'What's wrong with Karen?'

'Same as usual. They did another scan on her head three weeks ago, and couldn't find anything to worry about. But she gets awful headaches, and something's not right. I hardly know her sometimes.'

'What does she say about moving?'

'She won't even think about it.' His brow creased. 'If I try to remember how she was before the injury, I'm forced to accept that she's really not the same person at all. She functions well enough if everything's kept simple and superficial, but if a big change is threatened, or a big decision has to be made, she just retreats into herself like a child.'

'Sounds more like somebody who feels really frightened,' said Thea.

'Right! That's it. I haven't even told her I'm coming up here today. It'll worry her far too much.'

'But surely you can't think about moving if she's like that? How can you? And where does she think you are today, anyway?'

'I didn't really say.' His look was forlorn. 'I keep assuming she'll get better. Or maybe a move will jolt her out of this state she's in. But probably I'll have to give it all up,' he said again.

'Let's hope not,' said Thea doubtfully. 'That would be a waste.'

'The worst thing,' he burst out, 'is not being able to *talk* to anybody about it. Maggs is too protective of Karen to let me make any hard and fast arrangements, which is a real pain. The business is stagnating, while we dither about how to carry on. Other alternative funeral people are setting up and doing quite well, even though they charge double what I do. Those willow coffins are extortionate, for one thing. And the public are being stitched up just as badly as they always have been, even if it's got a lovely environmental ticket on it. I do it at rock-bottom prices, no frills, no fuss, and hardly anybody's interested any more.'

'Hey!' she soothed softly. 'Steady on. It'll come right, you see if it doesn't. I've never heard you talk like that before. Let's change the subject before we both end up in tears. Let me tell you a secret that nobody else knows.'

'Are you sure you should?' he asked anxiously.

'If you promise not to breathe a word to anybody within fifty miles of here.'

'I promise.'

She told him about the dog and her pups hidden away in the woods. At first he interrupted with irrelevant questions about the owner and whether the babies could hope to survive, but then he went quiet and something of Thea's delight got through to him.

'I know it's irresponsible of me to help her,' she admitted. 'But what else can I do? If I can keep her going while I'm here, she might rear at least some of them. She'll be able to leave them and go off to catch a rabbit or something. She's chosen a good time of year for it.'

'But then what? She's sure to be found eventually, even if she doesn't go back home.'

'I know. But there's no sense in worrying about that in advance. Who knows what'll happen?'

'It's a fairy tale story,' he smiled. 'My kids would be enchanted.'

'Maybe you should adopt one of the pups, then,' she flashed. 'Why don't you?'

He smiled again. 'Maybe I will,' he said recklessly. 'The kids would love that. How many are there, anyway? Maybe I should take all of them.'

'No more than six,' she said. 'As far as I could tell.'

'Fine.' He waved an airy hand. 'The more the merrier.'

'If I can find a home for one, when they're only a day or two old, then what's to stop me fixing it for all of them by the end of next week?'

He laughed away all residual worry about Karen and the business and being thwarted of the

116

Cranham funeral. 'Let me help with the cooking,' he insisted. 'What did you say we were having?'

Thea showed Drew the geckoes, which left him unimpressed, and then sent him into the garden with a fruit drink while she fed the dog and concocted a meal from the items available. When he had pleaded with her to let him help, she had flatly refused. 'It's not going to be anything elaborate,' she said. 'Baked potatoes, I think, and a meat sauce, with most of it out of a jar. Two minutes work for one person. Go outside, and I'll be with you before you've chosen where to sit.' She had gradually abandoned cooking as a serious activity over the past two or three years. Without Carl it had lost most of its purpose, and the short periods she had spent with Phil Hollis had generally included eating out, rather than home-cooked candlelit suppers.

As it turned out, she took rather longer than planned, because the cooker was so complicated to operate. Lights and buzzers and incomprehensible symbols defeated her at first. Feeling it was wasteful to turn it all on just for two potatoes, she also put in a ready-made apple pie that she had bought on a whim.

'It should be ready in about forty-five minutes, I think. I'm not a very capable cook, to be honest,' she confessed when she finally joined Drew. 'I'm ashamed to admit all the things I don't know how to do – or have never even tried.'

'It can be quite boring,' he said. 'Karen used to be brilliant at it. She grew all our own veg, and made amazing things.'

'But not now?'

He shook his head. 'It's funny how much has fallen away, without us properly noticing. To begin with, we were just terrified that she was going to die, or be in a coma for years. When she recovered, bit by bit, we treasured every returning memory and ability, without thinking of how she'd been before. If that makes sense,' he added. 'We just sort of forgot where the baseline had been. It's only in recent months that I've allowed myself to remember much about how she used to be, before the injury.'

'And the children? What about them?'

'They can't remember any of it, as far as I can tell. Stephanie was very puzzled and upset to start with, of course. Timmy was just happy to have the physical contact. He clung to her when she came home, like a baby monkey, burrowing into her. I think that did her a lot of good, actually. It made her feel needed and grounded. He was in our bed for the next year.'

'I can't imagine how traumatic it must have been for all of you.'

'People cope,' he said shortly. 'Everybody does.'

'Maybe they do. You'd know more about that than me.'

The phone in the house began to ring, as Thea took a generous swig of the gin and tonic she'd prepared for herself. 'Bother!' she said. 'I think I'll just leave it. It'll be somebody for Harriet.'

'Up to you,' he said, with a pointed look that clearly said he disapproved.

'What? You think I should answer it?'

'A man died close by, today, and you found the body. I think you might find there are people wanting to speak to you.'

'I doubt it. Anyway, it'll stop before I can get there, now.'

She was right. The ringing ceased and she sank back into her seat. 'I don't like telephones,' she said. 'They're so intrusive and badly timed. Mobiles are ghastly things.'

'They've transformed my business,' he said mildly. 'Maggs and I used to have to spend all our time at home, in case there was a call. Now we're free. Though we did take ages to take the risk. We thought we'd never give a proper service unless we had all the diaries and papers and stuff at our fingertips.'

'The diary must still be pretty important,' she said.

'Not really. We're not so busy we can't remember what we're committed to. At least –

most of the time,' he amended, recalling a very embarrassing omission he had made during his previous involvement with Thea in the Cotswolds.

The phone began again, and Thea stood up without any further prevarication. 'OK, I give in,' she said. 'They obviously mean business.'

It was a woman's voice, with plummy vowels that sounded familiar. 'Is that Harriet's house-sitter? I'm sorry, I haven't got your name. This is Edwina Satterthwaite. Perhaps you know who I am?'

'Oh, yes. My name is Thea Osborne. You must be Donny's friend. I met your sister.' She waited to glean the reason for the call, without asking directly.

'Did you? Now, I wonder whether you'd agree to meet me? I was hoping I could come up for a little talk.'

'When?'

'Now. If that would be convenient.'

'I have somebody here, and we're eating in a little while.'

'It is quite important.' A wobble came into the voice, and Thea reminded herself that Edwina had just lost somebody that she had been fond of, perhaps more than that. 'Donny told me you might arrange a natural burial for him. That's what I would like to discuss with you.'

'In that case, do come right away. I have the

undertaker here. He would be very happy to talk it over with you.'

'Thank you, my dear. Give me five minutes.'

She had expected a car, but two figures came walking up the drive, shortly afterwards. A woman and a man approached purposefully, the woman obviously lame, but moving fast nonetheless. Drew and Thea watched from the small front lawn. Thea had rapidly explained to Drew that he might yet find himself with a new burial for his cemetery, if Edwina's hints were to be believed. 'It's all very mysterious,' she said. 'I've not met the woman yet. I hope this won't lead to a fight with Jemima.'

Thyrza Hastings' sister turned out to have the same family mouth, but was several inches shorter, stouter and with none of the frizz to her hair. She was in her early seventies, and walked with a pronounced sideways lurch at every step.

The man with her was in his forties, ginger-haired and monosyllabic.

'This is Toby Brent,' said Edwina. 'He was married to Donny's daughter.'

'Cecilia?' Thea queried. 'You're Cecilia's husband?'

The man nodded, with a brief scowl. He gave the strong impression of wishing he was somewhere else. Thea hoped Drew would be able to keep up without a need for explanations. The wretched Cecilia with her failed heart transplant felt like an irrelevance to the more immediate matter of Donny's death. It seemed slightly bizarre that Edwina should have brought the widower with her, under the circumstances.

'It would appear that you know something of the family's recent history,' said Edwina, with the same archaic delivery as her sister. Thea found herself instinctively wanting to respond in a similar manner.

'Donny spent two afternoons with me here, and told me some of it,' she confirmed.

Edwina was wearing good-quality dark clothes over unmistakable corsets that must have been hot, given the season. Her grey hair was pulled back and coiled tidily on her neck. There was more than a hint of Queen Victoria about her. 'It was good of you to spend time with him,' she said.

'It was a pleasure. Really – I enjoyed his company. He was a nice man.'

'Yes,' said the older woman, averting her face. 'Yes, he was.'

'Donny was great,' endorsed Toby, with a flicker of spirit. 'Really great.'

'This is Drew Slocombe,' Thea made the introduction. 'He runs a natural burial ground in Somerset. Donny was due to meet with him this afternoon to discuss his funeral arrangements. I'm afraid it was all a bit clandestine because for some reason Jemima is against the idea.'

Edwina thrust out a hand for Drew to shake, and nodded acknowledgement of Thea's confession. Drew gave Thea a sharp look, reminding her of his disapproval of anything underhand. She grimaced apologetically at him. Only then did all three notice that Toby was turning red, anger clear on his face.

'What do you mean?' he demanded. 'How could he have been?' He was barely articulate for rage.

'Have been what, Toby dear?' Edwina asked placatingly.

'Planning to talk about his funeral? He wouldn't do that.'

'I'm sure he wanted to get it settled,' said Thea. 'He told me his family refused to discuss it, and he found that very frustrating.'

'Oh, did he?' The snarl was brief, to be replaced by a sudden slump of the shoulders. 'That was Mimm. She doesn't like morbid talk.'

'So I understand. Listen – Donny *asked* me, with no prompting at all, whether I knew somebody who might be able to help. And I did. I knew Drew. It all seemed to fit so well. But I'm sorry now. I was wrong to go behind Jemima's back.'

'And *mine*,' he insisted. 'He's *my* father-in-law. I've got a part in all this.'

Edwina patted him, plainly to his annoyance. 'Nobody's questioning that, dear,' she said. 'You know how grateful we all are for the way you've looked after him.'

The four of them had disposed themselves around the beautiful living room. There was seating for eight or nine people, arranged in smaller groupings. Toby and Edwina sat together on a wooden settle strewn with plump cushions. Thea took a window seat, with Drew across the room, near the fireplace, looking rather out of place. He and Thea were both very aware of their supper waiting for them. A cooking smell was filtering through from the kitchen.

After a short silence, in which everyone seemed to wonder why they were gathered there in the first place, Drew cleared his throat and produced a notebook. 'So am I right in thinking you'd like your . . . friend . . . to be buried in my ground?' he began. 'Obviously, it would have to be his daughter's decision, as next of kin.'

'No, she's not,' said Toby.

'Pardon?'

'Mimm isn't next of kin. That must be his wife.'

Drew's eyes widened and he looked to Thea for help. 'Wife?' he stuttered.

Thea tilted her chin at Edwina, reluctant to say the wrong thing, annoyed with herself

124

for forgetting to tell Drew there was a wife. Of course, this would be a crucial detail when it came to funeral arrangements. Edwina said nothing, either.

'Yes. Mrs Janet Davis,' Toby informed him. 'She's in a nursing home near Cirencester.'

'I see,' said Drew, clearly not seeing at all.

'She's senile,' said Edwina. 'Mimm has power of attorney. It comes to the same thing.'

'You mean, in effect the daughter makes the decisions,' said Drew.

'Precisely.'

'But Janet *is* the next of kin,' persisted Toby.

'All right, Toby. We know how fond you are of her. But the truth is – well, she hasn't been able to function for a long time now.' She looked from Thea to Drew and back. 'It's very sad.' There was no hint of embarrassment that she should have at least in part replaced Donny's wife as his female partner, nor was there any sign that Toby resented this, however loyal he might be to his mother-in-law. More briskly, Edwina went on, addressing Drew, 'How far away is your burial ground?'

'Nearly sixty miles from here, I would guess. I'm in the process of establishing a new one in Broad Campden, but it won't be ready for a long time yet.'

Edwina glared at Thea. 'But I understood from Donny that it was something local.'

Thea blinked. 'Hang on,' she said. 'You mentioned on the phone that he'd talked to you about it, as well. When did this talk take place? I thought you'd been away.'

Edwina widened her eyes at the sharp tone, but replied quite readily. 'Last night. As soon as I got back from my daughter's, I popped in to see him. I live barely a quarter of a mile away, after all.'

'Were you there at half past nine?'

'About that, probably. Why do you ask?'

'I heard you arguing with him,' said Thea rashly. 'He sounded very cross.'

Edwina waved this aside, without a shadow of unease. 'Rubbish. We were simply having the same sort of discussion we always have. It was our manner, that's all. Isn't that right, Toby?'

The son-in-law nodded. 'Always yelling at each other,' he confirmed.

'I'm going to miss all that,' Edwina continued, with a suppressed sniff, as if only then recalling how recently her friend had died. 'I knew he wasn't going to last a lot longer, but it's still been a dreadful shock. He was so . . . energetic . . . last night. He gave no hint at all of what he was planning to do.'

Thea was impressed at the total lack of self-reproach. Surely most people would be consumed with guilt if their last encounter with somebody had involved a row, in which words like *patronising* had been thrown about? She was also struck by how rapidly Edwina seemed to have absorbed the fact of Donny's demise despite her protestations of shock.

'So you were surprised when you heard the news?' Drew asked.

'Thunderstruck,' said Edwina. Her brow puckered, and her little body seemed to shrink into itself. 'You see, I was going to help him, when it came to the point. We had it all decided. The plastic bag and the pills. We'd come to the conclusion that I wouldn't get into any serious trouble, if he left a note, and told people he wanted to die. I still can't believe he would go ahead and do it on his own.'

The suffering in her face was well concealed, but still it leaked out, and cast a pall across the room.

'Come on, Weena,' murmured Toby, patting her tentatively on her arm. 'He's saved you a load of trouble, when you think about it.'

Edwina's head reared back, in just the same way as her sister's had done the day before. 'Trouble!' she hissed. 'When have I ever been afraid of a bit of trouble? I *wanted* to be there with him. It was something I could do for him. Nobody should die all alone like that.'

Drew cleared his throat. 'You know – most people prefer to be alone at the very end. It's strange to think of, but I'm sure it's true.'

'Well, it's my belief that something happened after I left him. A phone call or visit, or *something*. He was in such a lively mood, pleased that I was back, enjoying his chats up here with you . . .' she nodded at Thea. 'He was going to have another go at Jemima about the burial business. And they haven't found a single note. I would have expected him to leave each one of us our own long letter before he went.'

She was met by a long silence as the others absorbed the implications of what she was saying. Thea struggled to separate the facts from the feelings. 'What could possibly have happened that would drive him to commit suicide before he was ready?'

'You tell me,' said Edwina.

Outside the door, which led into the hall, a loud siren noise suddenly accosted them. 'Oh, God, it's the smoke alarm!' cried Thea. 'Something's burning.'

'Our supper, I imagine,' said Drew, hurrying after her into the kitchen. Smoke was billowing out of the cooker.

'That pie! Look – you can see it in there, all black.'

Sure enough, the contents of the oven could be seen through the glass panel at the front – two big baked potatoes and a charred fruit pie.

CHAPTER SEVEN

'It was only meant to be heated gently for twenty minutes,' said Drew, reading from the box that had contained the pie, after the visitors had left. 'And potatoes take the best part of an hour, on a much higher setting. What on earth were you thinking of?'

'Other things,' said Thea tightly. 'Maybe the dog in the woods will fancy it.'

'Poor thing – is she that desperate?'

'Shut up.' She relaxed into a rueful chuckle. 'Do you want me to take you to see her?'

'Not really. I'm not especially interested in dogs. I was bitten as a child and I never quite got over it.'

'It was probably your own fault. It's not fair to judge a whole species by one incident.'

'I'm sure you're right. When I have time, I'll go and get therapy for it.'

Another chuckle, and then she changed the subject. 'What did you think of Edwina Satterthwaite, then?'

'I think she's being very British and controlling her grief admirably.'

'You think grief ought to be controlled?'

'Not entirely. But it still is in our culture, and I have great respect for those who stick by that as a way of responding. I mean, it takes immense reserves of strength to hold yourself together like that. I like the dignity of it.'

'Hm. But is it *honest*? It can look as if you don't care.'

'Why should that matter? Besides, it's a sort of generosity, as well, to protect other people from all the mess and sentiment of your emotions. You just get on with it, inside yourself, in your own time. That's why we have the sort of funerals we do. It's all right to cry, but only quietly. Then there's the get-together afterwards, which is louder and often quite merry. It all tides you over the first week or so, and stops you falling apart.'

Thea watched his face, with its youthful openness and sincerity. She smiled at the fervour of his words. 'Thank you,' she said.

'What for?'

'Reminding me of how it goes. For setting me right. I needed to hear that.'

'I hadn't forgotten you've been through it yourself,' he said.

'But I had, sort of. It's so easy to slide into thinking the same conformist, superficial stuff that everyone else thinks.'

'Except they don't.'

'Pardon?'

'Real, actual people are amazing when there's a crisis. They don't follow stereotypes at all. That's one of the best things about my work – I can never lose my respect and admiration for ordinary people.'

'Because they're not really ordinary at all,' she supplied, feeling humbled by his wisdom. 'As I said, I needed to be reminded of that. You're absolutely right, of course, about grief and the rituals we've established. It helps to let the misery out a bit at a time.'

He nodded agreement, and then sighed. 'It doesn't look as if I'll be doing this one, though, does it? Was I right in assuming she thought I was too far away?'

'We got off the subject, rather, didn't we? I found that whole conversation fairly confusing. What was Toby doing, coming here, for a start? I couldn't get much sense of his relationship with Edwina – could you?'

'Moral support,' Drew shrugged. 'It's very common for somebody else to be roped in when it comes to arranging a funeral. If for nothing else, they can be useful for remembering everything that was decided.'

'He didn't say much.'

'Presumably he took time off work to be with her, which was probably enough. What does he do?'

'I have no idea. I don't think he lives around here, either.' She tried to recall everything Jemima had said about Cecilia and her husband. 'But I might have got that wrong,' she concluded. 'His wife had a heart transplant and died, not too long ago. It was a major trauma for the whole family, obviously.'

'She was Donny's daughter, right?'

'And Jemima's younger sister. It makes sense that they'd want to keep Toby close, I suppose. But Edwina isn't related – she's Donny's girlfriend, if you can use that word for a woman over seventy who looks like Queen Victoria.'

This time it was Drew who giggled. 'Did you think that as well? Do you think she does it on purpose, with the corsets and the hair and everything?'

'It's more as if she got stuck in a time warp fifty years ago.'

He shook his head. 'I don't think people looked like that in 1960, did they? She'd have been out of fashion even a hundred years ago.'

'Perhaps it's her idea of mourning clothes. When she heard Donny was dead, she fished out an old outfit that had belonged to her grandmother.'

'People do funny things,' he agreed. 'But I didn't detect any whiff of mothballs. I think she always looks like that.'

The baked potatoes made for a dull meal, despite the added sauce. Thea made no attempt to apologise and Drew made no complaint, having expressed his opinion of the burnt pie earlier. She questioned him about the proposed new burial ground in Broad Campden, eliciting a despondent account of all the hitches and complications.

'I'm not sure it's ever going to be worth it,' he repeated, clearly hoping to convince himself that the project was doomed. 'I can't see it really happening, if I'm honest.'

'Especially if your wife and partner are both lukewarm about it.'

'Maggs is positively cold. Karen won't discuss it. She can't really cope with something that big.'

Thea looked at him. 'So you can't do it, can you? Why are you even pursuing it, if things are as bad as that?'

'I've got to, don't you see? I own that property now. I can't just ignore it.'

'Is everything settled with the council, then? Last I heard, they were doing all in their power to stop you going ahead.'

'That's just it. I hate to walk away and let them think they've won. But it would help if I had some local people on my side. So far, they've all politely looked the other way when I've asked for some support.'

'I bet they have,' she nodded. 'They won't want to think about it.'

He sighed. 'I ought to be used to that by now. Five years ago, I was sure we were close to a breakthrough – that people would be more and more prepared to talk about the sort of funeral they wanted, and go for the most ecological burials.'

'And they're not?'

'Nope. Well, *some* are. But it's still a very small minority. With all the other pressures and worries, ecology or environmental concerns seem to have slipped right down the list of priorities. Cremations are in more demand than ever.'

'Well it's a shame about Donny, especially when Edwina made the effort to come and talk to you.'

Drew chewed his lower lip pensively. 'There's something rather odd about your Donny, don't you think? Something definitely doesn't add up.'

'How do you mean?'

'For a start, he and his lady friend had agreed on a suicide plan, so why did he go back on it?'

'Because she annoyed him so much last night.

He was really yelling at her. I was surprised he could manage to shout that loud. Perhaps he was so upset, he decided to end it all, right there and then.'

'To punish her, you mean?'

'I hadn't exactly thought of it like that, but maybe so, yes.'

'But there's more. He was supposed to be meeting me this afternoon. Why jump the gun, instead of waiting to arrange things as he wanted them?'

Thea's shoulders sagged, and she exhaled a long breath. 'That's what I've been wondering,' she said. 'Perhaps he forgot he was due to see you. I'm not sure how good his memory was – although it seemed perfectly fine when I was talking to him. He was really looking forward to it – going behind Jemima's back made him act like a naughty little boy. He was twinkling with mischief, the last time I saw him. We were conspirators, and it was *fun*.'

'It's much too early anyway to get anything resolved concerning the funeral. The timing is terrible.'

'I'm sorry. I ought to have called you this morning and put you off.'

'But you forgot about me. Yes, you said.'

'I did. And it was two o'clock before I got back here, what with all the goings-on at the Lodge. The time just disappeared.'

'Besides, I was in the area anyway. There's no harm done. I've met the family, and helped you cope with the shock. At least, I hope I have.'

'Yes, you have. Without you to talk to, I don't know what I would have done.'

'One thing puzzles me. Edwina and Toby phoned and asked to come and speak to you, before they knew I was here. And yet they did seem to want to discuss the funeral. Isn't that strange? I mean – they wouldn't talk it over with you, would they?'

She shrugged helplessly. 'I doubt it. Except – didn't she say that Donny had told her he was meeting you here? So she *did* expect you to be with me.'

He grimaced. 'It gives you the feeling of being talked about behind your back, as if they know exactly where we are and what we're doing. Don't you feel that?'

'A bit, maybe. It definitely makes me wonder just what happened between Donny and Edwina last night. I can't help feeling I was supposed to prevent this very thing from happening. Harriet did ask me to watch out for him.'

'Don't be daft. You couldn't be with him night and day.'

'I know. It isn't very rational. And it's too late now, anyway.' She sat up straighter, and went back to the question of Edwina. 'What if he did confirm that he'd like to be buried by you? In fact, thinking about it, that *is* how it sounded. She came here to see you because she'd had instructions from Donny before he died. Doesn't that suggest that she *did* help him with the plastic bag?'

'On the face of it, I guess it does.' He frowned. 'But she must be a damned good actor, if that's how it was.'

'If she thought she was carrying out his wishes, that would feel like justification, perhaps? By focusing on the funeral, she could avoid any thoughts of how he died.'

'Even if I did handle the burial, we would still need his daughter's permission,' he said thoughtfully, clearly prioritising his own role in the matter.

'Even if he wrote down what he wanted?'

'Then it would get complicated. Very few people go directly against the wishes of a dead person, if it's written down. Even in these secular days, there's still quite a fear of annoying the dead. You can never be entirely sure what they're capable of.'

'True.' She thought back to the days following her husband's sudden death, when she felt his presence in the house, heard his voice repeating her name, and even once thought she glimpsed him at the top of the stairs, one cold grey dawn when she couldn't sleep. 'I felt as if Carl was still watching over me for weeks after he died.'

'I'll have to go,' he said suddenly, having glanced at his watch. 'It's half past seven.'

'I'm sorry it hasn't worked out better,' she said, feeling slightly wistful. 'You'd have liked Donny.'

'I'm sure I would. But these things happen. How much longer will you be here?'

'Nearly two weeks, assuming Harriet doesn't come back early for Donny's funeral.'

'Have you told her what's happened?'

She shook her head. 'No, she said she wasn't contactable. Although I imagine that if the police wanted her, they'd soon figure out a way to get in touch. It isn't up to me . . . at least . . .'

Drew gave her a look as he realised she was floundering. 'What's the matter?' he asked gently.

'I don't know. I suppose it's just hit me, that I won't see him again, and that something isn't right. And I'm going to be here on my own trying to keep it all straight. Plus there's that dog in the woods. Why does everything happen to me?' she concluded with a wail.

'I rather fear it's because you go looking for things to happen to you,' he said dryly. 'If you got yourself a nice dull office job, and didn't spend your life intruding into other people's business, you'd be pretty sure that nothing would ever happen to you.'

'I don't *intrude*,' she protested. 'They want

me. They *pay* me. And I had no idea that I'd be required to entertain Donny when I took this commission.'

He shrugged, smiled and said nothing.

'You're right. It's too late to moan about it now. With any luck I can keep my head down and everything'll carry on without me, for the rest of my stay.'

'Except the dog,' he said.

'Right. Except the dog.'

Twenty minutes after Drew drove away, as Thea was sitting in the kitchen with a large mug of coffee, somebody knocked on the front door. She opened it to discover a red-haired man in a blue shirt. 'Oh!' she said. 'I know you, don't I? Last year . . .'

'Yes, Mrs Osborne. It was in Lower Slaughter. I'm Detective Inspector Jeremy Higgins.'

'So you are,' she said.

He followed her into the kitchen and accepted coffee from the still-warm pot. 'It seems a long time, doesn't it?' she said. 'I've been to a few other places since then.'

'So I understand – Hampnett and Broad Campden, if I remember rightly.'

She flushed, embarrassed to think the police were keeping track of her. Adventure had followed her from village to village, even after she had broken up with Detective Superintendent Phil Hollis. She had instead become friendly with DS Sonia Gladwin, from Cumbria; a thin, intelligent woman with her own quirky way of doing things.

'What can I do for you, then?' she demanded, impatient to get to the main point.

'Donald Davis, who died during the night. I understand you met him.'

'Twice,' she agreed. 'He came here for tea yesterday and the day before that.'

'Must have been a shock for you.'

'All the more so because I was with his daughter when she found his body. He was a sweet old man. I was looking forward to our daily chats.' For the first time, she felt a sense of failure. 'I was supposed to be looking after him, in a way. He was part of my duties as a house-sitter. I made a rubbish job of it, didn't I?'

Jeremy Higgins had a big head, and a slow manner. His colouring, which might have suggested somebody irascible or volatile, gave the lie to such stereotypes. Thea had found him to be kindly and sensitive in her brief dealings with him. He smiled consolingly, and said, 'I don't think you can blame yourself. We've had an anonymous call, to say that Mr Davis was assisted in his suicide. Technically, that's murder. DS Hollis suggested that I talk it over with you. "Knowing her, she's already met all the significant people in the story," he said.'

'Did he?' She felt a sharp pang of nostalgia for the intimate times she had spent with Phil, at his side in investigating earlier murders, questioning and suggesting – and sometimes interfering. Brushing it away, she continued, 'I thought the police were encouraged to turn a blind eye to that sort of thing nowadays.'

'Not if a direct accusation has been made. And not if it conflicts with the evidence we've been given.'

She had to think it through. 'There wasn't any sign of another person having been there. Wouldn't they have called to report the death, rather than leaving poor Jemima to find him like that?'

He shrugged and raised his eyebrows, as if to say, *your guess is as good as mine.* 'I'm just telling you how things stand.'

Thea was all too aware of a painful dilemma. Less than an hour before, Edwina Satterthwaite had been admitting to a plan in which she was to help Donny to kill himself. But she had been perfectly clear that this had not in fact happened. She had left him alive, after their argument, and been stunned to hear of his death the following day. Could there be any harm in revealing this to the police?

She decided to backtrack first. 'An anonymous phone call? Man or woman?'

'I probably shouldn't tell you, but it was a man.'

'Do you have the call on tape?'

'Unfortunately no. It was put through to the part-time local station, where they don't record all calls.'

'What time was it?'

'The middle of this afternoon. The girl who took it hadn't got any record of Mr Davis's death, and got herself so bogged down in spelling his name and other details, she can't remember anything helpful. He only said it once – something like: "Donald Davis was assisted to commit suicide by his friend Edwina." And then he put the phone down.'

'I see.'

He cocked his head at her. 'What do you see, Mrs Osborne?'

'Call me Thea,' she said, still thinking hard.

'OK – Thea. What does that suggest to you?'

'I might as well tell you, I suppose. Edwina was here this afternoon, and she told us she'd agreed to help Donny when the time came. But she didn't do it. I'm sure she didn't.' She explained how upset Edwina had been, and puzzled by Donny's precipitate action. She kept quiet about the words she had overheard the night before, her conscience paining her, but outweighed by the knowledge that words once said could not

142

be unsaid. She could reveal everything later, if it seemed necessary.

'Who else was here?'

'Drew Slocombe, the undertaker. Donny wanted to talk to him about his funeral.'

Higgins was sometimes a bit slow, she remembered. He rubbed his brow with a short forefinger. 'Mr Davis wanted to discuss his funeral today, but killed himself before meeting Mr Slocombe?'

'That's right.'

'Was anybody else here?'

'Toby something. Husband of Donny's dead daughter, Cecilia. They all seem very fond of him.' She wanted to add *he's got ginger hair, as well*, but it was obviously completely irrelevant.

He puffed out his cheeks in an expression of admiration. 'Phil was right, then. You *have* met all the main players already. Have we left anybody out?'

'Well, there's Thyrza. She's Edwina's sister. And she has a son, Philippe, who has a big grey poodle called Jasper. I've met all of them.'

He had extracted a notebook from a back pocket and was making hurried notes. 'Should I add Jasper to the list, do you think?' he asked, with a smile.

She thought of the dog in the woods, and shook her head. 'He's only useful if you need to identify

143

his master,' she judged. 'And that probably won't be too difficult. He wears pink clothes and a sort of Breton cap.'

'And they all live locally, do they?'

'Most of them. I think Toby's from further away, but I don't know where. And I'm not really sure about that. He might be staying here until Donny's funeral, anyway.' Again she tried to think back to exactly what Donny had said. 'I think it was just a vague impression to do with Cecilia being in and out of hospital. I gathered there was a lot of driving back and forth. Actually, Donny never mentioned that she had a husband.' She spread her hands self-deprecatingly at the muddle of relevant and irrelevant information. 'I don't imagine the source really matters,' she added, while at the same time wishing she could convey the fragile threads connecting the various individuals. The sad story of the failed heart transplant could not be pertinent to Donny's death, and yet she could not shake it from her mind. 'Poor Toby,' she sighed. 'I think he was very fond of Donny. They went through a lot together.'

'So – you think this phone call got it wrong, then?'

'Absolutely, I do. Possibly whoever it was heard something about the plan, and just assumed that's what happened. But it all points to a straightforward suicide without anybody there to help.' As she spoke, she felt doubt clouding her words. Could Edwina have stayed with Donny while he died, and then quietly slipped away when it was all over? She might have been putting on an act when she came to the Manor to see Thea and Drew. But then – why feign an interest in Donny's funeral when it was too late to be sure of getting what he wanted? Why not delay doing the irreversible deed until after talking it over with Drew?

Jeremy's head moved slowly from side to side. 'It's not, though, is it? Straightforward, I mean. We'll have the post-mortem tomorrow, which may or may not throw more light on the matter. But meanwhile, we have to assume there's reason for further investigation. You haven't said anything to change that.'

'Haven't I? That's a shame. I hate to think somebody's hiding what really happened. Donny deserves better than that. There ought not to be any deception going on.'

'Makes sense, though, if somebody did slip that bag over his head, without taking proper precautions first. They'd be scared of a murder rap.'

'Precautions? Like what?'

'Like getting everything written down and signed by the deceased. Like not benefiting from his will, or having the slightest accusation of

145

undue influence laid on them. And even then, it's a risk. The law in this country does not recognise assisted suicide.'

'So even with the precautions, it could still be seen as murder? Sounds like a no-win situation all round.'

He smiled tolerantly. 'Don't you think that just about sums up death itself? In the end, none of us can win, can we?'

She gave him a severe look. 'That's not the right attitude, is it? That's coming close to not caring how or why a sick old man finally dies, because it was sure to happen soon anyway.'

His expression changed completely, and an angry finger waved in front of her nose. 'Don't come that with me,' he snapped. 'Don't *ever* say anything like that to a police officer. I'd have thought you'd know better.'

'Sorry.' She held up her hands and backed away from him. 'I didn't mean it to sound like that. We're on the same side, of course we are.' The red hair was perhaps not so incongruous after all. For the first time, she had witnessed another side of DI Higgins, and learnt that he had deeper, stronger principles than she could ever have guessed.

'If this is a suspicious death, then the proper procedures will be gone through,' he insisted. 'His age and state of health make no difference to an investigation, if it comes to that.'

They do, though, thought Thea mulishly. *Of course they do.* It wouldn't be possible to raise the same head of steam as if a little girl had been raped and strangled, or a pregnant woman slowly tortured to death. Not all deaths were the same, and everybody knew it.

She decided to stand her ground. 'All I meant was, if Donny seriously wanted to die, because his outlook was so hopelessly grim, then somebody helping him could hardly be given the same treatment as a much more dreadful murderer.'

'That's not what you said just now.'

'No. We got off the subject, somehow. So – you'll be speaking to Edwina, then.'

He tipped his chin affirmatively, a gesture his body was not designed to make easily. His big head was set squarely on broad shoulders, with very little neck between. Thea examined him as the conversation ran dry. His ancestry appeared to combine sandy-haired Northerners with large-boned eastern Europeans, something Polish about his round cheeks and heavy hips and thighs. Few people would tag him as a plain clothes police detective, on first sighting.

'I don't think you should take what I say as important. I don't know the history, or how the people connect. I don't even know whether Jemima gets on with the sisters – or whether the sisters get on with each other, come to that. I'm beginning to think I might have got quite a lot wrong, making assumptions without much foundation.'

'It's plenty to be going on with,' he assured her. 'And you've got form when it comes to fingering the heart of the matter.'

The awkward metaphor recalled the tragic Cecilia and her transplant, yet again. An image of a probing finger delving behind the broken ribs to cut out the defective heart came to mind, and soured her stomach.

'Don't bank on it,' she muttered. 'I really have no idea what's what this time.'

It had been a very long day. She went to bed at ten-thirty, wondering whether she dared to hope for better things next morning. A sunny sky, a trouble-free visit to the mother dog in her burrow and no more visits from the police. But Donny would still be dead, and that in itself was cause for profound regret.

CHAPTER EIGHT

Wednesday was unarguably the middle of the week. It meant that her stay in Cranham had not much more than another week to run, and for that she felt rather thankful. The geckoes all appeared to be thriving when she visited them that morning, the eggs looking just as usual, and the gauges giving normal readings. The realisation that there was nothing more she had to attend to, no other duties, made her feel lazy and aimless. The lack of Donny did not diminish as teatime approached and there was little prospect of a visitor. She had no news about the post-mortem or the interview with Edwina, which came as something of a relief. A surreptitious trip to the woods with another bag of meat and milk for the runaway dog was achieved without incident. As recompense, she took Hepzie for a long walk in the other direction, wondering whether they might even get as far as the outskirts of Painswick before turning back again.

On the map, the walk looked feasible, but the reality was rather different. The rise and fall of the land, the uncertainty of the way at one or two junctures, and the absence of any other human beings combined to make the walk both tiring and dull. Every time she embarked on one of the house-sitting jobs, she dutifully examined the large-scale map and traced the surrounding footpaths with every intention of exploring them with the dog. Once or twice she had met her own targets, with mainly gratifying results, but she had to admit to herself that walking was not as much of a pleasure as she wished it to be. Unless there was an obvious goal, or a companion, it felt rather hollow, a pointless exercise. And now, the plan of reaching Painswick looked insanely ambitious. There and back was a walk of some miles, involving several hours, and however unreasonably, she felt unjustified in deserting Hollywell for the best part of the day.

'Enough,' she announced to the spaniel, after almost an hour of trudging along the inside of hedgerows and worrying about getting lost. 'Let's go back.'

She turned and walked up a slope and was suddenly confronted by a vista that left her gasping.

She was somewhere between Sheepscombe and Bulls Cross, looking westwards towards Painswick. The fact that she must have been heading east before she turned was disconcerting, when she had believed otherwise, but there was no room for concern in the face of the fabulous view before her. The whole town of Painswick lay before her, the church spire dominating the spread of houses interspersed with grand old trees. The colours were greens and greys under the thin white cloud, with frequent creamy-white facades catching the light. It was perhaps half a mile distant, with a long green slope stretching from her feet to the first houses of the town.

'Wow!' she breathed. 'Look at that!'

It did not alter her decision to return to Cranham, but it amply justified her excursion. The walk had acquired a point, after all. The joyful uplift caused by the perfect landscape presented so unexpectedly to her sight was worth a lot of weary tedium. The buildings, made of local materials, flowed up and down the natural slopes, sharing the space with vegetation and waterways, as aesthetically right as any trees or hills could be. Only the church struck a false note, she found, somewhat to her surprise. It was too obviously man-made, too tall, the shape all wrong for the setting. The eye had no need for such a thrusting focal point – she felt it a detraction from the scene's undulating form. She held up a thumb to blot out the spire, confirming to her own satisfaction that the town would look better without it. The small heresy amused her – without the church, the vision before her was much more inspiring and awesome. It felt like a discovery she should share, and the thought that there was nobody to confide in was momentarily lowering.

But her step was buoyant as she worked out the shortest way back to Cranham. She had glimpsed something magical, something that was always going to be there for the contemplating. It made her happy, in and of itself. It was both ordinary and mystical, common and unique. It was full of paradox and illusion, and it was nothing more than a little town settled into an English valley like dozens of others. She toyed with a swirl of poetical thoughts as her spaniel escorted her unreliably back to their temporary home. 'Have you read *Cider with Rosie*?' several people had asked her, since she began her regular visits to the Cotswolds. She had not, believing on the basis of almost no information that it was an old-fashioned, sentimental picture of the countryside that couldn't hope to have any relevance fifty years after it was written. She knew that Slad was the setting of the book – a place she had never seen. Now she realised that she was very close by, and probably ought to give it a look. It was possible, she conceded, that it was as beautiful and memorable as people said. If Painswick could present such an enchanting prospect, then perhaps Slad could, too.

'Maybe we'll go that way tomorrow,' she said to the dog.

Something of her elevated mood remained throughout the afternoon and evening. She chirruped at the geckoes, and then patrolled the unambitious garden, tweaking out a few weeds and training some clematis tendrils through the spars of a wooden fence as she went. Gardening had never been very high on her list of interests, but she could see various ways in which this one could be readily improved. The roses were its best feature, but there were other things that would flourish with a bit of encouragement. An old plum tree was reaching the end of its productive life, at the back of the house, surrounded by straggly grass and hogweed. It could be transformed into a colourful island bed, if the tree were removed, she mused. All it would take was a saw and some imagination.

The sky had cleared again, and the sinking sun filtered pleasingly through the branches of a silver birch that grew tall on the far side of Harriet's boundary fence. The next property was a detached house in two or three acres of well-tended grounds. Thus far Thea had seen nothing of its occupants. Now a man was cutting the grass on the enormous lawn, on a ride-on mower. He wore a floppy hat, obscuring his face, and cut-off jeans, exposing brown legs. Somehow she thought he was an employee, and not the householder. But he could easily be a wealthy young stockbroker or – more likely these days – a media consultant with one of those jobs that created something out of nothing on the Internet. Where a year before she had wondered whether harsh economic times would affect the nature of these Cotswold villages, now she concluded that most of them were occupied by rock-solid plutocrats, whose wealth was beyond the vagaries of the market.

He showed no sign of having seen her, and she turned away, letting him carry on with his perfectly straight lines. Harriet's poor lawn was dotted with daisies and dandelions, the grass much too long, and Thea greatly preferred it to next door for its character. She had not been asked to cut the grass, and she had no intention of doing so.

There were, of course, insistent thoughts about Donny Davis. It was less than two days ago that he had died, and she was more and more sorry to have known him so briefly before losing him. She went over their conversations for clues as to just why he had chosen that particular night to kill himself. She had been barely two hundred yards away as he gasped his last inside that awful plastic bag. She had not properly looked at the bag itself, but carried an impression of it being unusually sturdy. Certainly not one of those flimsy things they gave you for fruit in the supermarket. They would be too easy to puncture in that frenzy to survive that surely overcame everybody, however miserably determined they might be to end it all.

She thought, too, about Jemima, and how Thea had liked her despite her short temper and unreasonable objections to Drew and his funerals. A bond had formed between them over Donny's dead body, the experience shared for ever, like it or not. She should see her again as soon as she possibly could, for a bit of mutual debriefing. She knew how important it was to tell the story repeatedly, and how hard it could be to find people willing to listen. There was something hidden about Jemima, too. Some undercurrent in her relationship with her father that had removed any real surprise at his death, and thereby aroused Thea's curiosity.

But whether and when she saw Jemima was not within her control. She might find Hobson in the phone book, she supposed, and track down the precise location of her fruit farm, but that felt intrusive. Sooner or later she was confident that the woman would come to her. Whether or not Edwina Satterthwaite and Thyrza Hastings would turn up again as well was less certain. She had little reason to assume that they would, but it would be surprising if they didn't. They had said too much to her to just drop the connection now.

The visit from DI Higgins had given her plenty to think about, too. She could just hear Phil Hollis saying *Pop in on Thea, informally, and see what she's picked up.* Which was exactly what Jeremy had done. He, like Phil, understood the value of an outside eye, objectively assessing the individuals concerned without any prejudices or old grudges to cloud judgement.

The more she thought about it, the more probable it seemed that Edwina had in fact helped Donny in his suicide. The deed done, she must have lost her nerve, unable to face the police questioning and the prolonged deliberations about whether or not to prosecute her for a crime. She had bolted the back door and pulled the front door behind her with the catch down, so nobody could intrude on the body. Then she had walked home, gone to bed and acted normally the following day.

This scenario was seductively simple, although she stumbled over the fact that she still did not know where Edwina lived. It was somewhere close by, she supposed, from Thyrza's vague words on Monday night, within easy walking distance, even for somebody with a bad hip. The hypothesis also required a belief in impressive acting talent on Edwina's part, but Thea had seen people tell large lies with perfect aplomb before. It came more easily than anybody liked to think. Edwina only had to concentrate on her quite genuine grief, and pack away her secret knowledge of exactly how Donny had died. It wasn't that aspect that bothered Thea. It was the argument she had overheard on Monday evening that stuck scratchily in her mind. Would anybody be able to conduct the final act, with the love and respect and dignity it demanded, after such words had been exchanged? She did her best to imagine it – the reconciliation, the smiles of self-reproach on either side, the hugs and farewells. After all, Toby had confirmed that Edwina and Donny regularly shouted at each other, without meaning anything by it.

So had Edwina *forced* him in some way? Had she lost patience, or broken under the strain and decided it was time to end it, whether he was ready or not? That felt like a more natural consequence of the raised tempers and exasperation Thea had heard. That would explain Edwina's attempts to conceal her involvement: her fear that the police would not accept that all she was doing was helping Donny to achieve what he wanted.

And that, she realised with a shock of comprehension, was exactly why there could never be a credible or effective law that authorised assisted suicide. Who could ever know the precise facts of those final moments? There was a monumental difference between – on one side – a loving, regretful, gentle service to somebody who quite definitely had come to the end of his endurance, and an impatient jumping of the gun on the other, an act born of stress and exhaustion, understandable but contrary to the wishes of the victim. A huge difference that mattered crucially, and yet was virtually impossible to detect from outside, after the event.

'Phew!' she gasped aloud, finding herself wracked by these thoughts on what had to be the most important subject there was. It was one thing to examine it in theory, round a chattering dinner table amongst young and healthy people – quite another to consider it in relation to a single real person who had actually *died* the previous day. If Donny had gone to his death resisting, fighting against it, that was certainly murder. That was cruel and horrible and deserving of punishment. It was also a dreadful betrayal of trust, if performed by his close friend Edwina.

She wished she could share her deliberations with somebody, before the clarity was muddled and lost. It felt like an elusive insight that might just evaporate if not pinned down by being spoken aloud. The day was nearly over, and she had not spoken to a soul for close to twenty-four hours. Such was the fate of a house-sitter, she acknowledged. It was the reason her spaniel was of such significance – another familiar creature to link her to the living world. But Hepzie was no use at all when it came to philosophy. Thea could only think of one person who would listen and understand – and he was snugly at home with his wife and children.

She watched an old film on the television and went to bed early, feeling the day had been a necessary interlude in which to absorb the fact of Donny's death and let the implications work their way into some kind of logical shape. There had been at least two moments of major emotional impact – which was more than normally occurred in a month. Wherever the objective truth might lie, she would never abandon the two distinct certainties that had gripped her that day – that there was transcendent beauty to be found in this part of England, and that there could never be a fair and watertight means of legislating for one person to kill another, however benign the intention. It seemed like more than enough to be going on with.

She fell asleep within seconds of turning out the light, the dog at her feet as always.

* * *

Thursday dawned fair, sunlight flooding Thea's bedroom for the first time since she'd arrived. 'This is more like it,' she told Hepzie. It was not quite seven o'clock, but she decided to get up anyway. Perhaps Jemima's example on Monday had made more of an impression than she realised. There did, after all, seem to be something wasteful about lying in bed on such a lovely morning.

Thinking about Jemima, she glanced out of the window where the woman had been cutting roses on Monday morning. No reason to do that any more, of course. No more visits to the Lodge fitted into a busy farming life; no more worries about what would happen when Donny needed urgent medical treatment simply to alleviate pain or get nourishment into him. Was Jemima feeling relief, on this sunny morning, that such a large burden had been taken from her shoulders? Surely anybody would.

How much of a hole had Donny left in people's lives? What about Toby, who somehow gave the impression of a man who had put himself on hold, treading water while he worked out how to live without his Cecilia? Thea would like to learn more about Toby and why he had tagged along with Edwina. She would even be interested in meeting Philippe again and his big grey poodle, to check his reaction to Donny's death.

She recognised her symptoms. All alone in

this big house, still far from understanding the dynamics of the village community, shocked by the discovery of a dead man close by, she needed human contact. Whilst it was satisfying to have time for some serious thinking, too much time was destructive. Thoughts began to straggle into realms of fantasy, with no checks or balances from another person. False notions could flourish extravagantly, and take root when they really ought to be discarded.

She could email a few people – her daughter Jessica, her sister Jocelyn, for example – and tell the story of what had happened in Cranham. She could phone her mother or her friend Celia back in Witney where she had her cottage and her official life. But she and Celia had very much drifted apart since the house-sitting had begun. A stalwart confidante in the year after Carl died, Celia had since found herself a new man and been absorbed into couplehood. Thea's frequent absences had damaged the friendship more than expected, until there was little the two had left to talk about.

In any case, you couldn't phone people so early in the morning. After a leisurely breakfast she composed emails to daughter and sister, which said much less than she would have liked to convey, aware of a need to avoid worrying them. She permitted herself another pang of nostalgia for Phil Hollis, who would have talked through with her the whole matter of Donny's death, before she quashed it firmly.

She visited the geckoes, which were invisible again. They had eaten most of the mashed fruit from the day before, so she replaced it with a fresh helping, taking great care to fasten the catches of their tanks. Escaping animals, including a large snake, had caused trouble on more than one occasion in the past. These little reptiles would be impossible to find if once they got loose.

At eight-thirty, she took Hepzie for a short walk across a field or two behind the house. Then she shut her dog indoors and set out for the collie in the woods, which had been looming large in her thoughts for some time. The pups must be close to a week old by this time, growing rapidly and likely to start opening their eyes in another week or so. She hoped she would still be around to see them when that happened. Would Drew really take one? she wondered, remembering their slightly silly talk about him adopting the whole litter. Most probably not, she concluded. He wasn't even likely to get the chance. If she left Cranham at the end of the coming week, the whole thing would probably be out of her hands entirely.

She would examine them more closely this morning, making sure of the number in the litter, and whether they were male or female. With each day that passed, she felt more confident of their survival, whilst knowing this was an ill-founded optimism. The bitch's owner could still kill them all if he chose. He might even be so angry that he shot his collie as well, she thought wildly. It wouldn't be the first time. Farm dogs led a precarious existence, even in these more enlightened times. Cruelty was far from eradicated, and neglect seemed to be a growing plague, as people assessed the cost of keeping a dog and decided to fling the encumbrance out of their car on the motorway.

'Stop it,' she muttered to herself. She was all too susceptible to agonising about the ghastly fate of countless dogs, not only in Britain but around the world. It was a deep well of pain she kept inside herself, never quite forgotten. Not just dogs, of course, but other animals as well: elephants, baby seals, terrified suffering cows in American abattoirs – people could be appallingly savage in their treatment of other species, and it was never going to get better. The fact that many creatures could sometimes behave cruelly and viciously to each other was irrelevant. People ought to know better.

All of which contributed to a growing sense of foreboding as she approached the burrow. What if they'd been found, dragged out and hacked to pieces? What if they had just disappeared and she would never know what had happened to them? The situation was so insecure, the little family so vulnerable, that she could scarcely believe it when she found everything as normal. The mother dog came right out of the hole to greet her and sniff at the bag she carried. Small squeals came from the shadows, and while the dog ate the food, Thea gently reached in and brought the pups out, one by one.

There were five of them, three girls and two boys. One was substantially bigger than the others, a grey male with the rippled coat of the first one she had handled. They all had white feet and white noses, ranging in colour from black to grey. They seemed perfectly healthy, clean and dry with fat, full tummies.

'Well done, girl!' she applauded. 'You're making a very good job of them, aren't you?'

The dog trustingly wagged her tail, moved away a little to relieve herself, and then dived back into the hole to receive her offspring as Thea returned them to her. With a sense of virtue rewarded, Thea turned to leave.

She had only gone twenty or thirty yards before she heard somebody coming. Her heart leapt foolishly at the prospect of her secret being discovered. She glanced back, hoping there was no trace of the hidden dogs. The empty plastic bag in her hand might have to be explained. She couldn't pretend to be gathering mushrooms or nuts in June.

A large man came into view, between the trees. He carried a shotgun under his arm, and wore leather boots. His eyes were deep set and his cheeks pink. Thea felt a momentary terror at the sight of him, struck dumb by it, simply staring at him, wide-eyed.

'Morning,' he said pleasantly. 'Thought I heard a voice. Who're you talking to, then?'

She recovered her composure with an effort. 'Oh, nobody. Just muttering to myself, I suppose. It's a lovely morning, isn't it?' *Too lovely to be out here shooting things*, she wanted to add.

'Best day of the week, anyhow,' he agreed. 'It'll rain tomorrow, they say.'

'Really? That's bad news.'

'It is,' he affirmed.

'You live locally, do you?'

'Not far. And yourself?'

'I'm house-sitting at Hollywell, for Harriet Young.'

'Ah – I thought it must be you. But they said you'd got a dog.' He looked all round, eyes narrowed. 'Can't see it.'

'No. I left her behind.'

'Why'd you do that, then? Good for dogs, in these woods. Why would you leave it behind?'

Suspicion washed across his face like a

dye. Thea's mind went blank – what possible explanation could she give? The sight of his gun gave her an answer. 'Somebody said there was shooting going on, and I was worried she might get hurt.'

He shook his head slowly, like a teacher in despair at a pupil's pathetic response to a question. 'There's nobody around here would shoot a dog by mistake, least of all me,' he told her.

'So – what are you shooting?'

'Pigeons. Crows. Magpies. All the nuisances.'

'I see.'

'I'm missing a dog,' he said suddenly. 'Collie bitch, with a black face. Haven't see her, have you?'

The need to tell a direct lie was regrettable. Worse, it went against some deep principle that she had barely known existed until then. She played for time, pretending to think hard. 'Black face? No, I don't think so. How long has she been lost? You must be awfully worried.' She gabbled the words, convinced that he could see right through her. 'I'd be distraught if my Hepzie was lost.' It occurred to her that he might start calling his dog, and at such close quarters, she might well be unable to resist responding and showing herself. If Thea could keep him talking and convince him there was no trace of the animal in the woods, that disaster might be averted.

'Best part of a week,' the man replied to her question. 'I've a notion she was in pup, and has hidden herself away somewhere to keep them safe.'

'The poor thing!' Thea exclaimed. 'Why? What was she afraid of?'

'She knew I'd drown them if I found them. It's happened before.'

He showed no hint of shame at this admission. 'You cruel beast!' Thea accused him, too angry to mince her words. 'No wonder she's run away.'

'She's a working dog. Pups would keep her useless for a month or more.'

'Is it legal to drown puppies?'

He shrugged. 'So long as it's quick and they're newborn, it's nothing much.'

'But if you're right and she's been gone a week, they wouldn't be newborn now, would they?'

He tilted his head at her, still manifesting suspicion. 'I might be persuaded that she'd earned the right to keep one or two, at least,' he conceded. 'It's not so hard to manage without her, this time of year.'

It was tempting to believe him and disclose his dog's hiding place, but something prevented her. There could be a cruel game going on, in which he sought to entrap her into giving the dog away. And keeping 'one or two' pups really wasn't good enough.

'Are you fond of her?' she demanded. 'Do you have the slightest feelings for what she must be enduring, if you're right that she's trying to rear puppies all by herself?'

'She's a bright girl, I'll give her that. Doesn't have to be told twice. Never been disobedient in her life.' He was frowning at the question. 'We're a team, you might say.'

'So don't you think she deserves consideration? If you don't want pups, why the hell don't you have her spayed?' Anger had been rising since the admission about the drowning.

'Costs money,' he said shortly. 'Thought I'd kept her in this time, but some bloody dog broke in one night. Jumped right in through a window five feet off the ground.'

'You don't know who he was, then?'

'Something big, that's all I can say. There's a lurcher lives over towards Slad. Might be him.'

'Well, I'll tell you if I see her. Where do you live?'

He waved unhelpfully in the Sheepscombe direction. 'I walked there yesterday,' said Thea. 'With my dog. I saw the most fantastic view of Painswick from the top of a hill.'

He ducked his chin in agreement. 'Pretty enough,' he said shortly.

'I'll be getting back, then,' she said, afraid to leave the hidden dog when her master was so close by, but with little choice in the matter.

'And bring your animal next time,' he called after her. 'She's in no danger from me.'

It was a cleverly chosen parting remark, she guessed. He had a hunch that she was protecting his collie, and wanted her to believe everything would be all right if she revealed what she knew. Or perhaps she had penetrated his armour and made him see that he was behaving in a cruel way – not just by drowning puppies, but by shooting birds at a time when they had nests full of youngsters depending on them. The quick death of the parents would lead to slow starvation in the chicks. That was intolerable, to Thea's mind.

CHAPTER NINE

All she could do was hurry back to the Manor and liberate Hepzie, passing the Lodge with a mixture of unpleasant emotions. There was still such a lot she didn't know about Donny and his earlier life. Where had he lived before? What had his profession been? What would happen to his house now? She slowed her pace, in a vague gesture of respect, wishing she could bring him back to life again and resume their afternoon chats.

Hearing voices behind her, she turned to see two women coming through the gates towards her. They progressed slowly as she watched and wondered whether she should greet them. The distance was still slightly too great for conversation, so she used the moments before convergence to examine the two together. Jemima Hobson and Edwina Satterthwaite made a curious pair. They might have become stepmother and daughter, if Donny's senile wife had died and he had then married his lady friend – an awkward relationship at the best of times. Had his death brought them closer, or set them at odds, Thea wondered.

'Where's your little dog?' asked Edwina, her face level with Thea's, neither of them much over five feet tall.

'I left her in the house.'

'That's a shame on such a sunny day.'

'It was only for a little while. I'm going to fetch her now.'

Jemima seemed distracted, impatient. She was hovering beside the front door of her father's house, showing no inclination to talk, shifting restlessly from one foot to the other.

'I'll get out of your way,' said Thea, not at all wanting to leave them.

Edwina's face had sagged since the previous day and acquired an unhealthy colour. Her Victorian hair, previously so smooth and neat, was now escaping in wisps. Thea guessed that the woman had spent a sleepless night, and was feeling the sharp physical pains that nobody told you accompanied grief. By comparison, Jemima looked robust and efficient.

'No Toby today, then?' Thea said. 'I suppose he had to get back to work.'

Jemima snorted. 'What work?' she demanded. 'How did you come to meet him, anyway?'

Had there been something surreptitious in the visit that he and Edwina had paid her on Tuesday afternoon? Too late now, anyway. The older woman was not discernibly discomposed by the reference. 'It was Tuesday,' Thea said vaguely. Further remarks occurred to her, but were dismissed as potentially tactless or somehow treacherous. Perhaps because of her recent encounter in the woods, she felt that there were secrets on all sides, and she should be careful what she said.

'Toby's very upset,' Edwina put in, her voice toneless. 'So is Thyrza.'

'What!' Jemima's voice was strident. 'She couldn't *stand* him. Neither could that lunatic son of hers.'

The lunatic son must be Philippe, Thea noted. She opened her mouth to say she had met him as well, but closed it again, remembering her resolve to remain quiet. Any urge she might have to show off how well she was keeping up would have to be quashed. Besides, there was enough to interest her in this exchange between the two women.

'That isn't true,' mumbled Edwina unhappily. 'You just don't understand. You've never been any good at the more subtle things of life, Mimm.

172

It isn't your fault, but it can make you say very hurtful things sometimes.'

'How long have you two known each other?' Thea asked. After all, Donny still had a wife living. Had Edwina been his 'other woman' for decades?

'Twenty years or so,' said Jemima with an air of relief at being asked something factual. 'Dad and Weena worked together for ages.'

'Oh?' Thea did her best to imagine what sort of work would bring together a philosophical Donny and a Queen Victoria lookalike. 'What was it? The work, I mean.'

'He was a social worker, and I was a volunteer visitor.' Thea watched as Edwina focused briefly on earlier times when other people were sad and needy and she was the strong charitable one. A weak smile came and went, followed by a deep sigh. 'In West Bromwich.'

'Is that where you lived?' Neither Donny nor Edwina had anything like a Midlands accent. Nor did Jemima, come to that.

'At the time, yes.'

'And we were in Derbyshire, before moving to the Black Country,' said Jemima. 'Dad was promoted. Mum hated it. So did Cecilia. He moved down here the week after he retired.'

'Into the Lodge?' Thea eyed the little house doubtfully.

'No, no. They bought a bungalow up by the

church. But Mum's nursing home fees meant they had to sell it.' Jemima fixed a sharp gaze on the older woman, and added, 'And Edwina came too.'

Edwina bridled. 'It wasn't like that at all!' she objected. 'My family has lived here for centuries, and I wanted to return to my roots. It was Donny who followed me, not the other way around. I might remind you that Thyrza is still in the same house that we grew up in, and I found Donny the bungalow in the first place. Furthermore, when they had to sell up, I suggested the Lodge. That was before Harriet bought the Manor,' she added.

Thea was in her element. She loved piecing together the history of people's families and residences and where the turning points had come. Where women like her mother became obsessed by the names of people's children and the various ailments their friends were prone to, Thea wanted to know about reasons and connections and ambitions. Why did people move from one part of the country to another, and how did they settle in the new place? What made them happy? What were they most afraid of?

'So Thyrza stayed here all her life and you moved away – right?'

'Exactly. She was married twice, first to a local solicitor who died and then to a teacher who worked in Painswick. He used to walk to work across the fields in all weathers. People thought he was crazy. He's dead now as well. A sudden heart attack when he was fifty-nine.'

Thea made a suitable face at this unspectacular piece of cruel irony, and stored it up to report to Drew, if and when she saw him again. Already she had understood that he rather enjoyed swopping stories of noteworthy deaths, although they had shared only one or two thus far.

'It happens a lot, I think,' she said. 'It's not just the fat and lazy who have bad hearts.' Too late she remembered Cecilia, and her ghastly transplant. A glance at Jemima suggested that there was no call for remorse. Cecilia's sister was growing increasingly impatient, barely heeding the conversation. Thea accepted that she was not going to hear the story of Edwina's past, or what became of Mr Satterthwaite. She told herself not to be greedy – she already had a lot more detail than before.

'We ought to get on,' Jemima said. 'We've come to look for Dad's will. I thought his solicitor would have it, but apparently Dad insisted on keeping both copies here. Seems peculiar to me, but that's Dad for you.'

Edwina gave a little whimper of protest, but said nothing.

'And I must go and rescue my dog,' said Thea. 'I'm sure I'll see you again.'

Jemima evidently had a thought. 'There's no

date for the funeral yet. The coroner's officer is prevaricating over releasing the body.' Her staccato manner reached new heights. She seemed tight with frustration. 'You'd think they'd take my word for it, wouldn't you?'

Thea frowned slightly, wondering what that meant. 'Um . . .' she said.

'You can back me up, come to that. You'll probably have to, at the inquest. It's an obvious case of suicide. I don't know why they're wasting time and money in questioning it.'

'Are they?'

'Apparently.' Jemima looked at Edwina. 'But nothing's settled. And I've been thinking that perhaps we should think again about the funeral, especially if Dad's left a note about wanting a particular sort of burial. Mind you, I'd be surprised. It's just that Matt says we ought to keep an open mind.'

'Matt?'

'My husband. And there's Silas, of course. He's trying to force us to fix a date for the funeral, so he can book a flight. He won't come for more than the bare minimum, because his wife can't let him out of her sight.'

'Why doesn't she come as well, then?'

'She won't fly.' Jemima rolled her eyes in undisguised contempt. 'Can you believe it, in this day and age?'

'It's quite common,' said Edwina. Something

in her tone made Thea give her a close look. 'It's a sort of claustrophobia usually.'

'Don't *you* defend her, for heaven's sake,' snapped Jemima. 'That's taking saintliness a bit too far.'

Edwina gave an embarrassed little laugh. 'I've no reason to dislike Susan. It's Silas who's got the problem.'

'Um . . .' ventured Thea.

Both women looked at her. 'Silas feels a somewhat misplaced loyalty to his mother,' Edwina explained. 'It's perfectly natural.'

'He's an idiot,' said Jemima succinctly. She puffed out her cheeks in exasperation at all the demands piling on top of her. 'Now, come on, Ween, we've got work to do.'

Thea watched as they went to the front door. It was Edwina, she noted, who produced a key and unlocked it. Remembering the way Jemima had smashed her way in through the back door, it looked as if she still hadn't remembered to bring the one she had at home. She had not yet broken the habit whereby she took it for granted that the door would always be unlocked and she could walk in any time she liked. But Edwina could let herself in through the front, with a key. So which was the favoured visitor, Thea wondered – the daughter or the girlfriend?

* * *

It was still only half past ten, she noticed with surprise, when she got back inside the Manor. Hepzie jumped up at her in unreproachful greeting, and then ran outside to sniff around the front lawn as if tracking some wild creature. She always did that, Thea reminded herself. It did not necessarily mean that a badger or fallow deer had been there in the night; even less did it suggest that a human being had silently watched the house in the small hours. On the other hand, it *could* mean that. Just occasionally, the spaniel had tried to convey something important, which had only become apparent with hindsight. 'My next dog is going to be a beagle,' Thea told her. 'They're much more reliable informants than you.'

Time for some housework, she decided, with the sunshine highlighting dusty surfaces and demanding a polish to help create good reflections. The house was a pleasure to work in, with good-quality carpets and rugs on the floors and a general absence of clutter. The wood panelling was in excellent condition, waxed in the old-fashioned manner, without any crass varnish or synthetic polish. A light buffing with a soft cloth brought out the grains and colours of the wood like magic. A duster whisked over the window sills and shelves brought them up to scratch. The sofa cushions needed more attention, which seemed rather a wasted effort, given that

Hepzie would only flatten them again, and leave a veneer of her hair at the same time. There was no sign of any cobwebs in the corners, or scuffs on the skirting boards, which meant the whole project was completed well within the hour. It was a therapeutic interlude, in which Thea pretended she was living in 1860, working as chief parlourmaid to the wealthy and enlightened owners of the house. The Master was a publisher, she decided, producing liberal works by people like John Stuart Mill and Herbert Spencer – a man she had encountered in her youthful studies and always liked the sound of. The Mistress would be a bluestocking, reading everything her husband published and holding large dinner parties of highly intelligent people at which to discuss them. The servants would be contented and fairly treated. The delightful house, newly built, would be a joy to maintain.

The fantasy was rudely interrupted by the house telephone ringing. Somebody for Harriet, Thea assumed, putting down her duster and going to answer it. It had not rung since Edwina's call on Tuesday, and she fumbled it from its base, where it sat in the spacious hallway.

'Mrs Osborne?' The voice was familiar, but not immediately identifiable. 'It's DI Higgins again. Sorry to bother you.'

'No problem,' she said, wondering whether that

was true. The police often gave rise to problems, after all. She found herself unexpectedly wishing they would leave the whole matter of Donny Davis's death alone. What good would it do now to try to work out precisely what happened? It was a wish that must have been born from her meeting that morning with the two women who might be most aware of the secrets of Monday night and Tuesday morning. She had found herself liking them both, wanting things to go well for them in the aftermath of their loss. Even Jemima with her prickly stoicism must surely be experiencing some quiet relief at her father's death.

'Thank you,' said Higgins. 'I expect you can guess what I'm going to say?'

He overestimated her. 'Not really,' she said.

'The coroner's officer isn't satisfied with the circumstances of Mr Davis's death. He wants us to make further enquiries. Not surprising, of course, after that phone call we had, but a shame, in a way.'

'A terrible shame,' she confirmed. 'I can't believe anybody actually killed him against his wishes. It seems a waste of your time.'

'Right,' sighed Higgins. 'But ours is not to reason why. Rules are rules, as I think you and I agreed the other day.'

'So what do you want from me?'

'An objective assessment of Mr Davis's frame

of mind,' came the prompt reply. 'You saw him only hours before he died. Did he come across as a man about to kill himself?'

She took a deep breath. 'I can't answer that,' she said. 'I've never been with a suicide just before they did it. A whole lot of things might have happened after he left me.' She was dodging the question, and she knew it. The true answer was that, no, Donny had not seemed at all like a man contemplating suicide within the next twenty-four hours. She had been so surprised by his death that her brain had seized up on the day she and Jemima found him. Then she had struggled to convince herself that there was no good basis for her astonishment; that she hadn't really known the man and was in no position to judge his state of mind.

She found herself growing more and more certain that Edwina had been actively involved, probably at Donny's request. The woman's demeanour might be interpreted as that of a person carrying a guilty secret, a burden more complicated than simple grief.

Higgins grunted down the phone. 'And you've no other comment to make? Nothing else we ought to know?'

'I don't think so. I can see you've got a problem here, but I have no idea what you're supposed to do about it. How do you decide whether or not it's a murder investigation, anyway?'

'We piece together as much as we can of the picture, and take it from there.'

'Did the post-mortem show anything useful?'

'Nothing conclusive. No bruises or signs of any struggle.'

'Was he drugged?'

'Sedatives, dissolved in a drink. The sort of thing you'd self-administer.'

'Yes, but—' What had she been going to say? Her tongue had operated without conscious thought.

'But what?'

She thought hard. 'Donny wouldn't have had sedatives in the house, if I've understood him properly. He hated any kind of medication. He might have had a few aspirin and laxatives and Lemsip, but I can't imagine him taking sleeping pills.'

'As it happens, he did have a prescription for them, but not recently. We've checked with his doctor.'

'A local GP, I suppose?'

'Right. Not that he'd seen her for over two years.'

'That fits. He hated the whole medical profession, after what happened to his daughter. Maybe the pills were to get him through the awful time when she was dying.'

'I'm still not really getting it,' Higgins confessed. 'How does an old sick man manage not to see a doctor for so long? It's impossible.'

'He was stubborn. He'd boxed himself into a corner over it, and infuriated his daughter in the process.' It was coming more and more into focus for her as she spoke. 'He was convinced there was no possible good outcome for him, if he let himself fall into the hands of doctors. As he saw it, they'd just cut him up, or starve him slowly, or pump him full of drugs. He believed he would become subhuman and lose all control of his own destiny. He hadn't really any option but to take a short cut by killing himself.' She paused, surprised at her own detailed grasp of Donny's attitude. 'At least – I'm embellishing a bit, I think. He didn't quite say all that.'

Higgins grunted again. 'I imagine a lot of people feel like that – but they don't follow through on it, do they? If something hurts, they run to the doctor automatically. It's inevitable. We're all programmed that way.'

'Not Donny. He reprogrammed himself.'

'He must have had support. Somebody who was on his side.'

'Edwina,' said Thea promptly. 'That was Edwina.'

'Not Mrs Hobson, then?'

'She didn't like it, I told you. And she might have understood that she was on dangerous ground if she let herself be drawn in to what he said he wanted. She was effectively his next of kin, which I guess made it all more serious for her. She couldn't show herself to be in favour of him killing himself, when she presumably inherits his house and any money there might be.'

'Did he own the house?' Higgins could be heard rustling papers at the end of the phone. 'No – I thought not. He rented it from Miss Young. Three hundred quid a month.'

'Really? I suppose that's cheap for this area.'

'A nice little income, all the same.'

It was obvious, Thea realised on a moment's reflection. The Lodge would be part of the Hollywell estate in perpetuity, only available for rent. 'So there wasn't very much for Donny's family to inherit,' she concluded.

Higgins went on with his questions. 'What do you know about Mrs Davis?'

'His wife? Not as much as you, I imagine. She's in a home somewhere, more or less abandoned, by the sound of it. Lost her marbles when Cecilia died. Jemima shows no sign of caring about her. Toby visits, apparently.'

The detective inhaled sharply, as if that snippet was indeed new to him. 'Isn't that rather odd?'

'More like overload. Jemima has a husband, kids, a farm and a stubborn old dad. A batty mother probably feels like a burden too far.'

'I mean odd that the husband of a dead daughter should be the one to keep up the visits.'

'I don't see why. It isn't unusual, surely?'

'Maybe not. Thanks, anyway. You've been very helpful,' he congratulated her. 'This is absolutely the sort of thing we need.'

'You could find it out quite easily for yourself.' She felt a flash of resentment at being used in such a way. 'Just ask them all.'

'They wouldn't tell us, would they? Not the way you have. People hold very tightly to their self-esteem. They don't admit to neglecting their mothers or wishing their fathers dead. They assume we're looking for guilt, so they're defensive from the outset.'

'I know,' she conceded. 'But I can't see where all this is getting you.'

'I told you – it creates the big picture. It throws up anomalies. It gives us some background.'

'But it's only my take on it. I could be completely wrong.'

'Don't worry, that's understood. We're not going to quote you.'

She examined her conscience for any betrayals she might have inadvertently committed. There didn't seem to be any. 'OK, then,' she said. 'Can I go now?'

'Of course.'

* * *

The fact of Donny having taken ground-up sleeping pills niggled at her for the next hour or more. She tried to imagine him mixing them into a mug of black coffee and drinking it down, despite the bitter unnatural taste it surely had. What would his thoughts have been? Dogged determination that there could be no failure? Loneliness? Despair? Fear? Yes – fear must have been a large part of it. How could it not be? Sheer quivering terror, more likely. She could see his hands shaking even more than usual, the tremor in his neck keeping his head perpetually moving. At what point would he then have pulled the bag over his head and wound sticky tape several times around his own neck? When he felt himself slipping away? How in the world could anybody time it properly, all on their own? Too soon, and the instinct to survive would have you clawing at it, trying to pull it off again. Too late, and it would be impossible to do effectively. You'd be too woozy to get it all the way on.

Which indicated, yet again, that he had somebody there to help. And if she, Thea, could work that out, then the police would certainly arrive at the same conclusion, if they hadn't done so already.

The afternoon was even sunnier, the whole house warming up. It was a day for being outside and

Thea followed her instincts without hesitation. From the front garden, the Lodge was plainly visible, a fact that made her uncomfortable. She would rather forget Donny and his friends for a while. So she went around to the back, where there were large trees and a very neglected vegetable garden. She found a folding chair in the utility room at the back of the house, and erected it on a small level patch in dappled sunshine. She had a book with her, but found it difficult to concentrate on reading. Instead she found herself comparing this garden with others attached to houses she had been left in charge of. The variety could hardly be greater, from immaculately kept showpieces to muddy areas colonised by ducks and geese. In some cases the weather had prevented her from scarcely getting to know the outside areas at all.

The spaniel flopped lazily at her feet, content to spend an idle afternoon in the sunshine, if that was her mistress's choice. She had no better suggestions, needed nothing more to make life complete. If another person arrived, she would greet them cheerfully, but she had no craving for excitement. Thea watched her enviously, wishing she could so easily find satisfaction.

The adjacent property revealed no sign of life, the huge and perfectly cut lawn basking in the sunshine all by itself. On the other side, a track led away towards some fields, holding little of interest that Thea could see. A tractor had passed along it a few days earlier, and nothing more. Planes silently crossed the sky, leaving silver streaks now and then.

It was a very undemanding house-sit, by any standards. Only the geckoes, with their unregistered breeding programme, called for supervision. Harriet was paying her the usual rate, which was a not inconsiderable sum for two weeks. It seemed daft. But such daftness was far from unusual in Thea's experience. She had been similarly employed before, to do something a neighbour could easily have handled. There was some element of guarding, protecting, that was born of the general atmosphere of nervousness in British society. Burglars, vandals, marauders were lurking just out of sight, intent on intruding, wrecking and stealing your precious possessions. Hollywell Manor clearly had to be kept safe from any such predations. There was a large and beautiful stained glass window on the landing upstairs. It would be tragic if that got broken. The wood panelling was probably worth quite a lot on the reclamation market. There was good antique furniture and expensive carpets. There were oil paintings along the upstairs gallery. Perhaps in Harriet's place, Thea too would have wanted to know somebody was standing guard over it all.

She thought of nightwatchmen, expected to

stay awake from dusk to dawn, watching for robbers. They used television and all-night radio to pass the time, but how terribly long every night must seem to them. Did they phone their friends, and send emails and play computer games as well? At least Thea was allowed to go for walks and shopping trips and visits to any people she might befriend during her stay. At least she had her dog for company, and plenty to think about.

But still the afternoon crawled painfully slowly along. The sun hardly seemed to move across the sky, the shadows barely shifting. She got thirsty, her book failed to engage her, and annoying questions about Donny persistently intruded into her head.

It was not quite three o'clock when she got up and padded restlessly into the house for some fruit juice. She collected her mobile, to check whether anyone had sent a text. The only person who ever did so was Jessica, and that wasn't a frequent event. When she had been with Phil Hollis, he had nagged her relentlessly about keeping the phone switched on and within earshot, in case he needed to speak to her. Since they had parted, she saw little reason to maintain the regime. If Jessica needed her urgently, she would find a way of making contact. Thea routinely lodged the address of the current house she was sitting with her daughter, and left it at that. The mobile was superfluous, most of the time.

But there was a message on it. The voicemail icon was flashing. It took her a moment to remember what it meant, and how to access the recording. Eventually, she did it, and found herself listening to Drew Slocombe's voice.

'Thea? It's Drew. Sorry to do this. I hope it works. It's just that I've come across an interesting coincidence, and thought you'd like to know about it. It seems that your employer is a successful author of a book about funerals. At least I think it must be her. Call me if you're interested. Bye.'

Her employer? He could only mean Harriet. But she had seen nothing in the house to indicate that Harriet wrote books. There was nothing on the ground or first floors remotely resembling an office. A second floor remained unexplored, however. If Harriet had indeed produced a book about funerals, that might explain why Donny had paid such regular visits to her. He could have been consulting her special expertise – which could at a stretch surely extend to the subject of suicide. But why had he not long ago resolved the question of his own disposal, in that case? And where exactly had Harriet come by this particular interest? Had she worked as an undertaker, perhaps? Or had she been commissioned to write the book, as a freelance expected to turn her hand to anything that came along?

And why hadn't Donny said something, when the subject arose on his first visit? She thought back, trying to recapture every nuance of the short conversation on the doorstep as he departed on that first afternoon. She had described Drew's business and what he could offer, as she understood it. Donny had seemed excited, warmly receptive of the sort of service being offered. He had seized on her words, like a person finally getting something they had wanted for a long time. When he had come back the next day he was more restrained, but still eager to meet with Drew. So what had Thea suggested that was different from Harriet's contributions? She could hardly hope to answer that until she had seen the book itself.

She would have to phone Drew for more information. Was it a good time, she wondered, knowing little of his daily routines. His children would be arriving home from school – but did he stay away from the family, working in his little office until it was time for the evening meal? Was his wife capable of cooking? Where would his intriguing partner, Maggs, be?

Arriving at the conclusion that it was as good a time as any, she returned his call. He answered on the second ring, giving the impression that he had been sitting by the phone just waiting for it to summon him.

'Drew? It's Thea. Thanks for the message. I

only just found it. When did you ring?'

'First thing this morning. I found a review of the book in a magazine. It didn't mean anything to me until I noticed the name, Harriet Young. And it said she lives in the Cotswolds in a manor house, so I wondered if it could be her.'

'Yes, it must be. What else does it say?'

'Apparently the last chapter is highly controversial. It advocates a change in the law to permit assisted suicide, and people controlling the timing and manner of their death.'

'Which chimes with what Donny wanted,' said Thea, half to herself. 'Can we get a copy, do you think?'

'Already done. Maggs had heard of it anyway, and she dashed off to Yeovil to get one. She says the book's selling really well. She was quite scathing that I hadn't heard of it, actually,' he added ruefully.

'Even though it's only just being reviewed?'

'Oh . . . no. The magazine is six months old. They tend to pile up, and I was flipping through them before throwing them out. It's not very busy here at the moment.'

'It explains where her money comes from,' said Thea.

'Not really. At least, not unless she's been writing bestsellers for a while. And I think we'd know if she had.'

'Maybe she's some sort of consultant. Maybe she helps people who want to die, and charges for it.' It sounded unlikely, as she said it. Harriet had not struck her as any kind of consultant. 'But I have to admit I've never heard of such people.'

Drew knew better. 'Oh I have. There's a growing trend for that sort of thing. Like a sort of midwife, if you like. But they do have to be careful, obviously.'

'So now we have a dodgy suicide right here on Harriet's doorstep, which seems rather a coincidence, don't you think?' said Thea.

'Definitely. I said it was. But maybe there is a logical connection, a reason why it's all come together the way it has.'

She reminded Drew that somebody had called the police and said Edwina helped Donny to kill himself, which could lead to her being charged with murder.

'Who would do that?'

'Your guess is as good as mine. A man, is all I know. It could be anybody. I haven't met everyone who knew Donny and his family, obviously.'

'Just the main players,' he said shrewdly.

'Don't you start. That's what Higgins said. He's the police detective who's investigating.'

'Have you met him before?'

'Once or twice, yes. He's a nice man. Kind. A bit bovine.'

193

'What does the coroner say?'

'I have no idea.'

'He has to sign it off before the funeral can go ahead. And that means being entirely satisfied that there was no foul play. The phone call could scupper the whole thing. Probably has, from the sound of it.' She thought she could hear strain in his voice, an effort to concentrate on the remote events in Cranham when he had more pressing matters to attend to at home.

'Cheer up! You might yet get the funeral,' she said flippantly.

He made a sound like somebody in pain. 'No, Thea, that was never going to work. They're not going to want him buried all the way down here. Stop trying to rustle up business for me. It's never a good idea.'

'It is if the alternative is that you go bust,' she argued.

'I'll go bust all the quicker if people think I use shady practices to get customers. It all has to be totally transparent, don't you see? The subject is very delicate. People's suspicions are easily aroused.'

'I know. I wasn't being serious,' she apologised. 'So why did you call me, if you're not interested in Donny any more?'

'I didn't say I wasn't interested. I'm sorry I never met him. He sounded like a good man.'

194

'I don't know if he was good, but he was pleasant company. I'm lonely without him, to be honest.'

He made a clicking noise, part sympathy, part frustration. 'You can phone me any time,' he offered. 'For a chat.'

'Thanks. I expect I will.'

'Any news of your maverick dog in the woods?'

'Actually, yes.' She told him about meeting the rosy-cheeked man with the gun, who had to be the dog's owner.

'Was he going to shoot the dog?' Drew asked.

'No, of course not. He's not that angry with her.'

'But he wasn't calling for her?'

'He probably gave up days ago. Or maybe he was embarrassed.'

'What?'

'It's embarrassing shouting for your dog. It suggests poor discipline.' She paused and thought about it. 'And he might be a bit ashamed as well.'

'Mmm?' he prompted.

'Well, he drove her away, didn't he? He hasn't played fair by her. I told him he was cruel and he just took it, as if he knew I was right.'

'So you think it would be safe to tell him where she is?'

Her stomach jolted in protest at this. 'No, no. That would be a real betrayal. He said he'd only let her keep one or two pups. That's no good.'

'But she's going to need help . . . isn't she?'

'When I've gone, yes. But there's another week before I have to decide what to do.'

'Right. Meanwhile, you can research Harriet and her book sales. Have a look at her Amazon ranking.'

'Her what?'

Drew laughed. 'I'd never heard of it, either. Maggs told me. It's on the Internet. I'll leave you to figure it out. It'll give you something to do.'

'Thanks,' she said dryly.

'You're welcome. So – you don't sound as if you think my amazing discovery means anything much to the investigation.'

'I'm not sure. I think the biggest factor is the anonymous call to the police saying Edwina helped Donny to kill himself. Without that, there'd be no cause for suspicion.'

'And you haven't heard who's doing the funeral?'

'I doubt whether they've chosen anybody yet. They were looking through his papers this morning.'

'But we know he hadn't made any arrangements in advance, don't we?'

'I guess so, since he asked me if I knew anybody. That was a bit odd, actually. I mean – why me? You'd think Harriet would have sorted that out with him long since, if she's such an expert on the subject.'

'Do you think she knew about me?' he said slowly. 'That I'm trying to open a new burial ground in the Cotswolds?'

Thea found this idea decidedly unsettling. 'Possibly,' she said. 'Since it's obviously a special interest with her.'

'And could she have heard that you and I were both involved in the murder in Broad Campden?'

'I wasn't involved,' she protested.

'Yes you were.'

'Not publicly. I wasn't in the papers, like you were.'

'OK. But I think you underestimate your fame across the area. Your reputation as a house-sitter who always has some sort of crisis to deal with must be quite widespread.'

'Have you heard anything?' she asked suspiciously.

'Here and there,' he said vaguely.

'Hmm. I'm not sure what I think about that.' This was not quite true. She definitely did not like the feeling of being under surveillance by the people of the Cotswolds, engaged for house-sitting by somebody who knew much more about her than had been acknowledged. She felt manipulated and insecure. 'I'd rather maintain my privacy.'

'So I gathered back in March,' he said, with a short laugh. 'And I can see why you wouldn't like it. People don't really understand. They hear half a story and jump to conclusions. All the same, I think you should be pleased they don't regard you as a jinx. The way I heard it, you've got superhuman talents, and can solve mysterious crimes when the police are stuck. A kind of good fairy, restoring order out of chaos.'

'Rubbish,' she spluttered, feeling rather better. 'I don't believe a word of it.'

'Up to you. I'll have to go now. Maggs is flapping at me outside. She thinks I'm slacking in here.'

'I'd like to meet her sometime. She sounds nice.'

'She's a marvel.' He said it like a mantra, repeated too often for the meaning to remain. Thea suspected he had created a myth where his partner was concerned, and could just be in the process of doing the same thing with her.

'Thanks for the information, anyway,' she said. 'I'll keep you posted.'

'Bye then,' he said quickly and he was gone.

CHAPTER TEN

Drew had given her something fresh to think about, for which she was grateful. Donny's character and state of mind had been clarifying over the days since she had first met him. The picture was quite consistent, given the history of the family and the personalities involved. He had endured years in which his wife and daughter had been long-term patients, never entirely healthy. His wife had officially become a 'survivor', his daughter a more acutely ill patient, before she died. It had left him asking himself what value it all had, what the cost-benefit balance really was.

The discovery that Harriet was unusually knowledgeable about funerals had at first seemed like something Donny would find useful. But further thought cast doubt on this. Not everybody cared about their own funeral, thinking it quite irrelevant. Once you were dead, nothing else mattered. Even Donny, unafraid of the realities of dying, might have jibbed at exhaustive discussions about the disposal of his remains, especially if his daughter consistently refused to talk to him about it.

And yet he had quite readily agreed to a meeting with Drew Slocombe, to discuss his own grave. A terrible thought hit her at this point: had Donny killed himself in order to avoid the meeting? Had he been too polite to tell her he really didn't want to engage in it? Had Jemima or Edwina said something to strengthen this resistance? Had she, Thea, inadvertently driven him to kill himself weeks or months sooner than he would otherwise have done? It seemed all too dreadfully likely, as she recalled Jemima's horrified anger at her admission that she had contacted Drew on Donny's behalf. It was, after all, a dubious favour to do somebody – to arrange a meeting with an undertaker in anticipation of their death. Perhaps Harriet's interest had not been helpful at all, but frightening. If she believed in assisted suicide, would that not be rather alarming to a man in Donny's situation? Too close to being possible, too easy to get sucked in before you felt properly ready. Had she recruited Edwina against Donny's actual wishes, persuading him to make the living will, without ever properly listening to him?

So why had he died two days after Harriet went away?

Interference was always hazardous – she knew that. Especially coming into a new place, where everybody had their relationships established, and things were seldom what they seemed. Had she disrupted a delicate balance in some way, and precipitated Donny's suicide? If so, wouldn't Harriet have foreseen the consequences and made an effort to warn her? Instead, it felt as if the exact opposite had happened. Donny had broached the subject of dying and Thea had unhesitatingly jumped in with ill-considered assistance.

Harriet really ought to have warned her. How could she, Thea, have possibly understood the undercurrents? There was no need to feel guilty or reproach herself, nothing she might have done to affect something so massively momentous as choosing the moment to kill yourself. Or so she tried to persuade herself.

These musings made her restless. However vigorously she countered the arguments pushing into her mind, the logic seemed all too dreadfully clear. 'Come on, Heps,' she announced. 'We're going out.'

On the doorstep, she changed her plan from a walk to a drive. The car had hardly been used since she arrived, and there was still much to explore. They would meander through the little lanes, taking a route around three sides of a square, with the idea of familiarising herself more closely with the locality. The sun was still high, the shops would still be open, and there was no need to hurry back for anything. There was even the option of carrying on to Stroud, a town she barely knew at all apart from the supermarket she had found on Monday.

They did not get beyond Painswick. On a whim, seeing a clear space for parking in the main street, she got out and took the dog on a lead around the little streets. They didn't meet any familiar figures – not Phil's sister Linda or any of the few dozen people she had met during her various house-sits. The flash of disappointment this gave rise to made her realise how much she had hoped for a chance encounter with an old acquaintance. The church still struck her as incongruous, as it had when viewed from a distant hill. But the small jumbled streets were even more beautiful close up. Some were barely more than alleys, some sloped steeply. All the buildings were of the same perfectly cut stone, with low walls and barely protruding window sills effortlessly functional as well as utterly pleasing. Doors and windows were decorated with pediments and arches, shop signs were hand-painted and oddly shaped. She drifted slowly where the whim took her, savouring the visual glory of yet another confidently lovely small Cotswolds town.

CHAPTER ELEVEN

They returned to the hot car and drove away with the windows open, somehow enriched by the diversionary interlude, where nothing mattered but the images of an architecture that felt as if something greater than humankind had created it.

And then, standing in a gateway on the road back to Cranham, was a tall man with a grey dog and a small child. The child's face was exactly level with the dog's, which somehow emphasised the human qualities that poodles possess. Automatically, Thea slowed and stopped, pushing the excited spaniel off her lap. Hepzie always went into a frenzy at the sight of another dog when she was in the car. Outside, she was far more restrained.

Thea leant her head out of the window and gave the little group a broad smile. 'Hello again,' she said.

'The house-sitter!' Philippe gave her a friendly nod, wagging his head in a diagonal movement that suggested carefree bonhomie. 'Nice to see you again. This is Tamsin – my daughter.'

Oh. The only gay in the village had a *daughter*? Had it been a sperm donation for a pair of lesbians? Or what?

'Hello, Tamsin. Hello, Jasper,' said Thea politely. 'I've been exploring. Aren't these long evenings lovely? You forget that it gets dark at four in December. How is that possible?' She looked up at the sky, where the sun was still in full evidence at seven o'clock. 'We only got as far as Painswick and then drifted slowly back. I stopped once or twice on the way. The time just seemed to go.'

'I know just what you mean. Tam's mum must be wondering where we've got to by now. Jasper's such a keen walker, we just keep going.'

Tamsin had black hair and deep brown eyes, totally different from her father in colouring, but she had the same-shaped face, the long chin, low brow and familiar full lips. 'She looks like you,' said Thea.

'Nonsense!' he protested. 'She's the image of her mother.'

'Mummy has light-brown skin, Granny's pink, an' I'm coffee,' recited the child.

Thea had put the skin colour down to a few

204

weeks spent in the sunshine. 'Milky coffee,' she suggested. 'Cappuccino, maybe.'

'Are you OK up at the Manor?' asked Philippe, breaking into the chat about skin colour. 'With everything that's been happening?'

Thea remembered his uncharitable comments during their first meeting. Something to the effect that Donny was a nuisance and should get on with his suicide plans sooner rather than later. She had been left with an impression of a selfish, insensitive man, who took no account of Donny's feelings. This time he seemed a lot nicer.

'It was a big shock,' she said. 'A real surprise – to everyone, apparently.'

'Not to me. Inevitable, as I see it.'

'Yes, so you said before. I suppose you knew him better than I did. Even so . . .'

He glanced down at his little girl, who was probably no more than five, and Thea understood that she was not to pursue the subject in any detail. She would normally have few qualms about discussing death in front of a small child, but in this case it was not her decision. She ought to tread carefully until fully confident that she had the permission of the child's father.

What's more, this child was showing an unusual curiosity about the conversation. 'Did you have a surprise?' she asked Thea. 'Was it a nice one?'

'Not really.'

'We're talking about Donny,' said her father. 'He died. Remember we told you?'

'Oh yes.' The child was entirely matter-of-fact. 'Aunt Edwina was sad.'

'She still is, baby. She'll be sad for a long time.'

'I met your mother,' said Thea with a little frown, alerted by the reference to Aunt Edwina to the close links these people had with Jemima and Donny. 'And Toby.'

'I know you did,' he said as if this was obvious. 'You seem to have come across the full cast of characters in this little drama.'

'Except for your wife,' she pointed out. 'And Donny's, come to that.' The mysteriously banished Mrs Davis was beginning to niggle at her. She who ought to be the 'chief mourner', arranging the funeral and sitting in the front pew. By association, Drew Slocombe also came to mind.

'The wives are notable for their absence,' smiled Philippe. 'Especially poor old Janet. I don't think you need worry about her, though.'

'But . . .' The wholesale abandonment of the woman struck Thea for the first time as seriously unkind. 'Doesn't *anybody* other than Toby visit her?'

'Nope. It's much less awkward than it sounds. I mean – she has effectively been replaced by Aunt

Edwina, for quite a while now. She's done Donny a lot more good than Janet ever did.'

'Yes, but . . .' she tried again. 'What does *Jemima* think about it? Doesn't she feel any loyalty to her mother?'

'Jemima doesn't analyse things. That's to say, she never goes more than a millimetre below the surface. So she doesn't actually know what she feels about anything beyond the very simple basics. She sees no reason to resent Edwina. She reacts like an animal would – anger, pleasure, impatience, joy – she's perfectly honest about it.'

'Yes,' said Thea slowly. 'I noticed some of that. I was with her when we found Donny, you know.'

'I know you were. And how was she about it?'

'Efficient,' said Thea after a moment's reflection.

Philippe laughed. 'Good word,' he approved. 'Now, we have to get home. Come on, kidlet. Definitely past your bedtime.'

The little girl grasped his outstretched hand and gave Thea a proprietorial grin, as if to proclaim her good fortune in having such a father. After all, a lot of children didn't have one at all. Thea grinned back. 'See you again, I hope,' she said.

It had been a good day, on the whole, she judged. No further disasters, some social exchanges, and a deeper grasp of the interactions amongst the people around her – all slightly better than she might have hoped for when she awoke. The sunshine had been an omen, it seemed, bringing the beauty and goodwill that was part of the English June stereotype.

She went to bed in a calm mood, having visited the geckoes last thing. The eggs in their snug nests held a promise that she found exciting. She spent a few minutes conscientiously examining them. When they hatched, they would have to find food and shelter and companionship for themselves. It seemed a lot to expect. Harriet had written a brief list of instructions against the event of one hatching unexpectedly. *Make sure it can't escape. Give it a little bit of mashed fruit and a drop of water in a jam jar lid.*

It would be thrilling to witness a little hatchling emerge, of course, but the responsibility would probably outweigh the excitement.

Friday was sunny again and Thea felt a fresh responsibility to get outside and make the most of it. She could finally go and investigate Slad, rectifying an omission that seemed to have gone on for a long time. Or she could go to Gloucester and have a look at the cathedral or canal basin. She wasn't sure she'd ever actually been there at any time in her life. But that would make complications concerning the dog, and really she did not very much like cathedrals unless there was somebody with her to point out the main features. And a sunny day was more suited to open countryside, not city centres.

It was now three days since Donny had died, and there was a sense of limbo around the whole unhappy business. DI Higgins probably wouldn't contact her again. Nobody had mentioned a funeral to her. The people involved seemed to have melted away, forgetting all about the temporary house-sitter who had just happened to be present when the body was discovered. Suppressing a flicker of resentment, she gave a mental shrug and told herself she ought to be pleased.

But she was not pleased. She wanted to get to know Jemima better, for one thing, her curiosity piqued by something Philippe had said the previous evening. He had confirmed Thea's impression that Donny's daughter lived in fear of the deeper realities; that she evaded the dark side of life with all her strength. Such an attitude was perfectly common, of course. Nobody wanted to dwell excessively on death and disease and betrayal and loss, unless they were abnormally morbid. And perhaps Donny himself had been rather the same as his daughter. He refused medical help, in case it led to painful and undignified treatment, as it had in the case of Cecilia – and his wife, come to that. Jemima had said nothing to suggest that she disagreed with this approach. Nobody had mentioned that she put pressure on her father to see a doctor. If anything, it appeared that she colluded with him in his avoidance of any such action. Was that not wrong of her, Thea wondered. It was certainly unusual. All the stereotypes had the family urging their sick relative to get to the GP as fast as they could. There was actually something quite brave in giving their support in doing the opposite. Jemima might be frightened, but she wasn't a coward, it seemed. She had been prepared to stand by Donny's decision, even if it resulted in acrimony and accusations. Because it would. It was regarded as virtually criminal to fail to see a doctor if you knew there was good medical reason to do so. Thea felt a moment's rage at this idea. Doctors meant well, more or less, but they certainly had a very inflated idea of their own importance, thanks to society's wholesale reliance on them.

And Donny himself had been frightened, or revolted, or horrified by the prospect of a post-mortem on his dead body, according to Jemima. That was another factor in the balance against his having killed himself.

She tried to recall exactly how Jemima had reacted to the discovery of her father's dead body. *Efficient*, she had said to Philippe, but that wasn't quite accurate. Relief had been there, unmistakably. A dilemma resolved, a long and miserable end escaped. After the first shock – and Thea could swear there had been shock – the implications had all looked positive. It was sad, even painful, but not unbearably so. An old sick man had killed himself, seemingly without much suffering, seemingly in accord with what he had been wanting for some time.

So what was wrong? Somewhere, something was quite definitely wrong. The anonymous phone call accusing Edwina of manslaughter, if not murder, was at the heart of it. But Thea's own observations left her with profound misgivings. Donny had not wanted to die on that particular day. He had made an appointment with Drew. He was enjoying getting to know Thea. He was twinkly and spirited and witty. You didn't kill yourself while those words could still be applied to you. You just *didn't*. Drew himself had tried to suggest that, based on what he'd heard from her.

She should try to find Edwina again, and invite her to respond to the accusation that had been made against her. The police would surely have told her of it by this time; they had no choice but to confront her with it, albeit gently and non-judgementally. Quite how to arrange a meeting was tricky, however. She was not averse to simply walking up to the front door of a person's house and inviting herself in for a cup of tea when the situation seemed to demand it, but this did not quite feel like one of those situations. Edwina Satterthwaite was elderly and under police suspicion. Although she had been entirely civil to Thea, there had been no real relationship established between them. She could hardly be expected to readily open up and tell the house-sitter everything – especially if she really had helped Donny to kill himself and then panicked when the implications hit her.

Besides, Thea didn't know where Edwina lived, beyond the fact that it was somewhere in Cranham.

She opted for a stroll in the direction of the village centre and the pub, with Hepzie on a lead. She deliberately deferred another visit to the dog in the woods, in the hope of avoiding undue dependency on the part of the animal. If it could not rely on regular deliveries of food, then it might try a bit of hunting for itself – or even risk sneaking back to its own farmyard in the hope of finding something to eat.

Cranham had very few level stretches. The road took a dive downhill from the Manor, levelled briefly, and then surged uphill again. All the other roads similarly sloped upwards out of the hollow in which the core of the settlement had been positioned. The pub was up one of these smaller side roads, to the south of the main village street, and was as yet an unknown quantity. Perhaps she would be brave enough to call in and see if they provided coffee. It was not quite eleven o'clock, a time when village pubs would never have dreamt of opening in the past. Now some of them had embraced the relaxed regulations on opening times and invited people in from mid morning to late evening. In June especially, they were likely to want to attract any summer visitors who might fancy a drink.

It was a nice-looking little pub, unpretentious and tucked away. Across the street were a few classically lovely old buildings that she would have liked to examine more closely, if it hadn't been for an old man watching her with unashamed curiosity from the doorway of one of them. She smiled and waved at him, and walked on. The pub was evidently not yet open, but even if it had been, she wasn't sure she had the courage to go in alone. It probably didn't allow dogs anyway, she thought sourly, remembering the inhospitable establishment in Broad Campden, which hid cravenly behind spurious hygiene regulations when banning perfectly clean spaniels from their premises.

'Morning,' came a breathless voice behind her. 'Out for a walk?'

She turned to see Thyrza, mother of Philippe, grandmother of Tamsin, sister of Edwina. Like her sister, Thyrza had a faintly regal appearance, but was two or three inches taller than Edwina, with less covering on her hips. If you had to choose a queen with which to compare her, it would probably be the late Queen Mother, for the confident air and impression that her wish was most people's command. There was a directness to her gaze that Thea found engaging. She reminded herself that a great deal had happened since they had last met, and it was incumbent upon her to do her best to be diplomatic in the face of so much sensitive emotion amongst Donny's friends and relations.

'It's a lovely day for it,' she said with a smile.

'The pub doesn't open for an hour or more yet,' the older woman told her.

'No problem. I wasn't going in, anyway. I don't like sitting on my own in a pub. And I don't expect they allow dogs.'

'They do. Of course they do. My son comes here a lot with Jasper. I could sit with you,' Thyrza offered. 'If they had been open, that is.'

They both eyed the pub door as if they might force it open by sheer willpower. 'I'm not really thirsty,' Thea admitted. 'We just came out for a little stroll. Do you live in one of these lovely old houses?'

'Just around the corner. It's the house I told you about.'

In the family for three hundred years, Thea recalled. 'Oh, yes. It must be one of the oldest buildings in the village, then?'

'One of them, yes. There are a few that go back to the seventeenth century. Ours isn't quite that ancient. And of course, it's been so altered over the years, there is very little left that's really original.'

'I saw your son yesterday, with his little girl.' Again, she had to bite her tongue to prevent it from voicing an unacceptable comment or question. *It was such a surprise, because I thought he was gay.*

'Oh yes? He's off work for a week or two, although he's always on call. That's why he can never go right away. Dedicated,' she finished complacently. 'He's always been utterly dedicated.'

'What exactly is his speciality?' Thea asked, before recalling that Philippe had told her himself, days earlier.

'Cardiac surgery,' said Thyrza proudly. 'He's quite brilliant.'

'And he lives on this side of the common, does he?' Thea was still a bit shaky on the invisible delineations controlling the geography of Cranham.

'He's three hundred yards from my house, which is just far enough away for comfort. It wouldn't do to try and live in the same house as a daughter-in-law. That would be disastrous.'

Thea laughed politely. 'Very wise.' She was struggling to refrain from asking more questions, mindful of the objection Thyrza made when they last met. Besides, there was enough information emerging unprompted to keep her happy.

'And Edwina's right over the other side of the common, near the allotments,' Thyrza volunteered. 'There's more to the village than you might think at first. There are almost two hundred houses, you know. Doesn't seem like that many, does it?'

Thea stuck to the central point, trying to make it sound like a remark, rather than a question. 'But you both grew up in the house you now occupy.'

Thyrza turned her head away, her gaze on the rising ground to the east. 'That's right. Now, I think you're starting to ask questions again,' she said in a low voice. 'And I really can't see where it could get either of us. I did hear that you have close connections to the police, and I don't like to feel that I'm being surreptitiously cross-examined.'

'Oh!' Thea's heart thumped violently at the sudden change of mood and the familiar feeling of having gone too far yet again. 'No . . . I'm not. Honestly, there's none of that. I'm just nosy – I told you before. Interested. I'm sorry . . .' she tailed off unhappily.

'There are no mysteries or secrets in our family, I assure you. Neither my sister nor I have anything to hide. Nor does my son. We are ordinary, innocent residents of a small village. My sister had a very close friendship with Donny Davis for a great many years. She also knew his wife. She has nothing to feel guilty about, and has committed no crime. Can I make myself any clearer than that?'

'Yes. I mean, no. Of course. I'm sorry.' Thea felt as if she had been caught deliberately stirring up trouble, blunderingly making insinuations that couldn't help but be offensive. Except, when she thought back, she couldn't find anything she'd said that could actually be interpreted in that way. Thyrza Hastings was being impossibly oversensitive, for some reason.

'Apology accepted,' said Thyrza curtly. 'Just be aware that it doesn't always work to your credit when you barge in with your amateur sleuthing.'

'Oh, I see,' said Thea slowly. 'You've heard about my other involvements.'

Perhaps impressed by this piece of quick thinking, Thyrza softened and smiled. 'How clever of you! I am acquainted with a person by the name of Fiona who lives in Temple Guiting. I gather that you were there a year ago, with your senior-policeman boyfriend.'

'Fiona – Janey's friend? How are they now? I liked them both very much.' She paused. 'What did they tell you about me?'

'That you weren't as soft and sweet as you look,' said Thyrza with a painful directness. 'That you're not afraid of anything and won't rest until you've dug into people's private lives, merely to satisfy your own curiosity.'

'Gosh! I suppose most of that's true, more or less. Although you make me sound so interfering, when I truly don't believe that's fair. More than that, I'm not nearly as fearless as Fiona thinks. I was very scared six months ago, when I did a long sit in Hampnett, in the snow. There were moments when I was quite terrified.'

'I'm pleased to hear it. A person who doesn't know fear is a dangerous creature.'

'And quite annoying,' added Thea, with a smile she hoped was disarming. Her self-image was being battered repeatedly during her time in Cranham, and she badly needed to earn some approval from this woman, to compensate.

'Indeed,' said Thyrza, in a tone that was much too neutral for Thea's liking. 'Anyway, the news of Janey is good. She's putting the past behind her, at last, and has lost a lot of weight.'

Thea was thinking about the many people she had encountered over the past two years, her intimate entanglements with their lives, witnessing extreme emotion at times, and then leaving for another commission somewhere else, seldom if ever seeing them again. She had hardly ever wondered what they thought of her, when the dust finally settled.

'I should go and visit her,' she said. 'I'd love to catch up with her news.'

Thyrza's head tilted sceptically. 'Would that fit with your Flying Dutchman image, I wonder? Stay five minutes, wreak havoc, and move on without a backward glance – that's how it looks to me. And to others, I might add.'

'I don't wreak havoc. If anything, I do the exact opposite,' she protested hotly. 'None of the awful things that happen can be laid at my door. In Temple Guiting, especially, I was hardly involved at all. It was Phil – and he *is* a policeman. It's his *job* to solve crimes.'

'Calm down, dear,' said Thyrza in conscious parody of a famous television ad. 'It doesn't matter what I think, after all. Besides, there's nothing here in Cranham for you to get involved in. My sister's friend killed himself, as he had repeatedly warned that he would. His daughter refused to listen to him or take him seriously, which is for her to come to terms with. The man was always needing attention, overstating the case, broadcasting his troubles. Edwina understood him and did her best for him, but she couldn't be there for him every single moment of the day. As soon as she went to lend a hand with her own grandchildren, the wretched man gave in to his own self-pity and committed suicide. And now Edwina's under suspicion for having put the bag over his head. No wonder I'm angry,' she finished breathlessly. 'Anybody would be. It's a messy, selfish, unnecessary thing to have done – and all too typical of the silly old fool.'

'You didn't like him,' summarised Thea. 'But oddly enough, I did. And I didn't see the slightest hint of the man you've just described.' The image of Philippe swam before her mind's eye, and the things he had said about Donny on their first meeting in the woods. His mother's assessment chimed closely with his own, it seemed.

'I venture to suggest that I knew him very much better than you did,' said the older woman severely.

'Of course you did. But the fact remains that I thought he had a lot of energy and a capacity to enjoy life. That's what I saw, and I make a point of trusting my own judgement in this sort of thing.'

Thyrza rolled her eyes impatiently. 'I don't think there's any more to be said, then. Except – perhaps you'd be best advised to sit quietly up at the Manor for the rest of your stay and avoid the temptation to stir up any more trouble.'

'I'd love to,' said Thea tartly. 'I'll leave you alone if you leave me alone.' Even as she said it, she knew it wasn't going to happen. The police might well contact her again, for one thing – or the coroner's officer. She would inevitably bump into Philippe or Edwina or Jemima over the coming days, unless she cowered in the house the entire time – which she most definitely was *not* going to do. Thyrza Hastings was a touch too controlling for Thea's liking. Issuing something close to an order was guaranteed to provoke her into rebellion. But beneath that, her insides were spasming with anxiety. Finding herself the object of dislike and suspicion was an unfamiliar experience, and she hated it. The clear implication that it was the result of her own outspoken manner only made it worse. And yet she could not see how she might begin to remedy it.

'Well, then,' said the older woman. 'That's settled.' Thea thought she detected a hint of remorse at the open hostility she'd shown. Remorse or anxiety, she couldn't be sure which, but she seized on it as some small consolation. If she had been inquisitive, Thyrza had been almost rude, and that was a lapse of good manners, at the very least. Thea suspected that Thyrza and Edwina had been brought up to value manners above all else.

They parted with polite unsmiling nods and Thea meandered back to the Manor wishing herself a week forward in time, when she could leave Cranham and forget all about Donny Davis.

CHAPTER TWELVE

She was in the kitchen scrambling eggs when she heard a car draw up. 'Bother!' she muttered, unable to leave her cooking at such a delicate point. 'Who can that be?'

A minute later, she turned off the heat, gave a vigorous stir to the eggs and trotted out to the hall to see. She had left the front door standing open, letting the sun stream in. It was a quirk she had, a dislike of closed doors. Whenever possible, she left them open – a habit that had annoyed Phil Hollis, who had a policeman's opinion that an open door invited felonies of all kinds.

Drew Slocombe was getting out of his familiar car. The unexpected sight of his friendly face gave her a surge of pleasure. 'Come in!' she called. 'I'm doing something critical in the kitchen – just to prove to myself that I *can* cook when I try.'

Unhurriedly he followed her, sniffing the fresh coffee and warm toast appreciatively. 'I don't think there's enough for you as well,' she said regretfully. 'I only used two eggs, and I'm quite hungry. You can have a piece of toast if you like.'

'It smells like breakfast,' he said, glancing at his watch. It was one-fifteen.

'Well, it's not. I had breakfast about five hours ago and it's been a busy morning. What are you doing here on a Friday afternoon, and so soon after the last time?'

He flourished a hard-backed book. 'I thought you'd want to see this.'

'And you drove sixty-odd miles to show it to me?'

'Sort of. I've got to see the planning man in Stow as well. There's been a dramatic new development at Broad Campden, and everything's started to move. The burial ground seems to be taking off, just when I thought it was never going to work. I appear to have an ally on the council after all, and they've scheduled the application for Monday's meeting. I might have it all up and running in a few weeks, at this rate. I hardly know whether I'm coming or going.'

'Wow! Last I heard you weren't even sure you wanted it.'

'Seeing the land belongs to me and there's a grave in it already, I can't really back out if they tell me I can proceed. I could probably even bury your Donny chap there if that's what was really wanted. He'd have to hang around a while, but the family just might think it was worth waiting for.'

'Good God. I thought we'd completely abandoned that idea.'

'I expect we have. It was just a thought.' He casually made himself a mug of coffee while she tended to her cooking, then sat across the table from her as she piled her eggs onto toast, sat down and picked up the book. 'It's selling well, you say?'

'Apparently, yes. You can see why. It blows the whistle on the outrageous profits undertakers make, and talks you through how to do it all for yourself. She makes a few mistakes, but most of it's quite sound. Maggs thinks it's fantastic. She says it'll change everybody's mind, and we'll be snowed under with customers. And she does make a very passionate case for legalising assisted suicide.'

'Hm. Maggs agrees with that, does she?'

'Oh yes. Maggs is young and very straightforward.'

'And you?'

He tilted his head ambiguously, with a coy smile. 'I can't see how it could work legally. But it's no bad thing to argue the case. It's quite a brave thing to do, if you think about it. She'll have made a lot of enemies. Not just about that, but she's going to have an awful lot of undertakers gunning for her the way she's going.'

'Really? I can't believe people as dignified as undertakers would launch vendettas or engage a hitman. They probably don't know where she lives, anyway.'

'It's easy enough to find people. But I didn't mean they'd come and blow the house up. They'll stage a counter-movement, stressing the importance of tradition and pressurising people not to skimp on something so meaningful.'

'That doesn't sound too terrible.'

'No, and I definitely think she's right to expose it all. It's the other stuff that feels more relevant to what happened to Donny.' He took the book out of her hands and riffled through the pages. 'Listen to this: "It is a natural human wish to be able to control the timing and manner of our own dying. The uncertainty surrounding the final stages makes the arrangement of the funeral considerably more problematic than if everything were predictable and prearranged. Changes to the law in a few places around the world have led to emotionally richer and more considered funerals as a direct result. Many people are now campaigning for similar new laws in the UK."'

Thea frowned slightly as she digested this, along with her eggs. 'You think she does mean assisted suicide? Or some sort of legal euthanasia?'

'Either. Both. Probably the suicide thing is more what she means, because they're more likely to be still *compos mentis* and able to organise their own funeral.'

'Dodgy,' she agreed, with a nod. 'Almost like a piece of promotion for new laws.'

'The trouble is, she's right. It *is* what people want.'

'Of course it is. The same as they want sunshine every day, and painless childbirth. They want it but they can't have it. It's against the natural order. It's basically just a matter of luck when it comes right down to it.'

Drew puffed a small explosive laugh. 'You're speaking my lines,' he said. 'I used to give talks about the natural order.'

'Used to? Why did you stop?'

'I didn't deliberately. I suppose I got too busy, or thought everybody had heard it, or something. I'm not sure I'd be able to do it now. Some of the passion seems to have dried up.'

'I'm sure it'll come back,' she said carelessly.

'Mmm,' he said, his eyes fixed firmly on the book in his hands. 'So . . . do we have here some sort of clue as to what happened to your Donny?'

'Ah! I see. Of course.' She chewed a toast crust

and pondered. 'I hadn't realised that was what you were thinking.'

'Well?'

'Give me time. Let's sort this out. Firstly, Harriet isn't here, so she couldn't have been a direct influence on the night he died.'

'Unless she phoned him.'

'No. She made a point of not taking a phone. She's gone to Lindisfarne.'

'Very New Age,' he said dryly. 'But I assume they have phones there. She could call from a landline, or borrow a mobile.'

'True. But it's a bit contrived. What would be the point? Do you think she *wanted* him to kill himself?'

'No, no. At least . . . it feels so odd to me. The way you described him is so unlike a man on the verge of suicide. Something must have happened to tip him over the edge. Did he seem at all frightened to you, that afternoon?'

She thought back. 'No, I don't think so. Frightened of what?'

'Death,' said Drew flatly. 'If he already intended to do it when he did, he'd have been extremely afraid. And maybe he was a bit frightened of Harriet as well, if she was pushing this at him.'

'Really?' She drank some coffee and then rubbed a finger across her forehead. 'Is it always true that suicides are scared?'

'Perhaps not always, but he didn't sound to be seriously mentally ill, or facing some immediate danger or humiliation – anything even more frightening than dying. It's the timing, you see. The *timing* is all wrong.'

'I know it is. You're right. So Edwina must have done it, after all. Except everybody says she couldn't possibly have had the nerve to actually participate in his dying. She's quite a feeble old thing.'

'She didn't look feeble to me, apart from the limp.'

'You should see her sister, Thyrza. I met her this morning. She's much tougher. And she got cross with me. I suppose everybody's on edge, under the circumstances. It was her son I met on my first day here, with his poodle.'

She was scattering random remarks, still trying to fathom Harriet's place in the story, and why nobody had said anything about her book. 'There are no copies around the house,' she said aloud.

'Pardon?'

'The book. Wouldn't you think she'd have it on display, or boxes of them to give to friends?'

'Are you sure she hasn't? Have you searched?'

She laughed. 'Pretty well, yes. There are two or three spare bedrooms on the top floor that I haven't been into.'

'Well, I'll bet you there are stacks of books up there.'

'Why? Doesn't the publisher keep them in a warehouse or something?'

He gave her a look and turned to the first page of the book. 'Harriet *is* the publisher. Look.' He indicated the name of the imprint. 'Hollywell Press, Cranham. That's here. She self-published it.'

Thea blinked. 'And you say it's been selling well?'

'Fabulously well. She must be very good at publicity and all that stuff. She could probably teach me a few tricks.'

'Let's go and look, then,' said Thea, standing up. 'Come on.'

He followed her up the stairs and along a gallery that looked down into the living room, with a big stained glass window above. Four doors opened off it. 'That's her bedroom. Then there's mine, and the bathroom,' she pointed out. 'And another bedroom. And at the end, there's a little staircase to another floor, with two more rooms, I think. I haven't been up there.'

'How could you resist? It's like a fairy tale. Have you read *The Princess and the Goblin*? Where the fairy godmother sits spinning in a far-off room at the top of the castle? It's one of Stephanie's favourites.'

'Nope. Sorry. Never heard of it. I usually do explore the houses I'm in charge of, but somehow

I just never got around to it here.' She was standing in the middle of the gallery, which was furnished with antiques, mostly oak, and panelled with the same design as the downstairs rooms. A row of oil paintings decorated the wall between the bedroom doors. 'There's enough to keep me occupied right here,' she pointed out. 'I love these, don't you? I think they're the four seasons. It looks as if they're by one of the Pre-Raphaelites, or some minor hanger-on, more likely.'

'Original?'

'I think so, although I'm no expert.'

'Amazing! Did they come with the house?'

'I've no idea. I can't read the signature, although I haven't tried very hard.'

Drew peered at the bottom corner of the summer painting. 'Me neither,' he said. 'There might be an E and an M.'

'Come on, then. Let's explore,' she urged. He followed her to the foot of the narrow flight of stairs. 'This must have been the servants' quarters,' she said.

They emerged onto a small landing, with doors to the right and left. 'You go that way, I'll go this,' she ordered, her hand already on the knob of the door to the left. 'Quick before I lose my nerve. I feel like a burglar.'

'She'll have locked the doors if she doesn't want you to look,' he said.

'No keyholes, look. She couldn't if she wanted to.'

She pushed the door open and looked inside. The room was empty except for a small single bed, piled high with blankets and other bedding. The window sill was thick with dust, and on the floor a dingy rug could do with a thorough vacuuming. 'Nothing in here,' she reported.

'You got the short straw,' he replied, his voice muted by distance. 'Come and look in here.'

His room was slightly larger, and very full. A metal filing cabinet, a Victorian roll-top bureau, several large cardboard boxes and an office chair were ranged around two walls. There was also a laptop computer and a printer on a square table. Everything was clean and free of dust. 'Wow!' breathed Thea. 'Just as you thought. But why stash it all away up here?'

'Efficiency,' he said. 'She can take orders, print the invoice, package up the books and take them to the post.' He lifted a flap on one of the boxes. 'Padded envelopes,' he said. 'All perfectly businesslike.'

'Yes,' said Thea slowly. 'But it feels so *hidden*. As if she doesn't want anybody to know about it.'

'She uses her real name on the book. This address is printed in it. I don't call that being secretive.'

'But nobody's said anything about it to me. Isn't that odd?'

'They probably find it embarrassing. Haven't you noticed how uneasy English people are with writers? They regard the whole business as frivolous, self-indulgent, not serious.'

'Do they? How do you know?'

'I had an aunt,' he said vaguely. 'I remember she told us once how an old man at a whist drive told her she could hardly complain that her husband left her. "What sort of a wife is it that goes in for book-writing?" he said to her. She was so shocked, I still remember her face when she came round to tell my mother about it. We talked about it for ages afterwards, mainly because there was probably a bit of truth in it. Book writers put themselves outside normal society. Perhaps Harriet didn't want that to happen to her.'

'But she's American. She's already outside normal society.'

Drew laughed. 'You don't mean that, do you? I never had you down as xenophobic.'

She grimaced. 'That just came out, without conscious thought. I think everybody likes her, actually. I haven't heard a word against her. Not that anybody talks much about her. They might resent her having this house, I suppose.' She was trying to analyse her own reaction to their discovery. On one level, it meant very little. But as Drew located dozens of copies of the book on how to organise a funeral in the other cardboard boxes, she knew there had to be a greater significance – something connecting Harriet's writing to Donny Davis's death.

'What's happened with your rebel dog in the woods?' Drew asked her, half an hour later. 'Is it still there?'

'Gosh, yes! I haven't been to see her today. I should go this afternoon. The poor thing'll be starving.'

'Can I come?'

She looked at him. 'Don't you have to be somewhere?'

He shrugged. 'Not for a bit. I just have to go and check that the planning application's gone in properly. I could do it by phone, actually, but I thought I should turn up in person. Things so often go wrong when it comes to council offices.'

'Will they pass it, do you think?'

'You know, I think they might. It sounds as if I've got a few prominent residents on my side, which is likely to make all the difference. Opinion has suddenly changed in the past few days. I can't think why.'

'It's your boyish charm.'

'That must be it. It works every time.'

'Even Jessica changed her mind about you in the end.'

He groaned. 'I should hope so. I thought

I'd be dogged by your daughter for the rest of my life, trying to catch me out in some minor transgression. She's a scary woman.'

'Don't give me that. Your Maggs sounds every bit as bad.'

He raised his eyebrows. 'Maggs is a pussycat. What do you mean?'

They laughed easily, without saying more about the people closest to them. Their first meeting in Broad Campden had not ended happily for everyone, and it was an unspoken pact to stay off the subject. For a long time, Drew had not been at all sure he wanted to open a second natural burial ground there, given the associations.

'So show me your secret protégée,' he encouraged. 'Does Hepzie come as well?'

'Better not, although I hate to go without her.'

'Put her on the lead, then, and I can hold her,' he offered.

'Good idea. Hang on while I get something for the collie to eat.'

They set off five minutes later, in warm sunshine. 'What a splendid day,' Drew enthused. 'Sunshine makes such a difference to everything, don't you find?'

'It's only superficial, though,' she said thoughtfully. 'We had a lovely June last year, if you remember, and it didn't help much when I got embroiled in some trouble in Temple Guiting.'

'Oh? And in January you were caught in all that snow – right?'

She sighed. 'That was awful. OK – sunshine is better, regardless of the horrible things people might be doing to each other. You win.'

'I wasn't arguing,' he said mildly.

'No, but I was. I do it quite a lot.'

'Feel free,' he invited.

She laughed and led him down the path into the beech woods, Hepzie enjoying a free run for the first part of the walk. 'This woodland is quite famous, apparently,' she said. 'It extends for a long way.'

'It's fabulous,' he said, looking around admiringly. 'There's something so *English* about beech trees.'

'Really? I thought that was oaks.'

'And chestnuts, of course. The village smithy and all that.'

'Cold Aston,' she nodded. 'They've still got theirs, right in the middle of the village.'

'The smithy?'

'No, you fool. The tree.'

'Coffins always used to be made of elm, you know. I don't think I've ever seen an elm tree, and yet the whole country was dense with them at one time.'

'It just goes to show, you can't take anything for granted. I don't think I've ever seen one, either.

235

Will they come back, I wonder?'

'Probably. How far is this secret hideaway?'

'Ten minutes or less. I'll catch Hepzie before we get near. She's bound to cause trouble otherwise. But at least she's not suspicious by her absence.'

'Pardon?'

'Did I tell you I met the dog's owner last time I came here? He thought it was very strange that I was out here without my spaniel. I'm famous for my spaniel,' she added.

'But the man didn't find his missing dog?'

'I hope not. He'll drown the puppies if he gets a chance.'

'How old are they now?'

'About a week, I think. They're terribly sweet. I've always adored puppies. They smell so wonderful.'

'I've never been particularly close to a dog. I told you I've never got over being bitten as a child. We used to say we'd get one, because Karen likes them, but somehow never did. It's such a huge responsibility.'

'So you were joking when you said you'd take a puppy?' She tried to quell the flicker of disappointment.

'Not entirely. There's really no reason not to, apart from the mess and the expense and the responsibility.'

She stopped and faced him, her expression

serious. 'Don't just have it on a whim. You have to be sure you'll stick with it for its whole life. That might be fifteen years.'

He nodded with mock solemnity. 'No, ma'am.'

'Listen to me!' she exploded. 'When did I get to be so pompous?'

'No, but you're right. A lot of dogs get thrown out. Maggs was talking about it the other day. She gets in a real state about it, even though she's not especially fond of dogs. She's very idealistic in some ways. Bad behaviour upsets her.'

'Do you know you talk about Maggs more than you do about your wife?'

He grunted. 'Do I? There isn't a lot to say about Karen these days, that's the trouble. She's gone so *limp*. She used to be a real firebrand, campaigning for local food, and the farmers' market and all that. It seems a hundred years ago now.'

'So she was as idealistic as Maggs?'

'More, if anything. It's all very sad, although she seems happy enough. I'm not sure she understands how changed she is.'

'Difficult,' murmured Thea, carefully. 'And maybe not an ideal situation to introduce a puppy into.'

'The children would love it. Poor little things, they could do with something new to occupy them. Do you know – I think I might be able to talk myself into it.'

'No rush. There's six weeks or more until they can leave their mum.'

'By which time you'll have been long gone, and their fate will be in other hands. I think we have to admit it's all just a dream. The truth is, I can't really imagine myself with a dog.'

'Pity. Now, Hepzie, come here, girl. Time to put your lead on.'

The spaniel reluctantly presented herself, staring down at the ground with lowered head while Thea attached the lead. When she found herself being led by Drew, she shook her shoulders in a canine shrug and did her best to drag him through a clump of brambles.

'Hey! Steady on!' he pleaded. 'Whoa there!'

'Just give her a firm tug,' said Thea. 'She's trying it on.'

'It's just occurred to me that I won't be able to see the pups if I've got to stay clear with this creature,' he said. 'Bad planning.'

'I can go and feed her, then come back to take Hepzie, and then you can go and have a look,' she suggested. 'Except, I'm not sure how the mother dog will feel about a strange man showing up.'

'And I'm not entirely heartbroken to miss it,' he admitted. 'I mean – I don't expect there's very much to see, is there?'

'Up to you,' she said shortly. Something about the area surrounding the burrow had changed, and she quickened her pace, sliding down the steepest part of the approach on her backside. 'Hello, girl?' she called softly. 'Are you there?'

No answering whine came from the hidden nest. 'Oh!' Thea exclaimed, seeing the disturbed ground and shifted tree trunk. 'Somebody's found her. She's gone!'

Desperately she searched for signs of violence – half expecting to see dead puppies lying on the forest floor. She dropped the bag of meat and milk, and stood helplessly staring at the wrecked hideaway. 'Oh,' she said again.

'Gone?' repeated Drew, stupidly, from ten yards away. 'How?'

She ignored him, kneeling down and pushing her head and shoulders into the hole where the dogs had been. Its shape was all different, with the removal of the fallen tree that had comprised the roof. A few branches still remained and a lot of dead leaves. There was a smooth hollow where the family had been, and an unmistakable smell of dog.

Feeling like a distraught mother herself, she rummaged in the leaves, feeling for small cold bodies that she was sure must be there. 'They're not here,' she moaned. 'They've all gone.'

Slowly she got to her feet, swinging a leg to clear away bracken and other plants in a search for her lost protégés. 'What happened?' She faced Drew. 'Come and look.'

Assuming it no longer mattered what he did with the spaniel, he joined Thea, squinting bemusedly at the ground.

Surprising herself as much as him, Thea suddenly dissolved into tears and buried her face in the undertaker's chest. For half a minute she wept like a child, while he rubbed her back and made soothing noises. Then she pulled away, wiping a hand across her nose and sniffing forcefully. 'Sorry,' she said thickly. 'I didn't mean to do that.'

'Don't worry about it,' he said. 'People cry on me all the time.'

She giggled moistly. 'I bet they do,' she said. 'Comes with the territory. But not over lost puppies. It was what I'd been afraid of all along. It shouldn't have come as such a shock.'

'So you think the farmer found her and dragged her home?'

'Must have done. It was probably me that gave her away.' Her face crumpled again, but she fought back the tears. Enough was enough, she told herself. 'Poor little things.'

'Well, I guess that means I don't have to adopt a puppy after all,' he sighed. 'And there's not much we can do here, is there? Do you know where he lives? I mean – which farm is it?'

'I've no idea. Presumably he's got sheep, if he keeps a working dog. I might be able to find out.

But I can't just march in and accuse him of cruelty to dogs, can I?'

'Can't you? I imagine it wouldn't be the first time.'

She giggled again. 'That's true. But it is his dog, and I don't expect he'd listen to me.'

'I doubt if it's legal to kill puppies, though, is it?'

She wiped her face again, with both hands. 'I'm not reporting him to the RSPCA, if that's what you mean. Nobody deserves that.'

His eyebrows lifted. 'Why not?'

'They overreact terribly. Every farmer dreads coming to their attention. Horrible things happen to animals as a matter of course, with the best will in the world. The whole attitude of the authorities is hopelessly unfair and judgemental.'

'I'm amazed. I thought they were Britain's favourite charity. You sound as if you've had close encounters with them.'

'No, actually. It's just being around farming people on and off for much of my life. And reading local papers. They're like a branch of the social services – all that moral outrage because somebody left a dead sheep in a ditch. You don't have to be especially well informed to know that sheep die routinely, whatever you try and do for them. And they remove dogs and cats from their owners on little more than a whim. Most pet owners dread coming to their attention, let alone farmers.'

'I'm not sure I believe you,' he said, with a look of puzzlement. 'It sounds like gross exaggeration to me. Plus you're contradicting yourself. You were trying to save the dog from her master, but now he's found her, you're defending him.'

She chewed her lip, unhappy at being accused of exaggeration. 'Honestly, I could find people to back up what I said. But you might be right that I'm being inconsistent. I just think the farmer was basically fond of his dog, and had no intention of hurting her. It's a bit like Jemima and her father, come to think of it. She was trying to steer him away from thoughts of death and dying, but when he did die, she was almost glad. Things so often turn out to be much more complicated than we expect.'

He smiled, but she could see he was still confused. The fruitless expedition left her feeling thwarted and slightly foolish. 'We'd better go back, then,' she said, gathering up the unwanted mince and milk. 'At least I suppose he'll feed her properly. And he did say he might let her keep one or two pups. I'm going to miss her,' she admitted. 'I liked coming here to visit her.'

'That's obvious,' he said. 'She was lucky to have you.'

'I wonder. All I did was delay the inevitable.'

'What would she have done otherwise?'

'Stayed with the pups until hunger drove her to take bigger and bigger risks, I presume. She might have managed with rabbits and squirrels, if she could catch them. But there's no water for a long way. They do say that dogs can't survive without people any more. They've got too dependent on us.'

Drew led the way back to the main track through the woods. Hepzie zigzagged amongst the trees, impervious to her mistress's sadness. Thea said very little, her thoughts all on the bitch, trying to cling to a hope that all was well with her. Perhaps the farmer's heart was softer than it looked, and he would permit the whole litter to grow up.

The driveway up to Hollywell Manor looked steeper than before, the house slightly forbidding as it looked down on them. 'Funny little place, isn't it?' Thea said, pointing to the Lodge.

'I wonder what'll happen to it now,' he replied.

'Harriet will have to find a new tenant, I suppose.'

'Is Jemima his only child now?'

'No, there's a brother. Silas. He's in Africa. He'll come for the funeral.'

'I can see the appeal of your work,' he said slowly. 'All these new people to get to know. A whole new community to try and understand. It's a bit like what I do, but more so. I get very close to a family for a few days, and then they disappear.'

'Don't they come back to visit the graves?'

'Oh, yes, but there's seldom the same intimacy again as on that first visit, and the funeral itself.'

'I never considered myself as having anything in common with an undertaker.'

'Don't worry about it,' he advised. 'I'm just being fanciful.'

'You're right, though,' she said. 'Although I'm not sure other house-sitters would agree with you.'

'They don't have your curiosity – or your knack with people.'

She shrugged away the compliment, and waited for him to get back into his car and drive away. He did so unhurriedly, winding down the window to talk to her before starting the engine. 'It was nice to see you again,' he said.

'And you.' She smiled weakly, thinking of the long evening ahead with practically nothing to do.

'Let me know what happens,' he called, having turned the car and begun to move away. 'And good luck!'

CHAPTER THIRTEEN

She certainly had plenty to think about for the rest of the day, and the late afternoon was still warm enough for a lazy hour in the garden with a mug of tea. Hepzie crawled under the reclining chair, in pure contentment.

Drew had been sweet to bring Harriet's book in person and take such an interest in the Cranham happenings. He had lost a funeral, which must have been annoying, but he had not once mentioned it. His home life sounded rather joyless, despite the two children; a telltale air of making the best of it gave him away when he spoke about Karen. A sense of the best times being behind them, both in terms of family and business, cast a melancholy light on him as Thea replayed their encounters. She wished she hadn't cried on him – not so much for the lack of dignity as the relatively trivial reason for her tears. When he was accustomed to people weeping for their dead partner or parent, grief over the misplacing of a dog must have struck him as a piece of weak sentimentality. All the same, he had been exactly right in his response: neither stiff nor unduly sympathetic. He must be a perfect undertaker, she concluded. Safe, reassuring and efficient, without being distant or unctuous.

The disappearance of the dog and her pups was a nagging worry that refused to go away. There could be other explanations that she hadn't thought of: men illegally digging for badgers, for example. They might have mistaken the dog's lair for a sett quite easily. Or another dog walker, like Thea herself, alerted to the hideaway by their own animal, and dismantling it from overzealous curiosity. But what then? The bitch surely wouldn't run away and leave her brood. She would fight to defend them. Or would she? A trained sheepdog was viscerally subservient to human beings, whoever they might be. She might stand by, whining pitifully, as her offspring were removed and disposed of. Then she would probably slink home, the adventure over, and do her best to forget the whole miserable thing.

Hepzie had never had puppies. Thea had her spayed at a year old, almost without thought. She had never been especially interested in breeding.

There was enough life in the world already – more than enough, in her view. She felt no great urge to add to it. She had produced one child, because Carl had wanted it and she had no real objections. It was what you did, a year or two after getting married. And it got her out of having to go to work, which was a very considerable perk. She deeply pitied her contemporaries who struggled to juggle two full-time sets of responsibilities, with little sign of fulfilment. Carl had willingly taken on the role of provider, on condition that they lived frugally in their small cottage. She had been more than happy to cooperate, although never really immersing herself in self-sufficiency the way Drew's Karen seemed to have done before she was injured. Now all that early family life seemed a century ago. Jessica was grown up with a boyfriend and a career, and Thea hoped she wouldn't even think of maternity for at least another ten years. If ever. She had no desire for grandchildren, much as she enjoyed the company of little people. Her sister Jocelyn had produced five, who were great fun to visit once in a while. There were nine in Jessica's generation – the family seemed set to proliferate whatever Thea's little branch of the tree chose to do.

Hunger pangs sent her into the kitchen at seven o'clock to rustle up some kind of meal. There wasn't very much available, she discovered, so contented herself with a large sandwich stuffed with lettuce, cucumber, sliced cheese and mayonnaise. It was delicious.

Then she checked the geckoes, having learnt over the past days that they became more active as the daylight faded. One by one she peered into their tanks, where they would hide all day under leaves or inside the various tubes Harriet had provided for them. She found one large individual sitting in full view, its grey skin decorated with delicate patterns that were almost too subtle to see. The bulbous fingers and intelligent eyes gave it a genuine appeal, and Thea watched for some time, trying to imagine existence from a gecko's point of view.

The eggs looked exactly as usual. Twelve of them were ranged neatly in their incubator, much the same as birds' eggs in appearance. Harriet had given her a brief exposition of the life cycle of the creatures – the females laying two eggs a month, and the eggs taking a very unpredictable length of time to hatch. The survival rate was abysmal in the wild, apparently, with adults eating the hatchlings with appalling frequency. But somehow they grew up in sufficient numbers to ensure a healthy species, as everything did, most of the time – even those wretched little turtles being gobbled by voracious gulls in their first hour of life.

Breeding again, Thea realised, with a little

shock. Was she being unusually influenced by hormones – being at the age where the final chance of pregnancy was upon her? Did her body crave a late baby, while her mind considered any such thing completely out of the question? She had never for a moment contemplated having a baby with Phil Hollis. After the first inescapable exchange of information regarding each other's fertility, the topic had never again been mentioned.

Giving herself a shake, she left the cellar and wandered into the well-proportioned living room. It really was a beautiful space, which Harriet had successfully rendered comfortable as well as pleasing to the eye. She – or perhaps a designer she had employed – had really got to grips with the whole ethos of the Arts and Crafts movement. Earthy natural colours, warm welcoming surfaces, big botanical patterns on the rugs and cushions. It was a world away from stiff Georgian elegance, or cluttered Victorian busyness. There were no nasty little china knick-knacks or groups of elaborately framed photographs – just a large earthenware bowl overflowing with fragrant potpourri, which Thea always stirred when passing; a pair of pewter candlesticks holding chunky cream-coloured candles; a bronze of a young woman with flowing hair. Everything was perfectly in proportion, from the room itself to the long-piled rug in front of the fireplace.

But there was nothing to do in the room other than watch the television that stood defiantly in one corner, as if to proclaim that William Morris would have had no problem with it, had it existed in his day. And Thea wasn't in the mood for random murder dramas or wholesome documentaries about dolphins. She almost unconsciously opened the door to the stairway and climbed up to the gallery through which she had led Drew earlier in the day. Again, the proportions were impeccable, the furniture and decorations a delight. It would be a perfect spot for playing card games whilst listening to music, or sitting with some wine debating the politics of the day. As perfect in the twenty-first century as it must have been in the nineteenth, in fact. The thing about Hollywell Manor, Thea decided, was that it remained as fit for the daily pleasures and purposes of life now as it had been from the outset.

Although the computer and filing cabinet and boxes of books in the maid's room overhead would have seemed extremely strange to the first occupants of the house. As would the strange reptiles in the cellar, in all probability, despite the Victorian tendency to odd hobbies and amateur scientific pursuits. Harriet Young was a modern businesswoman, with an eye to the quirks and fears of contemporary society, quietly exploiting them in the less visible parts of her mansion.

Slowly, Thea mounted the second flight of stairs, and collected a copy of Harriet's book, Drew having taken his away with him. Glancing around the room, again noting its efficiency, she went back to the living room, where the light was rapidly fading. She chose an armchair with a reading lamp provided at the shoulder, and opened the book with a slight sense of transgression.

Not only had she borrowed a pristine copy intended for sale, but the subject matter itself carried hints of taboo. Of course, sooner or later almost everybody had to arrange a funeral. They had to make quick decisions about burial or cremation; whether to have hymns, and if so which; the quantity and ultimate destination of flowers – but already she understood that Harriet was not concerned with these universal choices, routinely presented by the undertaker who ticked a preprinted box according to the response. Harriet went much deeper, and was considerably more transparent about the implications than any undertaker Thea had ever met.

There were tables of costs, showing the percentage mark-up made by the funeral director. There were statistics about nursing homes and their loyalty to one particular local business, which could sometimes overrule the wishes of the family. There were quotes from suppliers of willow or cardboard coffins in which they refused to deal directly with members of the public. And, a few chapters into the book, there was a long diversion examining the Victorian origins of modern funeral practices. Harriet seemed to be saying that when people lost many of their children, and life expectancy was barely fifty, the attitude towards death and the disposal of bodies was a lot more wholesome. She made reference to rituals in which young children were taken to kiss the dead body of their relative, and how that rapidly swung to the opposite extreme, in which a child was not even informed that its mother or father had died. She quoted from novels and newspaper reports and diary entries, creating a dense forest of opinion and figures from which Thea found it hard to extract a central message. Skipping on, she arrived at the section on the present day, in which alternative undertakers were bravely swimming against the tide, making very little headway in twenty or thirty years.

None of it shed any light at all onto the death of Donny Davis. Increasingly, Thea suspected that he knew nothing about the book. Surely he would have mentioned it during one of their teatime chats, if he had read it. Instead, he had seized upon Thea as a lifeline, somebody it was at last safe to ask about funerals. He had wanted to meet with Drew. If Harriet had been involved, who better to talk him through the options and help him to make the arrangements? It seemed logical, then, to assume that Harriet had been on Jemima's side – had even perhaps been ordered to stay off the subject at all costs. The only person who had managed to talk about it with him was Edwina, and she had promised to assist him to die when he finally felt the time had come.

But then she found herself on the final chapter, having flipped through much of the book barely skimming the contents. 'The Future for Funerals' it was headed, and began with the sentence, 'And so this whole huge issue stands at a crossroads. Burial space in churchyards is almost full, cremations are increasingly seen as sterile and unsatisfying, while the cost of a grave in a municipal cemetery is spiralling higher by the week. To choose an alternative to these conventional means of disposal is to be catapulted into a hasty frustrating process, which is far from sure to succeed. Only with considerable advance planning can there be much realistic hope of having precisely what you want. And to plan your own funeral requires the courage to confront your own mortality. A major change in attitude is called for, in which it becomes standard practice to select the corner of your appointed field, the container in which you're to lie there, and the words to be said as the final farewell from those who love you. And, ultimately, we are all going to demand even greater control – we are going to want to choose the very moment at which we die.'

The rest of the chapter gave names and descriptions of organisations intent on achieving this glorious state of affairs. The tone was a clever mix of good sense and powerful polemic. There was no space for objections or arguments in favour of letting nature take its course, or having the courage to endure the final months of helplessness, as another part of the wheel of fortune, bringing you full circle from the dependent days of infancy. Nothing about the skills of doctors and nurses in palliative care, or the small insights to be gleaned from the final stages of life. Thea herself only recalled these factors when she put the book down and let its message sink in. It was past ten o'clock, the sky outside finally dark, the evening birds gone quiet. She let her thoughts wander unchecked, the unanswered questions rising insistently as she went over her brief acquaintance with Donny, the facts of her own father's death, the probable reactions to the book of all the people she knew.

She had few, if any, firm conclusions to draw, other than that she knew Harriet had omitted a major dimension from the pages of her book – and that a vulnerable reader might well be persuaded to act impulsively and contrary to their own interests. What, she asked herself insistently, would Donny have made of it, if he had read it?

* * *

Saturday came with a sense of relief, as the halfway stage of her commission. While still in bed, she asked herself whether this meant she was not enjoying Hollywell and Cranham. Was she impatient to return to her Witney cottage, and the dusty neglected possessions she kept there?

In a vague attempt to summarise the previous week to herself, she reran the scratchy conversation she had had with Thyrza Hastings, and the warning to mind her own business. Such warnings traditionally betrayed guilt, but in this instance, it had not felt like that. If anything, the woman had been protecting her sister, rather to her own credit. Thea went back further, to the visit from Edwina and Toby, curtailed as it had been by the burning pie. They had come with a view to arranging Donny's funeral with Drew, only to go cold on the idea when they realised where his burial ground was. But what made them think they had any control over the funeral anyway? That was surely Jemima's role.

Her summary amounted to a lot less than she had anticipated. She had spent very little time with any of the people of Cranham. An hour and a half with Donny, the sum of two encounters, with the sort of high-quality conversation she was good at, and which ordinary people seldom engaged in. A similar period with Jemima, perhaps, all added together. Much less with Edwina, Thyrza,

Philippe and Toby. She could not possibly expect to understand them on the basis of such brief acquaintance. Better by far to let everything take its course without any more intervention from her.

But at ten o'clock, just as she was wondering about an extended shopping expedition to Stroud, she heard footsteps approaching the house. The spaniel yapped, several seconds after Thea already knew they had a visitor, eliciting Thea's usual comment about her uselessness as a guard dog.

She went to the open door, to be met by the ginger-headed Toby, looking tousled and bleary.

'Goodness! Are you all right?' she burst out. 'Has something else happened?'

He rubbed his head. 'What? No, I don't think so. What do you mean?'

'Just that you look – well, dishevelled. Sorry. How rude of me. What can I do for you?'

'Is Mimm here? She said to meet her at the Lodge and there's no sign of her.'

A cold hand squeezed Thea's heart. Surely history couldn't be about to repeat itself? 'Is her car there?'

He shook his head.

'So she's probably just late, then. It's Saturday. She'll have her kids at home. Did she say a time?'

He rubbed his head again. 'I'm not sure. I think she said early.'

'Come in and have some coffee. Where's your car?'

'Outside the Lodge. I walked up here.' He seemed to be finding it difficult to construct whole thoughts, his brain muffled by sleeplessness or a bad hangover. He followed her into the house and through the hall into the kitchen.

'Where do you live?' she asked him, aware of this as a gap in her knowledge.

'Gloucester. I'm renting a flat.'

She looked searchingly at him. Something over forty, slight, awkward, he was the sort of man you overlooked in a group. And yet he had suffered the torment of losing his young wife, only a year previously. 'You must be terribly upset about Donny,' she ventured.

'Yeah.' He frowned. 'He was good to me. When Cissie was in hospital all the time, he was great. Paid for stuff. Sat with her when I was working.'

For the first time, Thea began to imagine how it might be to have a long-term relationship with a hospital when you had something as monumentally serious as a heart transplant. The place would become like a second home, the staff increasingly familiar, with emotional ups and downs as tests were run, results announced, predictions made. And the costs involved must be substantial. Never before had that occurred to her. 'What work do you do?' she asked.

He gave a twisted smile. 'I was a college lecturer,' he said. 'That's how I met Cissie, when she was a student. But I had to give it up when she was having her operation. I wasn't coping too well.'

'What subject did you teach?'

'Marketing.'

'Was Cecilia one of your students?'

'No, she was doing fine art. She fainted in the refectory one lunchtime and I caught her. I just happened to be standing right in front of her when she keeled over.'

How romantic, she wanted to say, but stopped herself. It didn't look as if Toby found it romantic at all. It looked as if he had come to the limits of his endurance. 'So what did you and Jemima have planned?'

He looked at her in bewilderment. 'What?'

'I mean, why were you meeting her?'

'Oh! She wants to give me his clothes. Should fit me, most of it.' His face crumpled fleetingly, which Thea took to be the natural resistance to wearing a dead man's things. But some people found it comforting, rather than morbid. She remembered her grandmother wearing a big Aran sweater that had belonged to her grandad, for years after he died.

'Well, she'll come and find you, I expect, when she sees the car.' He nodded dumbly, and she went on, 'Do you know Harriet at all?'

'Oh yes. I bought a couple of her geckoes. Dempsey and Makepeace. I've got them in the flat, even though you're not meant to have pets.'

'I imagine geckoes don't really count.'

'Right. Are you in charge of the eggs, then? How many are there now?'

He seemed more animated by this turn of the conversation, which she supposed made some kind of sense. 'Dozens. I just hope nothing hatches out before she gets back.'

'Why? It's fantastic when they do. You can't believe it could ever have fitted inside the shell, when they uncurl. I was here once when it happened. Magic.' He sighed. 'Not that mine'll ever work. I can't get them warm enough.'

Thea wondered about his financial situation, without a job and living in what sounded like a fairly basic flat. 'Will you go back to work soon?' she asked.

He shrugged. 'Have to, won't I? They stop the benefits if they think you're fit enough. The trouble is, I don't think I'll ever manage to face it again.'

'Oh? Not even in a different place? A different sort of teaching, maybe? You must be very employable. They always want teachers, don't they?'

He looked at her despairingly. 'You don't know

much about it, do you? It's all pressure and people ordering you about and everyone scared of getting it wrong. It's too much. I can't do it any more. I never was much good, anyhow,' he admitted with a grimace. 'I never could manage to engage their interest.'

'Perhaps you should do nurse training, then – after all your experience.'

It was completely the wrong thing to say. Toby's eyes bulged and he put a hand over his mouth as if to hide a snarl. 'I don't think so,' he grated. 'If you stopped for a minute, you'd realise what a mad idea that is.'

'Sorry,' she said. 'I was only . . .' *Trying to help?* That wasn't really true. She had, in fact, been flippant at precisely the wrong moment. Anybody less like a nurse than this man would be difficult to find. 'I expect you've had more than enough nursing already, with your wife, and then Donny.'

'I didn't *nurse* them,' he corrected her. 'I watched other people messing them about – Cissie, anyway. Donny quite rightly kept well out of their clutches.'

By some association, Thea thought of Donny's blocked bowel and the probable remedies that would be called for. Had Donny assumed that Toby would nurse him at the end of his life, keeping it in the family and avoiding any need for doctors and hospitals that way? They seemed to share a common attitude to hospitals, at least.

'I suppose they did their best for her?' she ventured.

'Who?'

'The hospital. After the transplant. I assume they did everything they could?'

He slumped in his chair, his head dropping until it almost touched the table. She expected him to remain silent, unable to bear the memories, or the implications of another death in the family. But gradually, he straightened, and began to speak. 'You know what? They used the heart of a sixty-nine-year-old man who'd smoked most of his life. They said her system was healthy and strong enough to make sure it worked, and it was only a muscle, after all. She wasn't supposed to know where it came from, but somebody told her, and that sent her over the edge. She flipped. She wasn't her usual self, anyway. Her brain was starved of oxygen in the operation, if you ask me, though they never admitted it. She tried to rip it out.' He said the final sentence in a husky whisper, increasing the horror of the image. 'I knew we'd lost her then.'

Thea remembered Donny's flat report: *They did a transplant and she died.* Did he know the full story of what Cecilia and Toby had had to endure?

'Surely the hospital . . . I mean, wouldn't they have talked all that through with her beforehand?'

He made a gesture of despair at her lack of comprehension. 'You're not meant to *talk* about stuff like that. You have to be grateful and compliant. Not just the patients, either. The *staff* have to stick to the same line as well. They have to lie to people all the time, for their own good – or so they tell you. They use baby talk and smile all the time, when in fact there's nothing at all to smile about. The patients *know* they're being lied to, but they can't get hold of what's true. So they feel confused all the time, and that frightens them. The nurses won't answer straight questions, because they worry the doctor will yell at them. When the doctor finally does tell you something important, it'll be in language you can't understand. So the patients make things up for themselves, trying to find some sense in what's going on, asking each other all the time.'

'It sounds nightmarish,' said Thea, shocked by the powerful images being conjured. 'But surely it isn't generally like that? You must have been unlucky.'

'Who knows? What difference would that make?'

'You should have had somebody to talk your feelings through with. You *and* Cissie. Surely somebody must have noticed how scared and confused you were?'

'It was always somebody else's job. There was a ward sister, called Abigail Williams, who we both loathed. She was totally disorganised, always on the phone about something, or yelling at the nurses. She wasn't cruel or mean, but just out of her depth. And you know something – that was *worse*, because you couldn't complain about her. You just had to watch her trying to stay in control, and worry that she was going to make some terrible mistake. Cissie actually felt sorry for her to start with, and tried to make things easier for her. But she took that as criticism and turned nasty. She wouldn't admit her failings. She never knew what was going to happen next, so it was no good trying to get anything out of her.

'You know what it reminded me of? – and I realise this is going to sound crazy – a book I read when I was nineteen and never got out of my head. About the Nazi concentration camps. *If This is a Man*. When they first arrive, the prisoners do nothing but ask questions, all the time. They're desperate to understand what's going on, what will happen to them. And nobody ever answers them. The people who've been there a while are scornful of these pathetic efforts to find a bit of sense when there just isn't any. Well, that was how I felt when I spent those weeks sitting with Cissie in that hospital.' His voice had risen and increased in volume, until the end, which was little more than a whisper.

Thea swallowed down an urge to dismiss everything he'd said as pure paranoia, or at least some sort of avoidance strategy to dodge the anguish of his young wife's death. The comparison between a hospital and a Nazi death camp went far beyond the rational, after all. But she could see no constructive way to respond, other than changing the subject. 'It's a shame you didn't know Philippe,' she remarked. 'He's a heart surgeon. He might have been able to explain everything to you.'

'Philippe Ferrier, you mean?' His face twisted again.

'I suppose so. I haven't heard his surname.'

Toby spoke over her. 'I knew him all right.'

'So? Wasn't he any help?'

'He might have been if we'd coughed up a small fortune for his services.'

'He's private?' Somehow it fitted, she realised. The sleek, well-groomed appearance, the patronising manner. NHS doctors had learnt to modify the patrician tones and behaviour that most surgeons had once possessed. But those in the private sector might well retain the old-fashioned ways.

Toby nodded exaggeratedly. 'You got it,' he said.

'What about Donny?' she asked. 'Was he there

when all this was happening?' She mentally traced the chain of relationships from Philippe to Cecilia, via Donny, Edwina and Thyrza. Not entirely surprising, she concluded, that the surgeon had failed to offer free care to the daughter of his aunt's gentleman friend.

It was as if he hadn't heard her. He drank his tepid coffee and stared blankly at the table. Finally, he said, in the same forced whisper, 'Donny wanted to die. Cissie didn't. It was all wrong.'

'But he's done it now,' she said, trying to follow the logic. 'And you can't make that sort of comparison, can you? After all, it comes to everybody sooner or later.'

The twisted smile returned. 'It's the "sooner or later" that matters, though, isn't it?'

She was suitably chastened. Ordinarily, that was the sort of thing she would have said, and she felt somehow trumped by this unhappy man. 'It is, of course,' she said. 'I'm sorry. I was being glib.'

'People are,' he nodded, as if aware of the point he had scored. 'Even Donny sometimes. And Edwina. She's been a lot of trouble to us.'

'Oh?' She visualised the woman, who had appeared to be uncontroversial in most of the ways that mattered. 'You mean because she said she'd assist his suicide, if he wanted her to?'

Toby's eyes bulged. 'What? No – that was just talk. She'd never have found the nerve. I mean about Cissie's mum – Janet. It was Edwina who got her into the home, and persuaded Donny she didn't need him to visit because she'd forgotten who he was.'

'You think she did that because she wanted him all to herself?'

He nodded irritably, as if that was too obvious to warrant verbalising.

'And what about Jemima? She seems to agree that her mother doesn't need anybody now.'

'They're wrong. All of them. Alzheimer's people don't forget everything. It comes and goes. She knows she's abandoned, and she's heartbroken about it.'

'Did you tell them that?'

'They wouldn't listen. It's all down to me. I have to carry it all on my shoulders. I went to tell her when Cissie died, and she was much the same as she'd always been. She understood, and she cried, and asked why they never visit. I'm the only one who sees her now. They act as if she's dead.'

'But Donny couldn't have got there on his own. Did you offer to take him?'

'Once or twice. Edwina always sabotaged it. She's good at that.'

'And yet you seemed quite friendly with her when the two of you came here the other day.'

'For his sake,' he explained shortly.

'So you don't think she did help him? That in effect she killed him?'

'Of course not.' His voice came loud and harsh, close to anger. 'Of *course* not. He did it himself.'

'You really think he could have done it all on his own? The tape and everything?'

'He wanted to die,' came the oblique reply. 'Donny wanted to die when Cissie died. It was only Jemima that stopped him. And Harriet.'

'Harriet? But—' She wanted to quote from Harriet's book, to reveal her assumption that Harriet was very much in favour of people controlling the manner and timing of their own death. That surely she'd have been in line as an assistant in the suicide, if it came to that. But she bit back the words. They were venturing onto dangerous ground, the shadowy figure of DI Higgins pushing itself forward in her mind.

'She kept on about how much life there was left in him, how he had his grandchildren to enjoy, and the Ugly Sisters to amuse him, and all the events of the world to follow. She told him he had to stay alive just to see whether the climate change thing was true or not. He was really interested in all that.' He gave her a penetrating look. 'It wasn't until she went away that he let himself go.'

'Really? But that was only a couple of days before he died.'

Toby's irritation was plain to see. 'She was busy for that whole week. He wasn't happy about it, that's what I mean. She ought not to have gone while Edwina was at her daughter's.'

A pang of startling remorse struck Thea. She had completely failed to fulfil Harriet's commission to keep Donny going. Instead she had listened with sympathy to his litany of self-pity, and even suggested he speak to an undertaker about his own funeral. 'Oh dear,' she said faintly. Then, with an effort, she said, 'Ugly Sisters? Is that Edwina and Thyrza?'

He nodded with a weak grin. 'And Philippe. We had some fun with him and his dog, as well.'

Toby looked as if he hardly knew the meaning of the word *fun*. There was something inconsistent somewhere, between his words and his manner. 'When did you last see him? Donny, I mean?'

He shifted on the wooden kitchen chair and turned to look out of the window at the view of the village church tucked amongst the trees. 'A month ago. I saw him a month ago. April 30th, it was. Cissie's birthday.'

'I think quite a lot might have happened since then,' she said gently. 'It's over five weeks.'

'That's what Edwina says,' he nodded.

They had not heard Jemima come in through the open front door. Not until she spoke, in the kitchen doorway, did they realise she was there.

'Well, this looks very cosy, I must say,' she remarked, nastily. 'I've been looking bloody everywhere for you, Toby. Can we get on with it, please? Now!'

Meekly he got up and followed her out of the house without a backward glance.

CHAPTER FOURTEEN

Jemima's abrupt rudeness was a lot more unsettling than it ought to have been. After all, it wasn't so very different from her manner on previous encounters – so why did Thea feel such a sense of injury? It had to do with the feeling of being sidelined, or, even worse, being regarded as a bad influence on Toby. That seemed unfair. So strong was her annoyance that she considered running after them, down to the Lodge, to remonstrate and demand an explanation.

But Jemima should be forgiven, Thea supposed, under the circumstances. After all, people did behave out of character when under the strain of a recent bereavement. Instead of following them she closed the front door with a decisive thump, and went down to the cellar to commune with the geckoes. Thoughts of Toby led her to wonder whether he might have used his expertise in marketing to help sell the creatures. He had, by his own account, two of Harriet's reptiles, thereby perhaps forging a closer link between the owner of Hollywell Manor and himself. Did Thyrza or Philippe Hastings also have pet geckoes? Did Harriet give them away as Christmas presents? Did every house in the village have its perspex tank full of exotic foliage and timid nocturnal creatures?

There was little to see on this sunny June day, except for the residents of one tank, which was labelled 'Gustave and Simonetta, 14th May'. This was presumably the date they were put in together, barely three weeks previously. There was definite activity on the floor of the cage, amongst a generous layer of woodchips. Two geckoes were apparently entwined, one considerably larger than the other. 'Oops – sorry!' Thea muttered, as she realised what was going on. Unable to see much in the way of erotic detail, it was still evident that gecko sex was taking place. Perhaps it had taken them three weeks to get to like each other, and this was the culmination of a long slow courtship.

'Good luck to them,' she said to the spaniel, who had followed her down to the cellar, only to stand aimlessly by the door, unable to detect anything of interest in the room. 'Fancy giving them such daft names.' The small labels had only come to her notice a few days into her time at Hollywell. They proclaimed geckoes by the names of Judith, Jezebel, Elijah, Bathsheba, Pandora, Panchouli, Norma, Mimi. When she paused to think about it, they seemed to fall into groupings: Biblical characters, names from classical literature and a scattering from opera. The great majority were female, which made good sense, she supposed. Somewhere there was probably a complex breeding programme planned out – although it was hard to believe that inbreeding would be much of a problem.

The morning sun beamed invitingly, and after a second mug of coffee, she went outside to consider her options for the day. There was still a vestige of regret for the weekends she had spent with Phil Hollis, when he would come and find her in whichever tucked-away little Cotswold village she was staying, and they would explore the byways together. It had not happened often, but there had been idyllic moments, for which she felt nostalgic.

Down at the Lodge, a little group of people had gathered. She could see Jemima, tall and somehow authoritative, with Toby submissively facing her, holding a large white bag. Another woman had joined them, it seemed, and was standing with her back to Thea, shoulders bowed. It took a moment to identify Edwina. As she watched, they separated. Toby went to a blue car, threw the bag onto the back seat and got behind the wheel. The two women watched him reverse and turn out into the road, but did not wave a farewell.

Then the women also parted company. At least, Jemima repeated Toby's moves, getting into a dirty white car and driving off. Edwina was left alone, having been given a hearty pat on the shoulder by the departing Mimm. Even from a distance of three hundred yards, Thea could read its message: *Pull yourself together, woman. There's nothing to be gained from self-pity.*

The view across Cranham Common, with the little chapel-like school and modest church to the south, was bathed in sunlight. At her back were the beech woods, all paths leading that way, as if ancient people had spent their time under the trees, gathering firewood or mushrooms or killing the wildlife. Scanning the entire vista, it was very clear to her that Cranham's only real merit lay in the woods. The houses were mostly post-war, many of them bungalows that were uncomfortably suburban in appearance. There was an impression of a settlement hastily expanded at a time before stringent planning laws came into force, no sense of design or cooperation between the various builders. Something must have gone quite badly wrong in the century between the building of Hollywell Manor and the arrival of all these undistinguished little houses, scattered amongst the slopes and troughs and tumps of the area.

But she remembered her first sight of the place, the little winding road diving bravely down to the hollow containing older houses, which she had initially assumed to be the entire sum of the village. There had been real excitement at that moment, a feeling of discovery and possibilities. Only gradually had she worked out the chaotic nature of the place, the split between 'north of the common' and 'south of the common'. And she had to wonder again how they coped in times of deep snow or torrential rain. There was something very vulnerable about Cranham, which made her feel uneasy.

She gave herself a shake. Edwina Satterthwaite was still standing forlornly outside the Lodge, obviously upset. With a brief sigh, Thea began to walk down to her. She did not regard herself as a rescuer by nature; she did not compulsively collect waifs and strays and set their lives to rights. But here in Cranham the strays were too insistent to ignore. Like the dog in the woods, she remembered with a bitter pang. And the malfunctioning Toby. And Donny himself, who had so obviously needed something, even if she had thoughtlessly provided quite the wrong kind of assistance. She had done her best, but it had not helped any of the sufferers. Maybe it would go better this time.

'Are you OK?' she asked quietly, a few feet from the woman. 'Tell me to go away if you like. I just thought—'

Without warning, Edwina broke into loud sobs. She did not, however, throw herself onto Thea's breast, as Thea herself had done with Drew. Instead, she buried her face in her hands, and stood there, swaying slightly.

'I'm sorry,' she choked indistinctly. 'I . . . I . . .'

'Come up to the Manor,' Thea urged. 'You need to sit down.'

'No, I have to stay here. The police want to talk to me again.' She blew her nose determinedly, and gained some control over her emotions.

'Here?' Thea looked around for unnoticed policemen. 'Now?'

'In a few minutes. They want something explaining, they said. I don't know why they don't ask Jemima. She was his daughter. I'm just a friend.'

'You said *again*? You've already been interviewed, then?'

Edwina nodded. 'Three days ago, it must be now. All about Donny's frame of mind and his wife. They were very kind, but it wasn't very nice.'

'No,' said Thea thoughtfully. 'They haven't taped off the house, so they obviously don't think it's a crime scene. That probably means you've got nothing to worry about.'

Edwina blinked red-rimmed eyes. 'Why should I be worried?'

'Upset, then. Look at you,' Thea corrected impatiently. 'You're clearly not happy about it.'

'Oh, you don't understand anything. All you can say is "probably" and "obviously". There's nothing obvious or probable about the way the police think. They just stick their noses into people's feelings and manage to get everything wrong.'

'They do, don't they,' Thea agreed mildly. 'And you're right, I should stay out of it. I was trying to make you feel better. Sorry.'

'No, I'm the one to be sorry. I miss Donny so terribly, I can hardly think about anything else. I just can't believe he would do what he did, without talking to me first.'

'But you were here, the night before.'

'Yes I was, and yes we argued, and shouted at each other, and I know the police have heard about that – from you, I assume.'

Thea remembered guiltily that she had indeed told Higgins about the raised voices on Monday evening. She flushed, and mumbled, 'I'm afraid so, yes.'

'Oh, don't worry about it. I would probably have done the same in your shoes. But that isn't what I mean. There was nothing unusual or different about that evening. So why did he choose to die a few hours later?' The tears had dried up completely, but her face showed the ravages of her misery.

'Well,' said Thea, groping for something that might console the woman, 'at least you shaved him. He looked much better for that.'

'What? I never did. I know he was awfully stubbly, but I never managed to say anything about it, with him being so cross with me.'

Before Thea could properly process this anomaly, a car engine alerted them to the arrival of DI Higgins. He got out quickly, his gaze on Thea. He did not seem pleased to see her, one eyebrow raised suspiciously. It was a familiar look, full of anxious questions as to how much she was disclosing to people the police would rather were kept in the dark. *Have you told her?* she could almost hear him asking. Did Edwina know that there had been an anonymous phone call accusing her of killing Donny? Thinking back through the long days since Monday, she could not be entirely sure just what she had said, and to whom. She did not think she had discussed Donny with anybody but Drew in any detail. With a reasonably clear conscience, she tried to indicate to Higgins that he had no need to worry, with a little shake of her head.

'Mrs Satterthwaite – thank you for coming so quickly,' he greeted Edwina. 'Will you come into the house with me, please?'

'I'd better go,' said Thea with reluctance. She quite badly wanted to know what Higgins had in mind. Was he planning to somehow re-enact Donny's death, hoping to push Edwina into a confession? If so, surely he should have a witness? It seemed odd that he had come here all on his own.

'No! Stay with me,' Edwina pleaded, much to Thea's surprise.

'Um . . .'

'Yes, all right,' said the detective. 'It might be useful to have somebody with you.'

'Why didn't you bring somebody, then?' Thea asked him. 'You couldn't rely on me being here. Or anyone else, come to that.'

He shook his head distractedly. 'Short-staffed. There's been a major incident in town. A kiddie never turned up at school as he should have done.'

Thea sighed. 'He'll be fine, of course. He just wanted some sunshine.'

'Let's hope so,' he said tightly. 'Meanwhile, practically everybody's out looking for him.'

'I'm impressed that *you've* given this case priority, then.' She glanced at Edwina, who stood passively near the front door of the Lodge, seemingly uninterested in Thea's evident acquaintance with the detective. Most people would have found it unsettling, at the very least. 'I don't know what you're planning to do, but I'm not sure I want to be a witness to it.'

'Chaperone, that's all. Mrs Satterthwaite seems upset. She'll be glad of a female friend, and she seems to trust you.'

Thea nodded uneasily. The matter of trust very probably lay at the heart of this whole business, and she was no closer to working out where it might justifiably be placed than she had been a week ago. She followed the others into the Lodge, wondering exactly what Edwina had been expecting, both now and before Donny died. How had she seen the future for herself and her friend? Had she believed him to be terminally ill, destined for helpless dependency while he slowly died? Had she been prepared to change his nappies, rub his bedsores, spoon food into him? She was apparently a competent person despite her bad hip, a committed grandmother, a close friend. But she had been involved with a married man for many years, had argued and fought with him as a routine part of their relationship. How did she feel about the abandoned Janet? How close had she been to the death of Cecilia? The questions swirled, effectively silencing her, as Higgins led Edwina along the passage to Donny's bedroom.

She waited for the woman to question the reasons for visiting the room, with its tragic associations, but Edwina said nothing, leaving Thea to fill the void. 'They've been clearing out his clothes already,' she said. 'Jemima and Toby. If you're letting them do that, you can't be expecting to find any clues as to what happened, can you?'

'We have all we need,' said Higgins. 'Now, I'd like you both to look out of this window, if you don't mind. That's if you can squeeze around this big old chair.'

'What?' demanded Thea. Higgins put a finger to his lips, almost playfully, and she lapsed into silence.

'Mr Davis enjoyed this view, didn't he?' The question was addressed to Edwina, who nodded. 'You can see across the valley to the south, to Sheepscombe nearly.'

It was the same view that Thea had paused to admire from the Manor, earlier that same day. Edwina went to the window and looked out. 'Yes,' she said.

'But from the bed, all you can see is the tops of trees. You have to sit just here, where the chair's been placed, and then you get the full panorama.'

So what? Thea was bursting to ask.

As if aware of her impatience, Higgins turned back into the room, and approached a framed piece of writing hanging on the wall. 'Have you noticed this?' he asked.

'No. What is it?'

'You could tell her,' he invited Edwina. 'Couldn't you?'

'It's one of his poems. He used to write them when I first knew him. This one is quite recent – since he came to live here. Harriet had a calligrapher copy it and frame it, for his birthday last year.'

'Shall I read it, or do you want to?' Higgins asked.

Edwina shrugged, and turned back to the window. Higgins read in a gentle voice:

'*May my final glimpse be the beech*
That crowns the hill by the square
churchtower
Or the mushroom yew by the
Horlicks grave.

May I sit at the window quietly, breathing
my last,
as Emily Brontë sat,
Vertically dying, dignity intact.
Or else in the garden with a rose in my
hand,
the big beech peering over the fence at me,
to bid me farewell.'

'Nice, don't you think?' he asked Thea.

'Very,' she said, with a surreptitious sniff. 'He almost got what he wanted. He was luckier than most.'

'He wanted to see the tree and the church, not the night sky distorted through a plastic bag. Don't you think that was a pretty poor substitute?'

'I don't know.' She peered at the text. 'What does "mushroom yew" mean?'

Edwina answered her. 'Have you not been to the church? The yew trees have mostly been trimmed so they're shaped like mushrooms.'

'Right,' nodded Thea doubtfully. 'I'm sure they look great.' She went back to the window. 'You can't quite see that from here.'

'You can if you know where to look.'

'Listen,' Higgins interrupted firmly. 'I see it as my job to try to understand as closely as I can exactly what happened here last week. I need to satisfy myself that Mr Davis freely and unaided took his own life, for reasons that make sense. I need to be able to assure the coroner at the inquest that there are no suspicious circumstances, no reason to think another person was here when he died, or that there was any coercion or violence used. I am finding it difficult to bring myself to that position, especially in the light of this poem, and one or two other anomalies. Am I making myself clear?'

Edwina spoke to him directly, almost for the first time. 'He was ill; he knew he could only get worse. He knew he would soon be too shaky to commit suicide by himself. It was a warm summer night, and he had put everything in order. You've got to believe he killed himself.'

'You believe it yourself, do you?'

'Yes, I do.'

'Mrs Satterthwaite, there are people who are suggesting that you assisted him. How do you respond to that accusation?'

'I know there are,' she said with composure. 'A lot of people know that I told him I would. It was no secret. My sister knew about it, and her son. They said I would never have the courage, and they were probably right. Jemima knows I did no such thing. So does Toby, as far as I can tell. I loved Donny. I don't think I could ever have watched him die.'

'When did you last see him?'

'You asked me that before, and I told you then – I was here on Monday evening. We argued about some small matters. I annoyed him, as I often do – did.'

'Exactly what did you argue about?'

'Food.'

'Food?'

'Yes, I said he wasn't eating properly, and if he was ever going to get right, he needed a lot more fruit. He said I was patronising.'

Thea opened her mouth to confirm this, only to shut it again. There was no reason for her to interfere any further than she had already.

'Get right?' repeated Higgins.

'His bowels were sluggish,' said Edwina repressively.

'That's true,' Thea felt it safe to endorse. 'He told me about it.'

Higgins tapped his lips again, but this time it seemed more as an aid to thought than a message for her to stay quiet. 'How was he in himself?' he asked. 'I mean, his mood, his manner, the way he came across.' He looked from one woman to the other, eyes bright.

'He was the same as usual,' said Edwina. 'Perhaps a bit restless. A bit bad-tempered, which I think was because of his problem. He knew I wanted him to see a doctor about it.'

Higgins turned to Thea, eyebrows raised.

'I only met him twice. He seemed . . .' She struggled to find words for her impressions of Donny. 'He seemed to be rather sorry for himself, perhaps. But not unbalanced or despairing or anything like that.'

'You mean, not like you imagine an imminent suicide would be?'

'Exactly,' she agreed.

'So, let me ask you directly, as well. Do you think he took his own life without anyone helping him?'

'I don't know,' she said. 'I don't think we *can* know for sure. But if there's no evidence that he didn't, I think you ought to put it down as suicide.'

'Oh, you do, do you?'

'I can't see any alternative.'

'Well luckily for the forces of justice, we do have evidence.' He looked searchingly from one woman to the other. 'We believe we do have evidence that Mr Davis was unlawfully killed.'

Edwina and Thea both remained quiet and still as the words echoed around the room. 'So what's all this charade been about, then?' Thea demanded eventually. 'All that baloney about needing to understand his final moments. It's not your job to play psychological games with the bereaved. *What* evidence, anyway? Are you accusing Edwina of murder?'

'I can't tell you anything about the evidence – obviously. And I am most certainly not accusing anybody.'

'He wasn't murdered,' said Edwina. 'Of course he wasn't. It's stupid to use that word.'

They both looked at her, expecting some sort of confession to tumble out. Higgins pushed his face towards her on his short thick neck, his eagerness rather unseemly to Thea's mind.

'Could you explain?' he urged her.

Her shoulders sagged, and tears filled her eyes. 'I shouldn't have argued with him. It must have upset him more than I realised. His last words to me were, "Go away and come back when you can

285

be a bit nicer."' Sobs forced themselves into the open, and Thea went to hold her. Muffled words emerged: 'So I went. I feel so terribly ashamed of myself. But I never intended him to do it. Perhaps he didn't, either. Perhaps he just thought it would frighten me and make me understand how he was feeling.'

'I don't think so,' said Higgins gently. 'I don't think you have anything to blame yourself for, if what you've just said is true.'

She raised her head from Thea's shoulder. 'It's unkind to call it murder. And wrong. Even if I had done as he asked, it would not have been murder. The law says so.'

'The current interpretation of the law is rather fluid,' Higgins told her, with a sigh. 'That's a big part of the problem.'

'You're advised to turn a blind eye to assisted suicide,' Thea elaborated. 'Why don't you go and look for that missing child, and let Donny rest in peace?'

'Because, as I just said, we have evidence that this was more than assisted suicide. I came here hoping to learn that Mrs Satterthwaite actually carried out the promise she made, and materially contributed to Mr Davis's death. But instead of that, I am very nearly satisfied that she did no such thing.' He took a few steps towards the bedroom door, then paused and looked down at the low bed. 'But somebody did, you see. I believe somebody killed him against his will.'

They processed slowly along the passageway and out to the sunlit driveway. 'I can tell you no more than that,' he said.

'I think your "clear evidence" is really just a red herring,' Thea accused him. 'Some small hint that doesn't fit the bigger picture.'

He widened his eyes, but said nothing.

'Like that poem. It means nothing. Nobody would regard that as evidence of anything. And if Donny had somebody's hair or skin under his fingernails, you'd have made an arrest by now. Besides, isn't it a bit late, after you've opened the Lodge to all and sundry and everything's been stirred up or taken away?'

Still he said nothing, but a smile played on his lips, suggesting an amused respect for Thea's impertinence. It only made her crosser.

'And I don't suppose the post-mortem was particularly thorough, either,' she went on. 'Stomach, lungs, heart – any visible signs of violence. I bet that was the extent of it. Wasn't it?'

Edwina moaned and laid a restraining hand on Thea's arm. 'Don't, dear,' she murmured. 'It's not doing any good.'

'Don't worry,' Higgins reassured her. 'Mrs Osborne is right, more or less. But there are other kinds of evidence.' He clamped his lips shut again, as if afraid of saying too much.

Thea's mind worked. Witnesses? Documents? Hearsay? What else could comprise evidence in a case like this? Why did she suddenly feel so worried, her insides griping? Why should it matter to her whether or not Donny died by his own hand?

'Edwina's right, though,' she insisted. 'This vagueness isn't doing anybody any good. Either it is a murder investigation or it isn't. Shouldn't you hurry up and make a decision?'

He would not be drawn. 'There's no rush,' he said calmly. 'I don't think anybody's going anywhere.'

'And if they do, you'll see that as evidence of guilt,' she flashed back at him, even more annoyed by his manner.

He smiled and shrugged infuriatingly, and headed for his car. 'Thank you, Mrs Satterthwaite,' he said. 'You know where to find me if you need to.'

'You don't think I killed Donny, do you?' The question burst out of her, giving Higgins pause, his hand on the door of his vehicle. 'Do you?'

He looked at her, the smile still on his lips. 'No, madam. I don't think you killed him.' He switched his gaze to Thea. 'Contrary to what you might think, this little meeting has certainly reassured me on that point.' Then he seemed to consider briefly, before adding, 'But we all know that somebody out there wants us to think you did.' To Thea's surprise, he went on, almost immediately, 'And you probably also know that if you *had* assisted him, and confessed to it, there's very little chance that you would have been prosecuted for it. Juries won't convict people for that these days. Do you see?'

Edwina stared at him, with more intelligence than Thea had so far given her credit for. 'I see,' she said. 'Thank you.'

'You're thinking it's a bit late,' he suggested. 'That something is not quite as you thought.'

'My thoughts are my own,' she said tartly. 'Goodbye, Inspector.'

The phone call must be the awkward, niggling piece of 'evidence' Higgins was holding on to, Thea concluded. Back in the Manor, she went over it obsessively, wondering why such a glaring fact had passed her by up to then. Higgins had plainly told her, days ago, that there had been an anonymous phone call, which had changed his thinking about how Donny had died, and put a stop on any firm conclusion that he committed suicide. While it had also altered Thea's own thinking, the identity of the caller remained a shadowy unvisited question. She had focused on the wrong people, the wrong questions, while the police had gone about their own methodical enquiries more or less out of sight.

It's none of your business, she adjured herself repeatedly. *Think about something else.* She could provide no material help in the investigation, had only been present by accident when Higgins had his meeting with Edwina. If Donny had been murdered, it could easily have been by somebody she had never met, and knew nothing about. Except she *had* met everybody close to him, everybody who might have their own good reasons for wanting to hasten his demise. Edwina wanted it for his own good, Thyrza for her sister's sake, Jemima because she had such trouble coping with illness and dependency. Even the absent Janet might not be quite as demented as Jemima had reported. According to Toby, she had lucid periods, when she knew quite well who she was and how cruelly she had been abandoned. And Philippe, the paradox, doting father and flamboyant exhibitionist, had made no secret of his opinion that Donny would be better off dead. Unusual for a doctor, she noted, to have such an attitude. But then many things about the man were unusual. Nor did she forget Harriet Young, who wrote about dying and must surely have regarded Donny as a useful example, if nothing more.

Increasingly she felt convinced that Donny had not wanted to die on that particular night.

Again and again she came back to the twinkling eyes and rueful grins she had witnessed when she met him. Her numbness on discovering his body had been born of total astonishment, she realised now. And yet Jemima had not been astonished. She said she had expected it. 'It's just what I've been afraid of,' she said. Perhaps she had been afraid that somebody would murder him, and not that he would end his life by his own hand.

She knew from past experience that such intensive hypothesising led to restless nights and great frustrations, unless she could share them with another person. She could so readily find herself drawing wrong conclusions, missing obvious connections – although more than once she had puzzled out an explanation that was at least close to the actual facts of the matter. With somebody to interrupt and challenge, it was a lot more enjoyable, and generally more accurate as well.

It was a year ago that things had begun to go wrong between Phil Hollis and her. She had failed him, even failed herself, when he had needed her understanding and support. The leap required had been too great for her: from Carl's wife to Phil's nursemaid. Carl had never asked that sort of role of her. If anything, he had been the supportive one, the capable breadwinner, full of certainty and strength. If there had been a problem, he would solve it cheerfully, explaining it all to her as he went. They had been a team, but Carl had been its leader. At first she had assumed that Detective Superintendent Phil Hollis would be similarly dominant. She had argued with him, defied his orders at times, but automatically expected him to be her protector when necessary. When he had physical problems, requiring her to drive, nurse and sympathise, she let him down by being impatient and annoyed with him. Only much later did she admit to herself that his sudden weakness had frightened her, the fear manifesting as bad temper and intolerance. By the time this realisation had dawned, however, Phil had moved away, unable to forgive the unkindness.

Now she would very much have liked to talk to him about Donny Davis, to share her suspicions and observations, and to hear his not entirely discreet disclosures about what the police were doing and thinking. Jeremy Higgins was friendly and comparatively open with her, knowing her associations with Phil, but it was nothing like the same.

Which left, of course, Drew Slocombe, undertaker and married man.

CHAPTER FIFTEEN

She could think of no justification for phoning Drew, despite all her efforts to come up with something. He had shown a polite interest in Donny, because he had thought he might be asked to perform the funeral. He had brought Harriet's book because it was obviously of relevance in more ways than one. But he had not offered himself as confidant, joint investigator or go-between in any way at all. He had not said *Call me if there are any interesting developments*. He had more than enough to deal with as it was, with his damaged wife and demanding children. She could not call him. Drew was nothing to her beyond a casual acquaintance with some basic qualities in common with hers. And even if he had been more important than that, he wasn't available. Thea believed in marriage without even needing to think about it. She came from one of those families where everybody stuck to their vows as a matter of course. It wasn't especially virtuous – it was simply the way you lived. There had been rocky marital moments for all her siblings, but infidelity had never been the reason for them, so far as she knew.

So the perennial answer to boredom or frustration or confusion presented itself again. She decided to go for a walk, even though the beech woods had lost much of their appeal since the disappearance of the collie dog and her pups. That small tragedy still nagged at her at odd moments, the sudden loss a mystery she would like to have solved.

Perhaps she could pursue it further, by locating the farm the dog had come from. The man with the gun obviously lived locally, and there were not so many working farms still remaining in the area. It shouldn't be difficult to work out the most likely ones and find a public footpath close by. Footpaths were everywhere, after all. Most of them ran from north to south, connecting Brockworth to Sheepscombe via the woods. In at least two instances she could see from the map that a path went right through a farmyard.

Despite a few unnerving experiences, she had little fear of farmers, or hesitation in venturing into their secretive worlds. For the majority of the population, there was an invisible but impenetrable barrier around the buildings and yards of a farm. The approach was often down a winding track between high hedges, with angry barking dogs at the end of them – or dangerous slurry pits, hostile cattle, loud machinery and the real probability of a defensive or aggressive man demanding an explanation for the intrusion. Very few people understood the workings of agriculture any more. Within two generations, a universal knowledge had been lost. When once almost everybody had a farmer somewhere in the family, now it was strange to the point where contact produced anxiety or bewilderment. Where once most institutions had given farmers precedence, consulting their convenience and serving their needs, now they were virtually forgotten. School terms had originally been constructed around the harvesting of potatoes, hay and corn. Weather forecasts had been aimed specifically at these same harvests. The timing of rent collection, the descriptions of engine size, the pattern and direction of roads had all been based on farming. Thea, as a historian, had a comprehensive knowledge of how things had once been. But she supposed that everybody knew it at some level. Or everybody over the age of around forty-five. Modern children did not learn that kind of history, although she had heard that fewer of them now believed that meat and eggs were made in factories, as they did a decade or so ago.

But, while not afraid, she was certainly cautious. She had no intention of marching up to the man from the woods, if she were lucky enough to find him, and accusing him of cruelty again. If he had retrieved his dog, he had every right to do so. It was even possible that he had spared the lives of her pups. All Thea wanted was to know what had happened, and that her interventions had not somehow made things worse for the animal.

Following some ill-defined instinct, she headed north on leaving the Manor. This meant crossing the common and passing the Black Horse pub. The woods rose majestically behind the buildings, the highest ridge running up towards Brockworth. Coopers Hill was the final flourish – a steep escarpment from which it was said the view was incomparable, despite several rivals within a few miles.

She saw very few people once in the woods, despite it being a sunny summer weekend. She had learnt that this was the norm for the Cotswolds. Coachloads of tourists were deposited in Stow and Broadway and Bourton, a lesser number of visitors ventured into towns such as Chipping Campden and Snowshill, with a dwindling trickle spreading as far as the smaller villages. The more remote corners remained almost entirely unvisited, which Thea found ridiculous. To her eyes, the most beautiful places in the area were Naunton, Northleach and tiny perfect villages like Duntisbourne Abbots, none of which appeared on the usual tourist routes. Whilst a wholesale onslaught would undoubtedly ruin them, it struck her as rather a waste that hardly anybody realised what they were missing.

The somewhat vague idea in her mind was that she could look down from the elevated ridge and identify possible farms to investigate. In reality this turned out to be a very poor plan. Trees obscured the views for much of the way, until she emerged an hour later on the summit of the famous Coopers Hill. The cheese-rolling contest had taken place less than two weeks earlier, despite an effort to cancel it by worried councillors. The crowds had swelled to alarming proportions over recent years, and a diligent risk assessment had concluded that it was impossibly dangerous. The angle of descent was almost vertical at times, the idea of hurtling down there with a crowd of other people very disconcerting, viewed in the calm light of day. The silliness of it struck her as perfectly, almost gloriously, English, although she suspected that other countries had their own versions of archaic rituals that were just as daft. Indeed, she had read somewhere recently that there was a town in America which staged a 'zombie festival' where people lurched around the streets with their faces painted white, bodies daubed in fake blood, uttering inarticulate cries. It was hard to come up with anything much sillier than that, especially as she doubted very much that there was the slightest vestige of historical significance to it. At least the cheese rolling could claim to stretch back, scarcely altered, through centuries of time.

Hepzie stood on the brink of the steep drop and looked over her shoulder at Thea, clearly asking *Are we going down there?*

'No,' said Thea decisively, turning back from the brink. 'Definitely not. We'll go back a different way, if we can find one, but not as steep as that.'

A footpath branched to the left, running parallel to the edge of the woods, and yielding glimpses of the fields below, which Thea thought must be in the direction of Great Witcombe – a settlement she had not yet seen. The prospect of another week in the area began to feel more enticing as she realised how much there was to explore, if she felt adventurous. The map showed a Roman villa on the same slope she was now observing, but experience had taught her that this often brought disappointment. There would be little or nothing to see, she was sure. There was also a suggestion that Witcombe Park might be worth a visit, laid out below the great hill of Birdlip, with its big road junction and special viewing areas.

It was one o'clock, and she began to reproach herself for not bringing food and drink with her. However many times she embarked on a walk, she seldom remembered to take provisions. Neither did she use proper footwear or carry a mobile phone. The increasingly burdensome palaver of setting out for a country stroll practised by serious walkers struck her as counterproductive and foolish. 'Just *go*,' she had always said, to anybody tempted to make excessive preparations. And to demonstrate, she habitually set out in sandals and T-shirt, admittedly with a large-scale map, but almost nothing else.

The sun was partly screened by a light layer of cloud, which kept the temperature pleasantly warm. There was also a slight breeze blowing. New paths regularly intersected with the one she had chosen, and with care she maintained a southerly trajectory, aware that the woods could be deceptive and it would not be difficult to get severely lost. A major track ran from east to west, broad and dry enough to allow vehicles to traverse it. It was clearly marked on the map, which was helpful. Rather to her surprise, she found one or two substantial houses tucked amongst the trees, in situations where modern planning officers would die rather than permit a new building. Perhaps, she mused, they had started life as tiny log cabins for gamekeepers or coppicers, and had gradually evolved into the much-prized residences they had now become.

And then, much more quickly than expected, she found herself once more in the middle of Cranham, the Black Horse unmistakable even from the back.

A quick inventory of her pockets assured her that she could afford a drink, and such was her thirst that she overcame her foolish shyness and went in to the main bar. It was only another few minutes to the Manor, but that felt more than she could comfortably manage. The inside of the pub was shadowy and her eyes took a moment to adjust. It was quite full, and she felt herself under scrutiny from several directions. Hepzie was securely on her lead, walking nicely to heel, and Thea hoped nobody was going to object to her presence. Other Cotswolds pubs had refused her entry in the past, much to her annoyance.

In an effort not to catch anybody's eye, she stared at the stag's head above the fireplace, its handsome antlers sporting a fine silk scarf, or so it appeared. 'Been there since they tried to cancel the cheese rolling,' said a voice in her ear. 'Things got a bit excitable here that day and Susie Powers threw her scarf at the stag in a fit of rage. Looks rather fetching, don't you think?'

It was Philippe, with his big grey poodle,

smiling down at her as if they were the best of friends. He wore a short-sleeved shirt the colour of stewed damsons, and a pair of jeans decorated with gold embroidery. 'I like the shirt,' said Thea faintly. 'Do you call it purple or puce?'

'I think it's burgundy, actually. My wife hates it, but Tamsin's a big fan.'

'Busy in here,' she remarked. 'You'd think they'd all want to sit outside.'

'There isn't much space out there. Can I get you a drink?'

'Oh! Well, you don't have to.'

'I want to. Jasper would be delighted if you and your little spaniel would come and sit with us. He's a great one for the ladies.'

'Just a lemonade, then. I've been for a long walk and I'm gasping. Thanks very much.'

The poodle gave no indication of enjoying Hepzibah's company. His aristocratic nose pointed in roughly the direction of the desecrated stag, as he sat stiffly beside his master.

'Where did you walk, then?' Philippe asked, as an obvious conversation opener.

'Coopers Hill. Have you ever taken part in the cheese rolling?'

'Certainly not. It's usually raining, for one thing. The mud must have been *unspeakable*.'

'I'm sure it gets horribly churned up,' she agreed, with a giggle she would have liked to stifle.

301

For some reason she disapproved of this man, and had no wish to encourage him.

'Funny little place, don't you think?' He looked round at the bar, but Thea imagined he was referring to Cranham in general.

'Surprising,' she corrected him.

'In what way?'

'Well . . .' she in turn looked round '. . . it isn't nearly so pretty as most Cotswold villages, is it? Those bungalows, for a start. They're completely out of place.'

'Oh, Miss Architectural Purism, is it?' he mocked. 'What's wrong with them? I'll have you know I live in one of them.'

'I don't believe you,' she said flatly.

'Clever old you. But I *might* have done. You ought to be more careful what you say.'

The glibness of his lie made Thea wonder what else he might have told her that was false. What *anybody* might have told her, come to that, over the past week. 'I expect you're right,' she said without repentance. 'But you did ask me what I thought.'

'And I do enjoy an argument. What else can we disagree about, I wonder?'

The obvious answer was Donny Davis, but she had no intention of giving him that satisfaction. Under that self-imposed restriction, she could think of nothing else to debate. She shrugged, and drained the lemonade. On the floor beside her, Hepzie squirmed restlessly, and Thea realised that she was probably thirsty as well. 'I think my dog wants a drink,' she said.

With no hesitation, Philippe jumped up, strode to the bar, and asked for a glass of tap water. Within thirty seconds he was back, pouring it into an anachronistic ashtray he had found on a window sill. Hepzie sniffed suspiciously at the offering, and took two half-hearted laps. He left the water on the floor beside her, and returned his attention to Thea.

'Thank you,' she said. 'That was very gallant.'

'Oh, but I *am* gallant.' He pronounced it with a French accent, which ought to have sounded pretentious, but instead made Thea feel like a country yokel with no finesse.

She took a deep breath and refused to be cowed. 'Do you have French connections?' she asked, remembering dimly that his surname was something French-sounding.

'French connections!' he repeated with a laugh. 'That sounds very funny. But yes, I had a French grandfather. I spent several summers there as a child.'

'Must be your father's father,' she said slowly, mentally sorting the family and recalling the various names they had claimed. 'But your mother's surname is Hastings.'

'Very true. Mr Hastings came after my Papa,

who was in fact named Ferrier, which is more or less the equivalent of Smith.'

'I see.'

'Do you?'

'Well, I think so. Your mother told me something about the house belonging to the family for centuries.'

'That's basically right. The house is actually nothing to get excited about. Its only claim to notoriety is its age. I'm sure you'd think it ugly.'

She forced herself to resist this provocation, telling herself he was quite wrong to think he could predict what she would think. But she had a feeling she had brought it on herself, making dogmatic comments about the local buildings. She should have known better. 'There are some really nice old houses just here, by the pub,' she said. 'As good as any in the Cotswolds.'

He pouted exaggeratedly. 'Too late,' he told her. 'The damage is done. Thea Osborne doesn't like Cranham. We'll never live down the shame.'

It ought to have been funny, but the sharpness beneath the jokey words could not be ignored. It hinted at anger or a threat of some kind. As if she came to the village to pass judgement on it. 'That's ridiculous,' she protested. 'What does it matter what I think?'

'You have friends in high places. You come trailing clouds of influence.'

'What? What on earth do you mean?' She was genuinely bemused. Was he talking about Phil Hollis?

He cocked his head. 'You really don't know? Do you remember a lady by the name of Cecilia Clifton, down Frampton Mansell way? Not a million miles from here, of course.'

Ah. She *knew* the name Cecilia had rung bells when Donny had spoken about his daughter. It had conjured a fleeting image of a sturdy capable woman, which she had not bothered to examine in detail.

'Now you mention it, I do. She was a college lecturer. My sister knew her ages ago.'

'You made a big impression on her. And she makes a big impression on most of the people living between Stroud and Minchinhampton. She's a veteran of a number of important councils and committees, let me tell you.'

Thea winced. Things had not ended very happily between her and Cecilia. 'Oh,' she said.

'And then there's Harry Richmond. I'm sure you remember him.'

'Yes, I saw him just a few months ago. But he doesn't live in the Cotswolds any more.'

'But a lot of people know him. He comes back from time to time, and he talks about you. He's been talking about you for two years now. And there are others.'

'Fiona,' she supplied. 'Yes. Your mother mentioned her.'

'So you see how it is. You've become rather a celebrity.'

The idea came as a startling revelation. She had somehow assumed that each house-sitting commission had been contained as a separate entity, with no overlap. The owners of the houses she occupied for a few weeks didn't know each other. They contacted her via a website she kept minimally updated, and a presence in one or two directories of house-sitters – the less professional ones, which asked for little by way of guarantee or endorsement, plainly washing their hands of any responsibility for the outcome. She had inserted advertisements in local newspapers once or twice, when work was slow to arrive.

Not only was it startling, it was rather unwelcome. 'Oh dear,' she said. 'I hope that isn't true.'

'Take Blockley,' he went on, plainly enjoying himself. 'Two deaths in the main street during your occupancy could hardly fail to raise your profile. And Cold Aston – now *that* was where you met the famous Ariadne Fletcher, if I'm not mistaken.'

'I wasn't house-sitting there,' she flashed, before catching herself up. 'Please stop it. I don't know what you're trying to do, but I don't like it.'

He raised his shoulders and spread his hands like a true Frenchman. 'All I'm doing is letting you know that I, and others, have been following your career with interest. Don't worry – nobody hates you, or wants you to stop what you're doing. It's fascinating. But you do make people nervous – which I'm sure you can understand.'

She smiled feebly. 'I think one or two positively hate me, actually.'

'Oh well – you can't please everybody. At least you've never been under suspicion yourself for any of the crimes you get involved in.'

Not yet, she thought ruefully, remembering Drew's recent difficulties in Broad Campden.

A thought struck her. 'Did Harriet know all this about me, before she engaged me?'

'Harriet makes it her business to know things,' he said obliquely. 'I think of her as a spider, watching from the centre of a web that very few people can see. Harriet loves to make things happen.'

Thea was feeling more and more unsteady at so many revelations. 'She knew about Drew as well, then? She knew it was likely that I'd introduce him to Donny.' She frowned. 'But how *could* she know that?'

He watched her face and said nothing. 'I liked Harriet,' Thea went on. 'She seemed open and genuine. And I can't believe she had any idea that

Donny would die while she was away. She was his friend.'

'She'll be very upset about it, I'm sure. But I don't think he was indispensable to her. There are plenty more where Donny came from.'

She frowned at him, wondering what he could possibly mean. 'You make it sound as if she's some sort of Frankenstein. Why does she need sick old men? What are you trying to say?'

'She doesn't *need* them. Don't be stupid. She just likes to collect people to take an interest in. Grist to her mill, so to speak. She likes to study human nature.'

'You've seen her book, I take it?'

His astonishment was gratifying. 'Have *you*?'

She tried to minimise the breadth of her smile. 'Oh yes.'

'I bet she didn't show it to you. Have you been snooping around the Manor? I'll tell on you if you have.' He said the last words with the sing-song lilt of a child in the playground. The fact that he was a heart surgeon returned to her with a sudden force. He simply could not be as frivolous and unengaged as he seemed. He was playing a manipulative game – and yet there was not the slightest hint that he cared about any of the people under discussion.

'Do what you like,' she said stiffly.

He seemed to catch himself up, giving himself

a perceptible little shake. 'No, but seriously – how did you find it?'

'A friend of mine noticed it. I had no idea it was a secret. She uses her own name on the front cover, after all.'

'True. But she felt confident that nobody in Cranham was going to come across it.'

'Except you.'

'I have special privileges where Harriet is concerned. Or rather, it's the other way around, I suppose. I owe my daughter's life to her, which tends to forge rather a substantial bond between us.'

'That's an interesting situation for a doctor,' she remarked lightly. 'What happened?'

'Oh, the peanut thing. We had no idea Tamsin was allergic until one day when she was in the playground with some little friends, while I stood guard with Jasper. The bloody dog distracted me, and I left my post for five minutes. Tam was offered a piece of Lion Bar by somebody's stupid mum, and by the time I got back she was in full-blown anaphylactic shock. Harriet was kneeling over her, keeping the airways open, while someone else's big sister produced the epinephrine that somebody always carries these days. There's me, a consultant surgeon, completely at a loss.'

The familiar sense of unfathomable connections and histories in the communities she touched for a week or two flowed through Thea. If she was lucky, she would be adopted by a knowledgeable individual and apprised of the basics, which helped her avoid some of the pitfalls. But in Cranham nobody had taken on that role. Never before could she remember being so at sea, so unable to judge truth from falsehood, benevolence from hostility. Never before had people's motives been so obscure and difficult to read.

She rubbed her head irritably, and gave up the attempt to discern patterns or meanings in the things Philippe was saying. 'I would ask you to tell me the whole story, but I don't feel strong enough at the moment. I've just walked three or four miles, and it's hot. Shouldn't you be somewhere as well?' For the first time, she wondered how it was he could escape from his family to go to the pub in the middle of a Saturday. She remembered her first impression of him, as a gay man, parading through Cranham with his peculiar dog, seeking to make an impression on whatever rare passers-by he might encounter. It seemed ludicrous now she knew that he had a wife and daughter and a very onerous profession.

'I know what. Do you have any plans for tomorrow?'

She shrugged warily. 'Not really.'

'Come to lunch, then. You should meet my wife, for one thing, and Tamsin already took to you. Plus Jasper has something to show you.'

'OK. Thanks very much. Tell me where you live, exactly.'

He gave her brief and easy directions. She felt a thread of anticipation at the prospect. She couldn't remember when she last had a normal Sunday lunch in a house with a family.

'Now I'm sure we should both get on,' she said, wondering at her own restlessness.

'I'm abandoned for the day,' he said. 'I've got all the time in the world.'

As if the Fates had been waiting for just this utterance, the pub door opened and a female figure appeared, quickly scanning the tables in the bar.

'Philip!' she cried, pronouncing the name in the English fashion, 'I've been looking everywhere for you. I need you to come and look at my computer. The drive thingummy isn't working again.'

'Coming, Mother,' he said brightly. 'Just give me one minute.'

Thea savoured this echo of the episode at the Manor when an impatient Jemima had summoned Toby every bit as imperiously. Was it the universal norm now for women to show no finesse when instructing their menfolk? Or was it particular to Cranham?

She wished she'd had the gumption to order a meal in the pub when she had the chance. Left alone with the dog in the still-crowded bar, she could not face eating in solitude. Besides, it was probably too late now, her watch informing her that it was almost half past two.

'Come on, then,' she muttered to the dog. 'Time to go home.'

It was true that she felt tired and somehow overloaded. Philippe had not been a comfortable companion, on the whole. He gave an impression of playing a game, acting a part, leaving his essential character unknowable. Thea disliked games of that sort. The older she got, the easier she found it to avoid them by deliberately turning passive and incurious. But this time, she had been drawn in further than she liked, to the point where she felt an imbalance, an unfairness, whereby the man was teasing her, exploiting her ignorance, while giving very little away. Even his dog had known better than to try to establish any kind of friendly relationship with Thea or Hepzibah. It appeared not to have much affection for its master, either, following him on its delicate little feet as if conferring a favour, its nose still aloofly pointing skywards.

There was, somewhere, a question of dignity. For a man of forty to be publicly summoned by his mother in such a way might be seen as humiliating. And yet he had responded cheerfully, somehow managing to make her appear the ridiculous one

– and even more cleverly, letting his dog maintain a regal air on his behalf. None of the people in the pub who had witnessed the little scene showed any sign of thinking it laughable or worthy of comment. Thea caught one or two exchanged glances, slight smiles, but nothing more than an acknowledgement that Mrs Hastings had come to find her son, and he had willingly gone to sort out her computer problem, as any decent man might do.

She took the path leading to the common, forking right to Hollywell, and tiredly walking up the drive to the Manor. She passed little girls sitting in a huddle beside the front gate of a house, examining something with absolute concentration. It was a scene all the more appealing for its rarity in these days of captive kids, seldom permitted outside without supervision. But in the light of the alarming story about Tamsin in the playground, she had to concede that supervision was frequently a good thing. Certainly it could be effectively employed as an argument on the side of the risk-averse. Every child was so indescribably precious that much was readily sacrificed in the interests of their safety. Thea did not like it, but she could barely remember a time when it had been any different. Idly, she wondered how historians would look back at this period. Would they calmly comment that the actual levels of safety were so unprecedentedly high that people had to invent dangers for themselves? Would psychologists point out that without some sense of hazard, human beings could not properly function? After all, the vast majority of living creatures spent their lives in a state of acute alertness to danger. Or would the collective memory focus on maverick individuals who ignored the conventions of the time and went in search of challenge and adventure?

As always when such musings gripped her, she conjured her husband Carl, who had taught her to notice social changes and to kick against them if they met with her disapproval. Carl would definitely point out the scepticism that sprang up in response to establishment edicts. The fact that the establishment always won in the end would not subdue him. 'It depends what you regard as *the end*,' he would say. 'In the end, right always prevails.'

Drew Slocombe would probably agree with him about that; she'd have to ask him sometime.

CHAPTER SIXTEEN

Saturday afternoon was half over, the sun intermittently breaking through the hazy cloud, only for a fresh bank of cumulus to stroll over the horizon from the west and obscure it again. It had been a long day already, with a great deal to process and try to understand – unless she chose to completely ignore the whole subject of Donny Davis and his unsatisfactory death. *Unsatisfactory* was precisely the way she regarded it. Nobody seemed quite satisfied with it, unless perhaps Jemima Hobson's evident relief counted as satisfaction. If it had been Donny's genuine and implacable desire to die, his end apparently painless, then wouldn't his circle of family and friends be feeling that something had been achieved? They might be sad to lose him, but surely they would quickly conclude that he had got what he wanted and they ought to be . . . well . . . *satisfied*? Not happy, or triumphant, but with a sense of the right thing having been done, and no lingering reasons for guilt or anger. Instead, there was an atmosphere of secrecy and defensiveness.

And it was all because somebody chose to telephone the police and make an accusation. Jeremy Higgins would never have been involved without that call. The paperwork would all have recorded a verdict of suicide, the funeral would be arranged and people would be clear about what had happened. As it was, there was doubt and confusion, everyone asking questions of each other, frowningly comparing their experience of Donny with the apparent fact that he killed himself.

The word *murder* had been uttered because of that phone call. Edwina had been accused by a person unknown. And nobody knew who had made the call. The foolproof, fail-safe system at the police switchboard had not functioned. From her close associations with the police, Thea did not find this surprising, but it was definitely frustrating. It could not be dismissed as some mischievous crank taking delight in stirring up trouble for its own sake, because Edwina Satterthwaite had been named specifically. At least, if it was a crank, he knew enough of the people involved to home in on the most sensitive spot. Edwina had, after all, agreed that she would one day help Donny to die. The intention had been there, however faintly, and that made the morality unclear.

The post-mortem results had not been disclosed to her, but she had an idea that if they had unambiguously indicated foul play, then Higgins would have told her. Instead, there were niggles, worries and suspicions. The Gloucestershire police were busy; they were bound to be tempted to file the Davis case away as settled, and concentrate on more pressing crimes. It even struck her now that they might be unofficially and delicately using her as their front-line investigator. She had met the man; she was good at seeing to the heart of things; she had form as a good amateur detective, in a time when such figures were assumed to have disappeared completely.

And Drew – he was another one. Before his wife was injured, he had been involved in suspicious deaths, missing persons, unduly hasty cremations. The serendipitous initial encounter with him in Broad Campden ought to be ensuring that between them they established exactly what had happened to Donny now. They should not be wasting their talents, but pooling resources and solving the puzzle together. Did they not both possess an unusual level of curiosity and sense of justice? Admittedly, Drew cared much less than

317

she did about civil rights and personal privacy, but he definitely had the right approach when it came to establishing the truth. She could tell that merely by looking at him.

Without further analysis, she phoned him at four o'clock.

He greeted her cheerfully. 'How's it going?' he asked. 'Did you find that dog?'

She had forgotten about the dog. 'No, I didn't. I set out this morning to see if I could locate its farm, but it was hopeless. There are too many trees.'

He laughed. 'I'm sure there's some sense in there somewhere. So . . . what's been happening, then?'

She described the episode in Donny's house, the poem and the window and the bed, and repeated her increasingly strong intuition that Donny had not died as he wanted to, which might mean he was coerced or worse, but that Edwina had been exonerated because Higgins had believed her protestations. She stressed the phone call, which felt increasingly malicious and important. She mentioned Toby and Jemima and Philippe, reminding Drew who they all were and what she thought about them. And Philippe's mother, who called him Philip.

'Wow!' he exclaimed. 'You *have* been busy. How many days is it since I saw you? It feels like ages.'

'It was yesterday, you fool. But I must admit a day can be a long time, especially in the summer.'

'I wish I lived closer,' he said easily. 'This is all so intriguing, I feel I'm missing an adventure.'

'Even after Broad Campden?' she quizzed him lightly. 'Was that an adventure as well?'

'That was different. I was much too deeply involved for comfort. This time, nobody can say I've got any sort of ulterior motive. I'd just like to help you sort it all out. He sounded like such a nice man.'

'That's it exactly. If somebody did kill him, they did a very bad thing, but because he was old and ill, nobody thinks it matters enough to raise a stink. That's horrible. It's a slippery slope. Although,' she added, 'to be fair, Higgins did get cross when I said something like that to him. He said every death matters, regardless of the circumstances – or words to that effect.'

'He's right,' said Drew with emphasis. 'Listen – maybe I could bring the family up tomorrow afternoon. We could visit a National Trust place or something, and have a meal with you in a pub afterwards. You could meet Karen.'

Did she want to meet Karen? she asked herself. Why wouldn't she? Ordinary human curiosity suggested that she should, but somehow it didn't feel entirely right. 'We could show her this house,' she said, before the *we* echoed loudly in her head and she wanted to kick herself.

'Better not. The kids might break something.'

'True. But yes, it would be fun to do something. I've been invited out for lunch, but I can meet you somewhere around half-three or four, if that's not too late. I'm not sure what there is to visit, though. I tend to avoid National Trust places, for some reason.'

'Well, it can be something a bit more downmarket. Isn't there a children's zoo somewhere, or a model village or something?'

'All of the above, yes. Mostly in Bourton-on-the-Water, I think. That's a good place to go with children. I could meet you there.'

'OK then. Assume that's on, and we'll check in with you tomorrow to confirm. Is that OK?'

'Fine,' she said, wondering how true that was. What chance would they have of a decent discussion about Donny, with his family tagging along? But what *did* she want, she asked herself. She had phoned him with an idea of forming a team, of updating him about events in Cranham, and he had responded more readily than she could ever have expected. 'I'll look forward to it. Shall I phone you, or you me?'

'I'd better call you. I think I've still got your number.'

'You must have – you phoned me about Harriet's book, remember?'

She had not thought it strange that he should have retained her mobile number for three months, since their first encounter. Now it made her wonder slightly. 'Of course,' he said.

'Will you need to go to Broad Campden as well? To see your burial field or something?'

'I might show it to Karen if there's time. She hasn't seen it yet. Who invited you to lunch?'

'Philippe, son of Thyrza Hastings. He wants me to meet his wife, apparently.'

'Really?'

'Maybe he's just being kind, although I hadn't thought of him like that. I think it's more that he regards me as some sort of rarity, and he wants to find out more about me. He knew about me before I even got here, and took great pleasure in telling me how famous I am.'

'And you didn't like that?'

'Not much, no. But his child is sweet, and it'll be a distraction. It never occurred to me to refuse.'

'Why would it?'

'Right,' she laughed. 'So I'll see you tomorrow.'

Which left a long Saturday evening to be got through, with no duties other than checking and feeding the geckoes – a task that took barely ten minutes, even including lingering to search out the invisible creatures. The food disappeared regularly, so she supposed everything must be in order. If she left her visit to nine o'clock or thereabouts, the animals were more active and she might find one clinging to the side of its tank, the large eyes apparently watching the room beyond, although probably not dreaming of freedom or adventure.

Restlessly she prowled around the Manor with a duster in her hand, slowly inspecting objects as she whisked the cloth over them; objects that she had overlooked before. The paintings in the gallery received a long examination, the signature in the corner suggesting all of a sudden that they could be the work of Evelyn De Morgan, a female painter whose name had been unfairly dropped from the canon of Pre-Raphaelites. This was obviously exciting, if true, and Thea reproached herself for failing to realise the importance of them sooner. Her sister Jocelyn would have been a lot quicker to identify them and explain their history. With very few interests in common, the sisters did at least share a relish for the whole Pre-Raphaelite experiment, an enthusiasm which had begun when they were barely into their teens. Athena posters of paintings by Burne-Jones and Millais adorned their bedroom walls for years. Almost by osmosis they acquired knowledge of the Brotherhood and its wider circle. But the De Morgans had never featured prominently – William and Evelyn, husband and wife, were always on the periphery.

Thea's initial assumption that these pictures

had come with the house seemed increasingly likely on reflection. If Harriet had purchased them, she would know them for what they were and be aware of their value. There would be issues of security and insurance. The fact that Harriet had not mentioned them seemed to suggest she regarded them as of little importance. Was it possible that she had no idea of their history? They were poorly displayed, on the shadowy side of the gallery, in urgent need of cleaning. Perhaps Thea was the first person to spot them in a hundred years or more. The idea thrilled her, despite its improbability.

For an hour or so she managed to forget about Donny and his circle, but inexorably it all broke through her defences again as soon as she went downstairs. In the kitchen, his ghost seemed to linger, sitting in his customary chair, clutching the coffee mug in shaking hands. More vividly than ever she remembered his words, his moving complaints about the unpleasantness of growing old, his emphatic rejection of the entire medical machine.

As if a voice spoke it clearly into her ear she understood that Donny Davis did not die by his own hand. He had done no more than utter the universal wishes of every sentient being nearing the end of life: to avoid pain and degradation, to remain fully human to the final moment, to cause minimal trouble to his loved ones, to be remembered for the energetic creative person he had been in his prime. In the wider world, such sentiments were being expressed on all sides, in speeches and articles and blogs and TV documentaries, until it felt as if there was some easy means by which to achieve this ideal. But Donny had known there was not. She saw it in his eyes. Donny had known that his actual fate was far more difficult and undignified than he wanted it to be – than *anybody* wanted it to be. From that knowledge to suicide might seem a small step, but Thea knew that it was far from being so easy.

She felt a sudden urgent need to talk to Jemima, the only blood relative Donny had left in the country, apart from her children, his grandchildren. The distant Silas and his needy wife had apparently severed all meaningful links long ago. Despite her denials and distractions, Thea suspected that Jemima understood most acutely the position her father was in. And because she knew that there was no solution, no possible truthful reassurance she could offer, she sensibly strove to divert him from it. And that was why she said *This is what I was afraid of* when she found his dead body. She believed that her efforts had failed, that he had sunk into a slough of despair that she ought to have been able to steer him from. And some of that was surely Thea's fault, in Jemima's eyes.

It was one thing to want to see the woman, and quite another to organise a meeting. Jemima was busy. She had a husband, a farm and a number of offspring. No doubt she did a lot of cooking, cleaning, shopping, washing. She might make pies and jams and chutneys as well, for the store cupboard, even if such activities had virtually died out in the popular imagination. It was the strawberry season, very nearly – an extra busy time for the Hobsons. In fact, hadn't Donny said something about people turning up to pick their own? If the berries were ripe already, that suggested polytunnels, which must entail a whole lot more work. What would Donny's daughter be doing on a Saturday evening?

On several occasions Thea had gone uninvited to the homes of people she wanted to speak to. She had done it right from the start, in Duntisbourne Abbots, where she had found herself unable to sit quietly alone in a big house close to the scene of a murder. On the whole the outcome had been positive, but there had been enough hostile receptions to make her more hesitant since then. Her spaniel had been attacked as well, once or twice, which had also taught her not to be too cavalier. She had developed a habit of circumspection, rehearsing cover stories, or trying to make her approach look casual or accidental.

And since the unsettling revelations from Philippe Ferrier, earlier in the day, she felt even more diffident about showing her face. If people regarded her as a celebrated amateur detective, they were unlikely to feel very pleased when she knocked on their front door and requested an interview.

But she and Jemima had a bond. They had found Donny's body together. Of the three women she had come to know in Cranham, Jemima was the one she most nearly regarded as a friend, despite her prickly manner and occasional rudeness. Jemima was the one she thought she understood. It was perfectly acceptable, therefore, to track down her number and make a phone call.

Except there was no sign of a telephone book in Hollywell Manor. People hardly ever used them any more, Thea had gradually realised. With the advent of universal mobile conversations, landline numbers were falling into disuse, except for businesses – and even they probably received more emails than phone calls. She rose cheerfully to the challenge. There was a free local paper in the neat stack of mail on the hall table. Turning its pages and scanning their contents, she soon found a display advertisement for Hobsons Farm Shop and Pick Your Own, with a phone number at the bottom. Easy, she congratulated herself.

Without much preparation, she dialled the

number on Harriet's phone. A boy answered.

'Is that the Hobson family?' asked Thea.

'Yeah. Who's that?'

'My name's Thea Osborne. Is your mother anywhere about? I'd like a word with her.'

'Yeah. Hang on.' She heard him shouting 'Mum!' at some distance from the phone. 'A woman for you. Don't remember her name.'

It was half a minute or so before Jemima's voice came through the receiver. 'Hello? Who is it?'

'It's Thea—'

'What do you want?' The words came sharp and unfriendly. Thea entertained a groundless image of floury hands and hot dank hair needing to be brushed aside.

'Just a chat. I'm all on my own here, and thought it would be nice to talk to somebody.'

'Shouldn't you have thought of that?'

'Pardon?'

'When you took on the job. You must have known what it would be like.'

'Well, yes. But with what happened . . . I feel all unsettled.'

Jemima gave an unsympathetic *tut*, as if an importunate child had interrupted her for no good reason. 'I've got Toby here,' she said, 'feeling all sorry for himself. I can't cope with any more whining Winnies, just at the moment.'

Whining Winnies? Was that how she came across? 'Oh,' she said.

Jemima sighed noisily. 'Oh bugger it. I didn't mean that. It's just . . . I don't know. Saturdayitis, or something. They're all milling about, trying to decide whether to go out or not, driving me mad. Matt's furious because some stupid punter drove into our sign and knocked it over. You'd better come round. Maybe you can help to calm things down. I dare say you're good at that.'

Thea was on the very brink of refusing, her pride damaged quite painfully. But she remembered why she had phoned in the first place, and accepted the grudging invitation. 'How do I find you?'

The directions were far from straightforward, particularly as she still had only a very hazy idea of how Cranham connected to its neighbouring settlements. 'I expect I can manage it,' she said, with only moderate confidence.

Jemima repeated the directions with impressive patience. 'It'll take you ten minutes at most,' she said.

Hobsons Farm was impossible to miss, once you got to the right road. For good measure, the sign announcing its presence, beside a wide gateway, was tilting alarmingly. Quite how anybody had managed to drive into it was hard to understand – but then accidents after the event seldom did make very much sense.

The sun had almost set by the time she arrived, but there was still a sense of a summer evening, designed for carefree gatherings on the lawn, with nibbles and Pimm's and some highbrow music playing softly somewhere. Or the gentle thwack of tennis racquets indicating the young things disporting themselves in the court behind the house. A scene Thea had to admit was no more recent than Edwardian times, a century ago, before Britain lost much of its self-confidence.

But as she drove up the long approach, there were definitely vestiges of just such an affluent lifestyle still lingering. The house was large and lovely, with a creeper over the facade for good measure. The expected polytunnels were an unavoidable blight, but she discovered that they could not be seen from the patio at the side of the house, where rustic tables and chairs were placed to catch the westering sun. Toby whatever-his-name-was sat at one of them, with a bottle of beer at his elbow. He watched Thea sullenly as she got out of her car and waved a greeting, giving no answering gesture. Three teenagers, aged roughly from fifteen to eighteen, sat at a separate table, two of them with mobile phones in their hands.

Nobody was playing tennis or drinking Pimm's, but there was a big old garden with big old shrubs and well-maintained stone walls. Matthew Hobson, it seemed, was doing all right, selling his summer fruits and whatever other agricultural pursuits he might be engaged in. There was a substantial flock of sheep in a big field behind the house, Thea noticed. She nodded and smiled at the youngsters, who nodded and smiled fleetingly back. There was a man standing in a doorway, broad-shouldered and complacent. He also watched her as she approached. When she reached the edge of the patio he called, 'Mimm! Your visitor's here.'

'Come on in,' Jemima's voice floated from the house. 'I'm a bit tied up . . .'

The man stepped aside and waved her into the big square room that opened onto the patio. As with Hollywell Manor, the proportions were perfect. It was an ordinary family room with a battered sofa and big rugs, television, and an oak table covered in papers, mugs, schoolbooks and a laptop computer, but the ceiling was high, the windows generous, lending an air of relaxed comfort and very little to worry about. 'Through here,' called Jemima. Thea followed the voice into a large kitchen, to find the lady of the house making sandwiches on a massive pine table.

'They had a perfectly good meal an hour ago, but now they want more,' she said with mock annoyance. 'Helen's friends are coming, apparently. She's gone to fetch them.'

Wordlessly, Thea stationed herself at Jemima's

elbow and started spreading pâté onto the sliced brown bread that was waiting. She added slivers of tomato and cucumber and pressed down the lid. She had the impression that none of the food was home-produced.

'They're all yours, out there, then?' she asked, after a few moments.

'Two of them are, last I noticed. The third one's a friend who never seems to go home. We've got a few casual workers in a caravan, as well. They join us now and then. It's all very informal. It means I never get a moment to myself, of course. They're always wanting something to eat.'

'Nice, all the same,' said Thea sincerely, finding a romance in the easy-going rural idyll she had stumbled into. 'That was your husband, I assume?'

'Matt, yes. The master of all he surveys. He loves it. In his element he is, this time of year.'

'A happy farmer! What a rarity!' said Thea, thinking of some of the hostile curmudgeons she had met over the past two years. Then she remembered a man called Henry in Lower Slaughter, who had been another exception.

'He was a swine when we had the cows. We never realised that his destiny was in fruit and veg and the sheep. He mostly keeps them for old times' sake, although the lamb prices have improved lately, and that's no bad thing. His father would be furious about selling up the herd, but we've got past that now. He's been dead for seven years.'

The reference to dead fathers was inopportune. They both fell silent as the spirit of Donny filled the room. Jemima was first to recover. 'My dad liked it here. He would have liked to move in, I think, but we never suggested it, and he never asked outright. There really isn't the space.'

'He seemed OK in the Lodge,' said Thea, trying to offer reassurance, assuming Jemima was feeling guilty about it.

'Much better,' Jemima nodded. 'Or so I thought. Maybe I was wrong.' Her eyes clouded, and Thea expected tears, but instead Jemima shook herself and handed Thea a large plate of sandwiches. 'Here. Can you take these out for me? Go and talk to Toby. He's driving me crazy.'

'What's the matter with him?'

'Oh, I don't know. Says he'll never work again, because the state won't finance any retraining, or something. It's all his own fault, pig-headed so-and-so.'

It was not the moment for eliciting the full story, but Thea was intrigued. 'OK, I'll try and cheer him up, then,' she offered.

'Good luck!' Jemima called after her, with a little laugh.

Toby gave her a weak smile when she sat down opposite him and proffered the plate of sandwiches. He took one with an air of weariness and nibbled half-heartedly at it. 'Isn't it nice here?' she began. 'Great views. What's that over there?'

'Painswick Beacon,' he said. 'You can see for about a hundred miles in every direction from up there when it's clear.'

'Really? I should go up for a look, then.'

He nodded inattentively.

'Are you staying here?'

'For the night, you mean? No way. There's no space here.' She eyed him carefully. Here was another man well into early middle age, who acted more like somebody twenty years younger. It was high time he gave up saying things like *No way.*

'Looks like a big house,' she said.

'Four bedrooms, two bathrooms,' he recited. 'They've got three teenagers, with a room each. Even when Helen goes off to college, she won't let anybody use her room.'

'Can't blame her, I s'pose.'

'No.' He frowned. 'Donny wanted to come and live here. Would have made things a lot easier if they'd have let him.'

She began to suspect that this had been a recent topic of conversation, with both Jemima and Toby telling her about it in the space of five minutes. Jemima had said something about Donny never directly asking her to house him, implying somehow that the old man's real feelings had

333

never been fully expressed to her. Perhaps he had confided in this son-in-law, who still maintained such a close connection. 'Did he ever ask them if they'd have him?'

Toby shrugged. 'Don't know. But they could see it was the obvious thing to do. Anybody could.'

'Instead of various relatives having to go and nurse him at the Lodge you mean?'

He grimaced unpleasantly. 'Right.'

'I see she put you to work, then,' came a voice behind her. She turned to see Matthew Hobson eyeing the plate of sandwiches. 'Feeding the five thousand.'

'I volunteered.'

'Good for you.' He turned to look at the youngsters at the other table. 'Gets more like a pub garden here by the day.'

Thea laughed, thinking she had been trying to work out what the set-up reminded her of. 'Could be worse, I suppose.'

'Certainly it could. I'm not complaining. You could say we've been having a bit of a wake for poor old Donny, in advance of the funeral. Should be an open coffin and all the grandchildren kissing the body, by rights I suppose. I quite like the idea of all that old-fashioned sentimentality.'

Toby made a small noise, attracting the attention of the other two. 'What?' said Matthew.

'Nothing. Just . . .'

'I don't expect you agree with him, do you?' she said.

He stared at her, his light-blue eyes bulging slightly. 'Why shouldn't I? What d'you mean?'

'Sorry. That was stupid of me. I was thinking about what you were saying to me this morning . . . but ignore me. I don't know anything about anything.'

Toby shrugged as if she was making no sense at all, and he didn't really care anyway.

'At least the police don't seem to be bothering you. Maybe they've changed their minds about Donny being murdered.' As soon as she said it, she wondered how she could possibly have been such an idiot. Had she, deep down, felt a mischievous urge to shake these people up? Were they coming across as just a bit too complacent for comfort? If so, she had achieved the desired effect.

'*Murdered?*' Both men uttered the word in shocked disbelief. Hobson went on to demand, 'What the bloody hell are you saying, woman?'

She gazed from one to the other, aware of a sudden hush on the other table, and Jemima just then coming to the door with two more plates of sandwiches. 'Well – the phone call. Edwina . . . You know. Edwina saying she'd help him, if . . . I mean . . .' She tailed off under the collective stares, harsher than any spotlight. Much

335

too late she tried to recall just who would know about the phone call, and Edwina's promise, and what each person had said to her over the past week. 'Sorry,' she faltered. 'I'm completely out of order. Ignore me.'

'You are, rather,' said Jemima wryly. '*Bloody* out of order, if I may say so.'

'Donny committed suicide,' said Toby, loudly. 'He said he would and he did. End of.'

Nobody looked at him, instead acting as if he had given them permission to carry on as before, as if nothing had been said to spoil their summer evening. Jemima met Thea's eyes warily, giving the impression she wished she had never invited her.

'Edwina's not well, apparently. She's gone down with some sort of summer flu.'

'Oh dear,' said Thea flatly. 'Poor thing.' She remembered that she was due for lunch with Edwina's nephew and his family the next day. The temptation to reveal this to the Hobson gathering was quickly suppressed. Much better say nothing for a bit, eat a couple of sandwiches and go.

But Jemima was more forgiving than expected. 'We found Donny's will, you know,' she said chattily. 'Rather a surprise, actually.'

'Oh?'

'He's left everything to my mother, for her care. Once his things are sold, we can upgrade her to a better place, even if only a modest improvement.'

'Things?'

'Not much, admittedly, but he did have some useful bits of silver, that he collected years ago. We had it all valued when he moved, and it's mounted up quite dramatically.'

Thea recalled the unlocked house and the spartan furnishings. 'Oh?' she said.

'They're all in a safe-deposit box in Gloucester,' Jemima informed her, with a raised eyebrow. 'If that's relevant.'

'I'm sorry,' Thea smiled feebly. 'You really don't have to tell me.'

'No reason not to, after all that's happened,' Jemima shrugged. 'We did go through something big together, after all.'

'Yes, we did.' It felt as if permission had been granted, so she risked a further question. 'And you didn't know about his will?' How was that possible, she wondered. Didn't Jemima have power of attorney, or something? Wasn't she the executor of the will?

'We had no idea. I never read the thing, just taking it for granted it would come to me and Silas. With something for Edwina. She's not even mentioned.'

'That'll be why she's sick,' said Toby, with a hollow laugh. 'Sick as a parrot, most likely.'

Matthew echoed the laugh. 'Right,' he said.

'Serves her right for not moving in and doing the decent thing. Leaving the poor old bugger fending for himself like that, she should be ashamed.'

A silence followed, during which Jemima flushed and Toby stared into his empty beer bottle, twisting it in his hands. Thea wanted to make some comment on Jemima's faithful visits to her father, when she had so many other claims on her time. Even Toby had appeared to be more attentive than the average son-in-law. Jemima spoke first.

'Edwina did her best, Matt. You're both being unfair on her. Dad would never have let her go and live with him. There was nowhere near enough *space*.'

'I suppose his wife is the official next of kin,' said Thea. 'He would want to be sure she was well looked after.'

'At least it comes to you when she's gone,' said Matthew. 'And you have control of it now. It's much the same thing, if you ask me.'

Jemima rolled her eyes. 'I don't think so. If she lives another ten years, there won't be a penny of it left.'

Toby kept his gaze on the bottle in his hands. 'She won't, though,' he muttered. 'You know she won't.'

'She might if she's moved to some palatial home that tends to her every need. There's nothing much wrong with her physically.'

'There is, though,' Toby insisted. 'You don't go to see her, remember. Not like me.'

The Hobsons exchanged a long questioning glance. 'They would have told us if she was ill,' said Jemima.

'It's not something easy like that. It's not cancer or angina.'

'So what is it?'

Toby's hands twisted together, the bottle abandoned. 'Go and see for yourself. She's not eating, for a start. She's miserable and scared. She won't be any better in a new place, either. Worse, if anything. Donny was daft to think money would make her any better.'

'Did he think that, though?' Thea asked slowly. 'Or was he just making a point?' She looked at Jemima, trying not to seem accusing.

'Point? What point?'

'Something about being looked after, maybe. If he felt he wasn't being properly cared for, he thought at least he could make sure his wife didn't miss out.'

She wasn't prepared for the abrupt flare of rage from Jemima's husband. '*Didn't miss out?*' he repeated furiously. 'What the hell do you know about it, Miss Interfering House-sitter? Mimm goes over there practically every bloody day, washing his sheets and leaving him everything he needs to eat, even when she's got a thousand other things to do. She spoilt him rotten. What a damned stupid, mean-spirited thing to say.' He turned from her in disgust, and she got shakily to her feet.

'You're absolutely right,' she said, the words emerging jerkily from a tight throat. 'I don't know what I was thinking of. I didn't mean it to sound the way it did. I'm terribly sorry.' She looked at Toby, half hoping he would come to her rescue. 'I'd better go.'

Nobody tried to stop her. She struggled to keep her head high as she went back to her car, all the while knowing she had been rude and hurtful. She was tempted to see the whole episode as Toby's fault: he had paved the way for her, raising the question of just how well the older generation were being looked after. But Jemima had obviously been doing her best, and to suggest otherwise was wrong. She, Thea, had been wrong, whichever way you looked at it. Her words had emerged thoughtlessly and had been badly chosen. She had not meant to hurt anybody, but had not taken enough care to ensure she didn't. The family were still suffering from the shock of Donny's death, still vulnerable to any suggestion of neglect or culpability. Despite the fact that she had only been trying to see things from Donny's viewpoint, she had been grossly insensitive. Aware of the teenagers watching the whole episode with mute fascination, she got in her car and drove back to Cranham.

At least she *tried* to drive back to Cranham. At some point she turned the wrong way, finding herself in the middle of Painswick, having failed to locate a small right turn in the twilight. Crossly she forced her attention onto the geography of the area, visualising how the various villages sat in relation to each other. Cranham was behind her, more or less. If she turned right and right again, she'd get there eventually. The road signs weren't bad, on the whole. She'd been lost like this before, and had learnt not to charge heedlessly on, getting further and further away from where she wanted to be.

The right turn took her along a rising street of handsome old buildings to which she gave little attention. Lights were on in people's front rooms, the curtains mostly still open, and she passed them feeling very much an outsider. She had no welcoming lights waiting for her back at Hollywell. Only a cellar full of geckoes who had no interest in the lives of human beings. And, of course, the dog. Hepzibah would be on Harriet's best sofa, curled up trustingly, waiting for the return of her mistress. Without her, Thea might have simply driven at random, hundreds of miles in a meandering excursion of England, easily reaching places like Nottingham and Stoke and Derby, if she kept on going, working off the bitter thoughts of self-dislike that filled her head.

Instead she concentrated, and found a sign mentioning Sheepscombe, which led in turn to a familiar approach to Cranham. The village hall welcomed her like a squat little friend, the common was still there, the hidden road to the Lodge and the drive up to the Manor were all just as before.

'What a day!' she exclaimed to the dog, which flew at her with absolute joy the moment she opened the front door. 'What a bloody day it's been.'

CHAPTER SEVENTEEN

As soon as she opened her eyes, she knew that Sunday was going to be cloudless, hot and beautiful. It was June, and a high-pressure system had condescended to pay a visit for a change. Where in January this had led to hard frosts and icy roads, five months later it brought the sunshine that every sane person craved.

Drew was coming, she remembered, but not until she had enjoyed the hospitality of the Ferrier family – not an entirely appealing prospect after the previous evening. Who could guarantee that she would not alienate those people as well with some reckless remark? She couldn't trust herself to say the right thing if they got onto the subject of Donny Davis. She had plunged too deeply into the matter of his death, and was starting to feel a real urgency to understand precisely what had happened to him. She had witnessed too much, carelessly allowing herself to be present for too many crucial junctures, the discovery of his body being the main one, of course.

With every passing month, Sunday became less and less of a special day. It was still a surprise that people had no resistance to being asked to work on a Sunday just the same as any other day. Jessica had recently mentioned that a man had come to install her new Sky TV paraphernalia at 8.30 on a Sunday morning. You could phone an electrician or a plumber any day of the week now, as if they were all equal. Shops were open, call centres were manned, and nobody got a proper guaranteed rest.

Even Drew, she supposed, had to be on call every hour of every day. She had no very clear idea of just how he managed it, or how urgently he might be needed, but she had gained an impression of a man who could never fully relax, when she had first met him. At any moment, his phone was liable to go off and summon him to switch into undertaker mode, without warning.

So when a car drove up to the Manor at nine forty-five, she should not have been surprised to recognise DI Jeremy Higgins, who could hardly be exempt from Sunday working, either.

He approached her without speaking, searching her face intently. 'Morning,' she said, encouragingly. 'What can I do for you?'

'I hear you got into a bit of a disagreement, at the Hobsons' last night. So I came to find out what it was all about.'

She stared at him. Had there been CCTV cameras, with sound, linked to the Gloucester police station? Was one of the teenagers a police informer? Had Higgins himself been hiding under one of the tables?

'How?' she demanded.

It seemed her second guess was closest to the truth. 'My daughter, Alice, is friendly with Helen Hobson, who Twittered all about it.'

The surprising thing was that Alice had proceeded to tell her father, surely. 'You all moved very quickly,' she said. 'It was barely twelve hours ago.'

He brushed this aside. 'So what happened?'

'I thought you knew all about it.'

'I exaggerated. Twitters are quite short. I think the exact words were: *Bad atmosphere at the Hobsons. Parents angry with visiting house-sitter woman. Fighting over Grandad Donny. Sick or what!*'

Surprisingly succinct, thought Thea, who had yet to experience Twitter at first hand.

'Well, it's true, as far as it goes,' she admitted. 'I did make them angry.'

'Can you tell me why?'

'I didn't *mean* to,' she said childishly. 'Toby was talking about Jemima's mother, and I was just trying to see things from Donny's point of view. I made it sound as if Jemima neglected him, but that wasn't what I meant. I still feel awful about it. Obviously she didn't neglect him at all. But I think he wanted more from her. I think he really did feel he wasn't being taken care of very well.' She stopped herself, hearing the defensive note in her voice and fearing it might sound like whining.

Higgins thought about this. 'You only saw him twice. You must be basing your opinions on very flimsy evidence.'

'That's true, but it did get quite intense, very quickly.'

'From what people have told me, I got the distinct impression that he was fiercely independent. I thought the whole point was that he didn't *want* anybody looking after him.'

She paused, aware of a contradiction. 'That is true, up to a point, yes. But it was mainly hospitals he dreaded, and total dependency. It was all rather subtle, but I think he was a bit scared of Jemima, scared of asking too much and annoying her. She can be quite fierce. So can her husband. Actually, you know, I don't think he wanted anything different from what everybody wants.' It kept coming back to this, she realised.

'Which is?'

'To be in control of your own destiny, while at the same time feeling there are people who love you and who'd drop everything for you if necessary.'

'Which Mrs Hobson would, I assume?'

'If it really was necessary, of course. But I'm not sure she'd be very gracious about it. She isn't exactly *kind*.'

'Ah – he wanted a *kind* person to be on permanent standby. I see.'

She shook her head gently, feeling exhausted by the effort of getting it right. 'Everybody does,' she repeated. 'We all want that sort of guardian angel standing right behind us to watch over us.'

Higgins groaned dramatically. 'Don't get started on angels,' he begged. 'It's all my girls ever talk about these days.'

'Really? I thought it was vampires.'

He cast his eyes to the sky. 'No, *no*. That's *so* last year,' he fluted, in a parody of a teenage daughter. Then he quickly switched back to serious mode. 'I'm not sure where this is getting us.' He smacked his hands together as if deciding to be yet more businesslike. 'We still don't know for sure whether this is a homicide enquiry.'

'After all this time? Isn't there a lot of pressure to just let it go, then? There has to be a deadline, surely?'

He shook his head reprovingly. 'By no means.

You ought to know that. It takes as long as it takes. The file stays open.'

'But he has to be buried eventually. You can't hold onto the body indefinitely.'

'That's a different matter. We're releasing it tomorrow.'

'And still no evidence of another person there when he died? Even with all your forensics and DNAs and so forth? That must be conclusive in itself, I'd have thought.'

He took a long calming breath. 'Thea – if I can call you that? – if you stop a minute to think about it, you'll understand that when a person dies in his own bed, where he's been visited by the same people over the past weeks and months, there will be traces of those people all over the room, without it having any sinister implications. Forensics is great for a lot of things, but in this instance, it isn't worth bothering. Nobody thinks a total stranger broke in and killed him by taping a bag over his head.'

'Which means it must have been Jemima or Edwina, in effect – if anybody, that is.'

He pursed his lips. 'Plus two or three others, maybe. At least. He wasn't short of people.'

She smiled. 'He certainly made friends easily. I suppose Jemima's children went to see him, and Toby, and probably little Tamsin. They all seem to have been fond of him, except—' She stopped,

348

mindful of her big mouth and the trouble it could cause.

'Except . . . ?'

'Well, Thyrza and her son, Philippe. I don't think either of them got on well with Donny. Philippe said some rather harsh things about him the first time I met him. I don't expect he meant them. He's nicer than I first thought. I'm invited there for lunch today, actually,' she added proudly, wanting him to see that *she* made friends easily as well.

'Good,' he said, with surprising emphasis. In a flash she was transported to Duntisbourne Abbots, two years earlier, when her brother-in-law had pulled strings to get her the house-sitting commission, knowing she might be useful to the police. Ever since then, she had nursed a secret suspicion that some of her experiences had been engineered behind her back, explaining the terrible things that happened, at least in part. She suppressed these thoughts as much as she could, preferring to believe in coincidence if possible. She embarked on each new job with the blithe hope that this time it would all be entirely normal and straightforward, but events somehow always conspired, even if the West Midlands police didn't. If the people behaved, the dogs didn't. Dogs had got her into a lot of trouble, one way and another.

'I'm not going to spy for you,' she said, with

matching emphasis. 'Not this time.'

He put up his hands, eyes wide. 'Of course not,' he said.

He only stayed a few more minutes after that, strolling into the lounge and admiring the wood panelling. 'Nice place,' he said. 'She's a lucky woman.'

'I think she knows it. It's very well cared for.'

'She'll have to find a new tenant for the Lodge now. She won't like that.'

'Donny must have hated renting, when he'd worked all his life, and had his own house, and a pension. He must have assumed he was secure for life.'

'And then his daughter's illness happened. And his wife's.' He smiled, as if to say – *Look how efficient I've been in investigating his background.* 'They sold the family house to pay for all the medical stuff. Terrible luck.'

'Maybe that's why Harriet took him on. She felt bad about being so lucky herself.'

Higgins shrugged. 'It's possible,' he said.

'Donny's left his collection of antique silver to be sold for Janet's care – did you know? Funny, now I think of it, that he hadn't sold it already, if she's in such a bad way.'

'Maybe he thought he might need it for himself,' Higgins suggested, with a meaningful look.

Thea groaned. 'Whatever he thought, he should have told poor old Jemima about it. He let her discover the contents of the will for herself, after he died. A bit mean of him, don't you think?'

'It's my hunch he did tell her, or tried to, but she wouldn't talk about it.'

She could have hugged him. 'Yes!' she whooped. 'That's exactly how it must have been. She would never let him talk about dying, or funerals or wills or anything. Seemed to think she was protecting him by being like that.'

'It's very common. More or less the norm, you might say.'

She blinked at him. 'Don't say that,' she begged. 'That would be awful.'

'Why?'

'It means everybody lives in fear and denial for most of the time. What a waste! What *dishonesty*!'

'I must go,' he said, already in the hall. 'No time for philosophy just now. And you need to get ready for your lunch engagement.'

'It's not for ages yet.' She sounded sulky, even to her own ears. A bit of philosophy would have been just the thing for a Sunday morning.

He would not be delayed, but as she followed him out to his car, he paused and said, 'It's not dishonest, you know. Not really. Didn't somebody once say people can't endure very much reality? That's the truth of it. You shouldn't judge.'

'You sound just like Phil Hollis,' she told him crossly. 'But thanks for coming. It was kind of you – I think.'

He laughed softly and drove away.

Ten minutes later, Drew called her on her mobile. 'Still on for this afternoon?' he asked.

'I am if you are. It's a nice day for it. Where are you going – have you decided?'

'It's still under discussion. Do you have any fresh suggestions?'

'Somebody told me about Painswick Beacon, near here, which might have more to offer, in a wild sort of way. Bourton will be awfully touristy. I wondered whether we should meet there, say four o'clock? I don't know how high it is. You might be a bit too tired for a steep climb. But they say the views are spectacular.'

'I don't know,' he hesitated. 'Kids aren't too keen on views, in my experience. Isn't there a place near you with a funny name – Prinknash, or something? Have you been there?'

'No. It's a Benedictine monastery, isn't it? I expect they do have a café, but I doubt whether your children would find much of interest there. They pronounce it "Prinnash", actually, just for the record. It's practically on the doorstep here, but I don't think it would fit the bill, from what I know of it.' She was groping for everything she knew about the place, odd snippets gleaned from time to time.

Drew sounded disappointed. 'We could have tea there and find somewhere for the kids to run about. I rather like monasteries.'

'Well I don't think I do, to be honest. I'd feel uncomfortable there, especially on a Sunday.'

'Hmm. That's a shame.'

She was doing it again, she realised with a sick feeling – riding carelessly over other people's feelings. 'I'm sorry, Drew,' she said. 'I'm being inconsiderate. We can go there if you really want to. Or stick to Plan A and go to Bourton-on-the-Water.'

'No, no. You know best. Where else do you suggest?'

'You could go to the wildlife park first, maybe? Furry animals never fail to amuse, after all. And then we can go and look at Painswick Beacon. Toby told me about it yesterday. It sounds great. It's on the A46, just north of Painswick itself.'

'OK, except I'll have to go to Broad Campden at some point, I suppose. As cover.'

She felt a different chill go through her. 'Cover?' she repeated faintly.

'For the tax man,' he added. 'I can claim back the cost of fuel, if it's business-related.'

'Oh.' The suspicion, if that was what it was, slowly receded. 'You'll be doing a lot of driving, then. Can you fit it all in?'

'I can if I set off right away. Assume the Beacon at four unless I phone you to change it. Is that all right?'

'Absolutely fine,' she said, wondering why she felt so heavy about it. She had been looking forward to it, eager to bring Drew up to date with all the local developments, but suddenly it felt doomed to embarrassment and complication. After all, Drew could not possibly be as pure and squeaky clean as she imagined him. And if he was, she herself was definitely not. Her flaws were becoming more and more evident to her: she was impulsive and insensitive and unworthy of Drew's friendship. He was certainly decent and friendly, willing to give full attention to other people's troubles, as well as sharing much of her outlook on the world. Quite how much they had in common was only slowly dawning on her, forming a bond of friendship that she valued more highly every time she met him. But he was married, he had a fragile business that required most of his energy, and a person called Maggs who sounded like a kind of alter ego, welded to him in a fashion that Thea had not yet understood.

'See you then,' he said quickly, and rang off.

The Ferrier household was predictably unpredictable. Before she got there, Thea was prepared for pink walls, plastic chairs, Persian rugs, prayer mats or pouffes. Anything was possible. And the wife – what was she going to be like? And the poodle – was it allowed on the furniture, or kept in its own separate outhouse? Or what? The curiosity behind the hypothesising was pleasurably distracting from gloomy self-recriminations, as she walked the half-mile in an easterly direction, without her spaniel. She would be very nice, she vowed – very careful about what she said.

Initially she had assumed the village to be divided into two sections, but slowly she had worked out that there was a third cluster of houses, in a deep hollow sheltered by the woods to the north. Sheltered, protected, and perhaps rather threatened on dark winter days. Philippe lived in this third area, in a square stone house at a remove from the others, further up the easterly slope. She found it easily, pausing to admire the jumbled garden boasting a swing and a trampoline as well as a big old fig tree which looked to be bearing fruit in some quantity.

The door was festooned with a yellow Mermaid rose, which immediately reminded Thea of her own cottage, where Carl had planted just the same thing, which continued to drape itself all around the porch at the front. The reminder came with a pang, a flashback more complicated than usual. This was not the moment to remember her dead husband, with all the sensations of abandonment and helplessness that came with the memories. She took a deep breath and reached out to pull the strange oriental-looking contraption that was the doorbell. Before she could connect, the door opened, and two faces beamed out at her.

'Welcome!' said Philippe expansively. 'What good timing! We've just finished the fruit punch.'

'I cut up the peaches,' chirped Tamsin, displaying fingers covered in juice and sticky pieces of peach skin.

'Messy job,' said Thea. 'I'm afraid I come empty-handed, which is very rude of me. I should have cut some of Harriet's roses for you, but that seemed a bit—'

'Perish the thought!' exclaimed Philippe. 'That would be grand larceny.'

The child beside him giggled, and repeated, 'Grand larceny,' with obvious relish, turning the syllables into mere sounds without meaning.

The wife was still invisible, but as they went into the house, Thea could hear glass clinking in a room at the end of the hall. 'She'll appear in a minute,' said Philippe. 'I do let her out of the kitchen on special occasions.'

It wasn't a joke that any self-respecting independent woman could possibly laugh at, which he must surely realise. Thea said nothing, instead making a point of inspecting the hallway, which was windowless and stone-floored. The flags were polished, highlighting beautiful swirling marbled patterns contained in the stones themselves. It definitely wasn't anything local.

'Chinese marble,' said the man of the house, seeing the direction of her gaze. 'Aren't the colours amazing?'

'Fabulous,' she agreed. 'But I guess you have to work hard to keep them as shiny as this.'

A large wall hanging was the next cause for admiration. Apparently Indian, it was an explosion of textures and colours, with small mirrors sewn in at random intervals, gold thread stitched into swirling shapes, and raised quilted sections crying out to be fingered.

'Come through,' he urged her. 'There's much more to see.'

He led her into a living room almost as big as the one at Hollywell. There was no wood panelling, but instead three walls were papered in a design that Thea recognised as William Morris's 'Acanthus' in shades of blue. The sheer perverse unfashionableness of it endeared it to her. Always a fan of William Morris and his many different products, she had made a study of his Cotswold connections. A big open fireplace was decorated with ceramic tiles, also carrying Morris designs. On the floor a pair of tufted wool rugs boasted further evidence of the same theme – flowers and leaves on a winding trellis with smaller leaves sprinkled all over the background.

'Deborah made them,' said Philippe. 'She's made a lot of the furnishings, actually.'

There was a portentousness to his tone that alerted her. 'I'm impressed,' she said. 'It's all lovely. I'm very keen on William Morris myself, as it happens. That's the Acanthus design, isn't it?'

He nodded. 'And the rugs are Windrush. Very appropriate, don't you think?'

'Definitely. The blues and golds are gorgeous.'

Tamsin had flopped down in the middle of one of the rugs, and was stroking the pile. 'Mummy's rugs are famous,' she said. 'Did you know that?'

'I'm not sure,' Thea hesitated, then took the risk. 'She's not Debbie Fawcett, is she?'

Father and daughter grinned delightedly. 'Got it in one!' cried Philippe. 'Most people need a few more clues than that.'

'Wow! Now I'm *really* impressed,' she breathed. Debbie Fawcett was close to becoming a household name with her Victorian revivals. Cushions, hangings, rugs, curtains, wallpapers and tiles – everything that Morris had designed, she built on, making her own variants, altering some of the colours, but using nothing but natural materials. People mocked, and insisted there was no market for such retro furnishings, but somehow they bought them anyway, seduced by the feel of real wool and cotton, heedless of the astronomical prices. *They must be minted*, she thought. *With him being a private heart surgeon as well.*

'Don't be,' came a voice. 'It's pure plagiarism, when it comes down to it.'

A grey-haired woman with Mediterranean skin was standing in the doorway, smiling calmly. She looked to be at least fifty, tall and straight-backed, but with telltale grooves on her face, and inelastic skin at the base of her neck. She wore a beige embroidered dress that almost reached the ground, sleeveless and shapeless. The embroidery depicted similar leaves and flowers to those on the Windrush rugs. The beige colour was almost exactly the same as her skin, giving the impression that she was naked apart from the patterns.

Thea made no move to greet her, paralysed by her charismatic presence. She had registered that the child had some darker blood than her father, leading her to expect an Asian mother, if not African. The serendipity of racial mixtures always interested her. In this case, the result was a beautiful child with classic colouring that might have come directly from Helen of Troy.

'It's good to be appreciated,' Deborah said in creamy English tones. 'Now, can I get you a drink? We've made a rather extravagant fruit punch. We'll be eating in the conservatory, if that's all right?'

'The punch sounds wonderful,' said Thea, thinking of Tamsin's sticky fingers on the fabulous handmade rug. 'Your daughter has been telling me about it.'

'Tam! Did you wash your hands?' The normality of the question was somehow reassuring. 'You were covered in peach juice last time I looked.'

The child sighed, and spread her fingers. 'It's dry now,' she said optimistically.

'Fibber. Go and wash.'

Obediently, Tamsin left the room, looking at her hands with exaggerated scepticism, throwing her mother a glance full of weary frustration laced with affection and a sort of wise understanding that some children possessed, to the discomfort of many adults. She returned within two minutes.

'Now can we – you know?' said the little girl, with a sideways look at Thea. 'Can we *show* her?'

'You'll have to ask Jasper,' said Philippe, who had been quietly watching the women as they met for the first time. There was something orchestrated in the whole encounter, Thea suspected.

Tamsin laughed, a joyous musical peal that made all the adults smile. 'Come on, then,' she trilled.

She led a little procession out of the room, and down the hall to the back of the house. Thea had time to register a big oak chest covered in scars and dents, with carved panels. On it stood a telephone and a scatter of papers. It filled an alcove next to a door, through which they all trooped.

They were in a large light kitchen, boasting a huge old pine table, almost the twin of Jemima's. The walls were bright yellow, the floor covered in black and white tiles. Unhesitatingly, Tamsin took them through another door, into an area that must once have been a dairy. The wide slate slab where butter was once made, cheese and eggs stored, cold meat carved, remained as evidence of more self-sufficient times.

'Here she is!' crowed the child, kneeling in a corner where something alive stirred. 'Hello, Lady. How are you today?'

Debbie and Philippe stood back to give Thea a clear view. She focused on a sharp nose, pricked black ears and a tangle of little bodies against a furry side. 'Oh!' she cried. 'It's my dog from the woods.' She knelt down beside Tamsin, and let the dog sniff her proffered hand. 'How did she get here?'

Nobody spoke, and for a moment Thea had no sense of tension or surprise. She rubbed the dog's soft head, between the ears, letting the relief and gladness flow through her, to the exclusion of all else. Only at that moment did she understand how miserable she had been about the sudden disappearance. All five pups had survived, and grown to nearly double the size they were when she last saw them. Gently she picked up the biggest one, a shaggy-coated grey animal, whose eyes were just coming unglued. He squinted at her as she held him close to her face. She inhaled the drenchingly sweet scent of him, aware of the incomparable instinctive protective love people felt for baby things, and perhaps puppies above all else.

'You've seen them before?' came Philippe's voice, oddly tight.

'Yes, yes. My spaniel found the burrow in the woods. I took food for her. I suppose your poodle did the same thing.' She fondled the bitch again. 'Silly girl – you weren't as well hidden as you thought, were you?'

'We hid her there, as it happens,' said Philippe. 'And you ruined it.'

Finally she detected the anger in his voice. Awkwardly she turned to look up at him. 'What?'

'We knew old Sam would never let her keep the pups, so we hid her. It wasn't easy, but she settled down after a day or so.'

'So *you* were feeding her as well? But she seemed so hungry. And thirsty.'

'No, we couldn't do that. She would have followed us home. It's only a field away from here. She'd have brought the pups one by one.'

'I don't get it. Why not keep her here from the start?'

'Because this is the first place Sam looked when she went missing.'

'Why?'

A big, warm, grey body appeared from nowhere, and pushed between Thea and the mother dog. The shade of grey on the poodle was exactly the same as on the pup she held. 'Oh! Now I see. They're his. And Sam would have realised.'

'Right. And no way does he want a mongrel litter of poodles. He despises the entire breed, for some reason.'

'So what happens next?'

'We'll have to tell him eventually. We keep the pups and he gets his bitch back.'

'But – why are you so cross with me? Didn't I save her? She would have starved if I hadn't taken food for her. And why did I ruin anything? What happened?'

'You left a trail as obvious as the M4 to a dog. Jasper came across it, and followed it to the burrow. He wouldn't leave her alone, so we had no choice but to move the whole lot here.'

'But nothing's ruined. This is better for all concerned.'

He shook his head. 'It makes us into criminals. We've stolen Lady, in the eyes of the law.'

Thea blew out her cheeks in a puff of amused

disbelief. 'Rubbish. Anybody would have done the same.'

Deborah spoke for the first time. 'The law doesn't see that as a very good excuse, though, does it? Even when you act out of kindness, or ordinary human sensitivity, you can still be breaking the law.'

It sounded as if she was speaking about more than the dog. Thea looked at her consideringly. 'I suppose that's true,' she agreed slowly.

CHAPTER EIGHTEEN

The lunch with the Ferrier family was ample, original and not entirely comfortable. Although Philippe appeared to be trying his best to recapture the easy friendliness that had characterised roughly half of Thea's dealings with him, she had seen too much of his other side to be seduced any further. She concentrated on Deborah and the child, with the Arts and Crafts movement the chief topic of conversation. Thea's background in historical studies proved useful. She expanded on her somewhat rusty knowledge of canals and railways, topic of a dissertation written twenty years earlier, with a brief account of her time in Frampton Mansell, where she was embroiled in local hostilities arising from the renovation of the Cotswold Canal.

Tamsin listened avidly to Thea's description of

a holiday spent on a narrowboat, one gloriously sunny July, with her daughter Jessica who was five at the time. It had been idyllic by any standards, and for the second time that day, Thea was transported back to her life as a wife and mother, when the world had been warm and easy. 'Can we do that one day, Mummy?' the child pleaded. 'We could take Jasper.'

'Dogs usually like it,' Thea confirmed. 'We had two when we went, and they were fine – except for the locks. One of them went crazy when the water started flooding in and the boat rocked. She knocked a whole lot of things into the sink and broke a plate.'

Tamsin uttered her contagious squeal of laughter, clearly knowing how endearing the adults found her.

Deborah had prepared a substantial game pie for the meal, containing rabbit, pheasant and venison. 'All wild,' she asserted. 'And local.'

'Wow!' Thea wasn't quite sure she approved of the implications. 'Who killed them?'

'Not me,' said Philippe, with a camp shudder, reminding Thea of her first impression of him. 'It's all perfectly kosher. I hope,' he added with a smile. 'There is a slight question mark over the venison, to be honest.'

'No there isn't, Phil. Don't be silly,' his wife admonished. She looked at Thea. 'There's a lot of poaching of deer going on, because the meat's selling so well at the moment. Awful townies coming into the countryside and making a real mess of it. Barbaric stuff we wish we didn't know about.'

'But aren't you encouraging it, by buying the meat?' Thea couldn't resist asking. 'I mean – it's a bit like buying ivory, isn't it?'

'Probably. But it's nice, isn't it?' The glimpse of Philippe's character that these words revealed again reminded Thea of her reservations about him. He was lacking in integrity, she decided. Irresponsible, not a serious person. A fair-weather friend. Deborah evidently chose the furnishings for their house and exerted discipline over their daughter. What was left for him to do around the house, other than behave as a handsome drone in his flamboyant shirts?

Donny Davis was not mentioned once, although he had not disappeared from Thea's thoughts. She bit back outrageous questions about Cecilia's heart condition and Philippe's reported failure to offer his services for nothing. She censored any references to Jemima or Toby or Harriet Young. *Be nice*, she repeated to herself at regular intervals. *Don't upset anybody.*

At three o'clock, after a large serving of home-made ice cream full of pieces of honeycomb, followed by a rich nutty coffee, Thea made a move to leave. 'I'm meeting someone in a little while,' she said. 'It has been a magnificent meal. Really wonderful.' She looked at Philippe, sitting with his big woolly dog between his knees. 'I'm sorry about the dog and her pups. I know I shouldn't have interfered. But I think anybody would have done the same. I hope you find good homes for the puppies.'

'Think no more about it. It's done now, and I expect it'll come right in the end. Things usually do.'

Thea thought of Donny. Had it come right in the end for him?

She thought not.

Only by prolonged use of their mobile phones did she and Drew find each other in the parking area near Painswick Beacon. Vehicles straggled along a rough wide track, angled into the edge of the woods wherever they could find a space. On a sunny Sunday afternoon, it was packed. Thea had to drive along the track for a considerable way and walk back, the spaniel pulling ahead on the lead.

She was looking for a family comprising two parents and two children, but when she finally saw Drew waving vigorously at her from the top of a slope, there was only him and the children. She unclipped the dog and climbed up to them, pausing for breath and to admire the view before saying, 'Where's your wife?'

'She didn't come,' he said. 'This is Stephanie, and this is Timmy.' He patted each child lightly on the shoulder, and they both stared at her, unsmiling.

'Hello there,' she said heartily. 'This is Hepzibah. Are you having a nice day out?'

They glanced indifferently at the dog. 'Timmy dropped his ice cream,' said Stephanie. 'And Daddy wouldn't buy him another one.'

'The queue was a mile long,' Drew protested. 'And he'd had about half of it.'

'Where did you go?'

'The wildlife park. It was bedlam.'

'Like here,' remarked Thea. 'I suppose it's the sunshine, bringing them all out.'

There were knots of people on all sides, scrambling down into an old quarry or walking around its edge. 'Have you been here long?'

'Ten minutes. We were lucky and got a parking space just as somebody was leaving.'

'So let's walk to the top, shall we? It's an old hill fort, according to my map. Two hundred and eighty-three metres above sea level.'

'Is that a lot?' Drew asked the question in all sincerity, it seemed, not simply wanting the information for his children, who had begun to take more interest in their surroundings.

'It must be something like nine hundred feet,

I suppose. I always think a thousand feet is quite high, so yes, it's respectably elevated.'

'Which way?'

She looked around, and consulted the Explorer Map she'd brought with her. 'Due north of here,' she said with authority. 'And the sun's in the west, more or less, so it must be that way.' She pointed to the far side of the quarry. 'Where everybody's coming back from.'

The children waited passively for instructions, and Thea wondered whether they had the energy for a climb. 'I don't think it's very far,' she said encouragingly. 'Follow me.'

It was further than it looked on the map, with a long straight path leading towards the earthworks that were all that remained of the fort. Just as she was bracing herself for complaints and resistance, she heard Stephanie say, 'Daddy, this is like Maiden Castle, isn't it?'

'It is a bit, yes. Well done, Steph. That's very clever of you.'

'Maiden Castle?' Thea echoed.

'You know – the big hill near Dorchester. We've been there three times. Steph loves it. She says she saw a ghost there.'

'Gosh! And how is it like this?'

'These banked-up ridges are much the same. They had wooden fences on top. It was all fiercely fortified.'

'And stakes,' said Timmy. 'They put sharp stakes to stop the army coming in.'

'Well, it looks as if this was a good choice, then,' said Thea with relief. 'You know more about it than I do.'

They progressed up the long sloping walkway to the very top, where a circular plate indicated the places that could be seen on a clear day – which this was. The children were less interested in the view than the imagined warfare that raged a thousand years ago. 'Roughly speaking,' said Drew apologetically. 'I'm not at all sure of the dates, are you?'

'A lot more than a thousand years, I think. If I remember rightly, it's BC, which means it's more than *two* thousand years old. They call it Kimsbury Camp in some of the books.'

With impressive energy, Stephanie and Timmy began to re-enact their idea of Dark Ages politics, with horses and swords. Hepzie was encouraged to join in, with modest success. Thea found Drew's children disconcerting on the whole, mainly due to a worry about her role in the little group and what they might tell their mother. Seizing the opportunity, she told Drew that the mystery of the missing dog in the woods had been solved.

'I was so happy to see her again. The puppies have grown amazingly.'

'You were so upset when she went missing.'

The memory of weeping on Drew's chest ought to have been embarrassing, but somehow it wasn't. 'I know. I was terrified for their welfare.'

'So what about Donny?' Drew changed the subject. 'What's been happening about him?'

'Loads of theories and suspicions, but nothing concrete.' She met his eyes and made another switch of topic. 'Why isn't Karen with you?' she asked him outright.

'She's not well enough. She hasn't been right for a week or more. I wasn't sure I should leave her, really, but there are neighbours she can call on if necessary.'

'What's the problem?'

'Oh, I don't know. More of the same. They're talking about doing a brain scan, to see what's going on. She's just so *flat* all the time.'

'It sounds like ME – though nobody seems to get that any more, do they?'

'It's similar, I suppose. But we're sure it's all a result of being shot in the head. There must have been more damage than we first assumed.'

'I can't imagine what it must have been like, for all of you, not just her.'

'Neither can I, now. We seemed to come through it really well at the time. The kids weren't especially upset, and once Karen got home from hospital they were fine. We all were, for months. But it slowly dawned on us that she was never going to be the same as before. Even if she'd made a complete physical recovery, the trauma would never entirely disappear.'

'Does she know you're meeting me?' The question had been on her mind since she'd realised Karen wasn't there. It had taken an effort to voice it.

He took a few seconds to reply. 'No, actually. It was all a bit chaotic this morning. She was going to come, right up to the last minute. Then I said I'd cancel it and stay with her, but Timmy made such a fuss it seemed easier just to stick to the plan.'

'So when they tell her you came up to the Beacon with a strange lady, what's Karen going to think?'

'Your guess is probably better than mine,' he said. He sounded so despondent and helpless that she almost put her arms round him in an effort to comfort him. 'She's very unpredictable,' he explained. 'The most likely reaction is complete indifference.'

'Oh dear. She really doesn't sound right.'

'No. And not telling her is definitely the best thing. For her, I mean. If I force her to listen, it'll seem as if I'm making a big issue of it – an important announcement of some sort.'

It was a problem that Thea had not encountered before, despite its ordinariness. When a married man spent time with an attractive single woman, there were implications and reverberations that took over, however innocent the intentions. Men never did tell their wives, she supposed, just in case things went out of control and there was reason to deceive after all. But in this case, the children would inevitably complicate matters. She knew Drew well enough to be sure that he would never ask them to keep a secret from their mother. So why had he taken such a risk?

They were still at the top of the Beacon, gazing at the compelling panorama stretching for many miles in each direction. Conscientiously, they called the children and pointed out the landmarks as indicated on the metal plate. The roofs of Painswick were a fairy-tale jumble, the smaller villages comfortably rooted in their cosy valleys, roads barely discernible until a big lorry crawling along showed where they were. Gradually, as they obediently looked, the spreading patchwork below them caught their imagination.

'It's a kingdom!' said Timmy. 'And I'm the king.'

'The ruler of all you survey,' said Drew. 'What a marvellous spot for a fort. Clever people they had in those days.'

'They killed everybody,' Stephanie objected solemnly. 'Fighting and killing.'

'Not all the time,' Thea said. 'They had plenty of peace as well.'

'Did they?' said Drew. 'Are you sure?'

'It isn't possible to fight all the time. There would have been long recovery periods, where the women put it all back together, growing vegetables and making new clothes for everybody, and seeing that the wounds healed. Besides, they call it a "camp", which suggests it was peaceful most of the time.'

'Sounds rather nice,' he agreed. 'But I'm not sure I believe you about recovery periods.'

'I'm right, all the same. It's obvious. It's the same now. War is exhausting in all sorts of ways. It has to stop eventually.'

'But people are still dead,' said the little girl. '*Thousands* of them.'

'True,' admitted Thea, wondering at the child's insistence.

'Daddy buries dead people,' said Timmy – something Thea had temporarily forgotten.

'So he does,' she smiled. 'So you know all about it.'

'Not *all*,' frowned the undertaker's son. 'But I will when I get bigger.'

'Time to get back,' Drew announced, with a palpable heaviness. 'Bedtime is already going to be late, and there's school tomorrow.'

Thea waited for the customary remark about an impatient Mummy chastising them for staying out too long, but nothing came.

'I'm thirsty,' said Timmy. 'And hot.'

'I expect we all are,' said Drew with an air of helplessness. 'There's some water in the car.'

The children went ahead, scampering down the long incline to the foot of the hill fort. Thea was aware that Drew wanted to talk to her, that he was frustrated at not having time or space for a prolonged conversation. Whilst happy in his company, she was unsure about his evident need for something more. It was unclear where his priorities lay – what was the most urgent topic for him amongst the things they had spoken of so far?

It was soon revealed. 'Listen,' he said. 'This man who died. I can't stop thinking about it. I've discussed it with Maggs as well. We're both convinced he didn't kill himself. It just shouts out that it couldn't possibly have been suicide. I think you have to contact the police and explain about his appointment with me. People don't make appointments the day before they take their own life.'

'I know. But there's no *evidence*. The police can't do anything on suspicion or hunches. They've questioned everybody concerned, and been back to the house. I think Higgins has been a lot more thorough than anybody would expect. He's not at all convinced that it was suicide, either. He came to see me again this morning. Really I don't think there's anything more I can tell him.'

'Has he checked the phone? Did Donny have email? Does anyone inherit anything of value? Did he make *any* provisions for his funeral?'

'He didn't have email. He left everything in trust for his wife. I'm not sure about the other things.' She spread her hands. 'I can't see what else we can do. Harriet will come home on Saturday, and maybe have something to add. Oh – and Deborah Fawcett said a funny thing, about kind acts sometimes being against the law. It felt as if she was trying to tell me something important.'

'Deborah Fawcett? Who's she?'

'She's a famous designer of soft furnishings. Married to Philippe, where I had lunch.'

'Did she know Donny?'

'I assume so. Her mother-in-law is his lady friend's sister.'

'Yes,' he said. 'So she is.'

'Do you mean you really are keeping up with all the names and connections, after only a couple of visits?'

'It's second nature,' he grinned. 'A vital part of my profession, if you think about it. You only confuse somebody's wife with his daughter once, before you learn to be extremely meticulous about family relationships, I promise you.' He paused, then said, 'So she thinks Donny was killed out of kindness.'

'Apparently. But she was very oblique about it.'

'Could she mean that her husband did it, but she couldn't say that outright? Did she try to take you to one side and elaborate?'

'Not at all. Why would she?'

'Did he give her a sharp look when she said that about kind acts?'

'Not that I noticed. I don't see why it would be him, anyway. He's not very kind, and has nothing to gain.'

'As far as we know,' Drew corrected her.

'OK. But I can't see it. She's much more likely to have been talking about Edwina.'

'Maggs thinks that book is significant. The one your employer wrote.'

'I don't see how.'

'She could have come with me today. She wanted to.'

'Why didn't she, then? I'd like to meet her.'

'I'm not sure I could cope with both of you at once.' He said it lightly, again leaving Thea wondering just what was going on inside his head. 'I told her about the Manor. She'd love to see it.'

'Oh – you know those paintings in the gallery? Well, I think they're by Evelyn De Morgan. She was quite famous in her time, although always overshadowed by the men. She was quite prolific. It's possible nobody knows about them. They might even have been in the house since soon after it was built.' Even as she spoke, she knew it was nothing more than foolish fantasy.

Drew evidently saw it like that, too. 'Surely not. There'd have been inventories for probate and so forth every time it changed hands.'

But she persisted with her fancies, for no better reason than to enjoy a gentle argument. 'They could have been tucked away in an attic and Harriet only just found them. They are quite grimy.'

He looked at her sternly, glancing away at the children, waiting obediently in the distance. 'Is this relevant?' he asked.

'Almost certainly not. But I bet Maggs would be interested.'

'She said she was going to read every single word about Harriet's book, on the Internet. There's quite a lot.'

'But nothing from Donny, because he didn't have a computer.'

'She's not just looking for him,' Drew said.

'Does she know the names of every person involved? What does she expect to find?'

'I jotted them down. Thyrza Hastings. Edwina Satterthwaite. Philippe Hastings. Toby Brent. Jemima Hobson.'

'Stop it. You're showing off. How do you know Toby's surname?'

'Edwina introduced him on Tuesday. Don't you remember?'

'No,' she sighed. 'But you're not quite perfect: it isn't Philippe Hastings. His father was called Ferrier. Thyrza was married twice.'

'Drat!'

'Don't let it worry you. I already told you I can't imagine it was him.'

'Only because you don't think he's kind, and you've got the idea it was meant as an act of kindness. What if Donny was killed by somebody *unkind*?'

'That would be horrible. Poor Donny.' She tried to think it through again. 'It might well have been, of course. If it wasn't assisted suicide, then it was outright murder, for selfish motives.' She frowned. 'Nobody's really behaving as if that was it. If one of the people I've met did it, they're showing no signs of guilt – or even of satisfaction that they've got whatever it is they wanted.'

'Most people can put on a pretty convincing act if their freedom depends on it. Or their good name.'

'Maybe,' she agreed doubtfully. 'I can't see how any of this is getting us anywhere.'

'It isn't until some evidence turns up.'

'And you think it will?'

'I think it might.'

'Look, Drew, I've seen them all over the past few days. I've been to their houses and met their kids. It's an ordinary family, who've had two deaths in a year. Nobody's behaving strangely or eyeing each other suspiciously. What if there was a conspiracy and they're all in it? Jemima, Edwina, Toby, Thyrza and Philippe all banded together and murdered Donny because they thought it was for the best. That would confuse the police dreadfully, wouldn't it?'

'You forget the most important detail.'

She closed her eyes, scanning her memory. 'The phone call! Somebody broke ranks and accused Edwina, and was lucky enough to catch a moment when the police recording machine was out of action and the number of the call wasn't logged.'

'Is that what the detective bloke told you?'

'Yes. He's embarrassed about it.'

'Without that call, would it just have been written up as a suicide, do you think?'

'Highly likely. There was nothing else to arouse suspicion.'

The children were squatting on a patch of grass, peering intently at the ground, showing no signs of impatience despite Timmy's thirst. Hepzie was sniffing at a hole in the roots of a tree some distance away. 'Aren't they good!' Thea approved.

'For the moment. They're obviously in no hurry to get home.' His expression was rueful, and she wondered about the atmosphere in the house, with Karen's ill-defined malaise casting a pall over everything. 'OK, kids?' he called from the point some yards away where he and Thea stood talking.

'Higgins told Edwina there was evidence that it was murder, but he didn't say anything about a phone call. She seemed to expect people to think she'd helped him to kill himself.'

'And she doesn't deny that she promised to help him to kill himself when the time came?'

'Right.'

'And this was not the time.'

'Right again.'

'So somebody killed him.'

'I suppose they must have done.'

CHAPTER NINETEEN

It was well past five o'clock as they drifted back to Drew's car, still talking, the children diverting from the path to examine items of interest. 'I really should get them home,' he said, more than once. 'They'll be hungry.'

'I hope you had a big lunch?'

'Not very. There was a café at the wildlife park, but we only had a snack. They weren't in the mood for eating.'

'Will Karen have a meal waiting?'

'I doubt it. We might have to stop somewhere on the way.' He was beginning to look harassed, running a hand through his floppy hair. 'I'm always getting the timing wrong when it comes to food.'

'Why don't you phone her, say you'll be late and come back to the Manor with me? I've got some sausages and eggs and bread. I can do a fry-up or something.'

'That's a great offer, but it'll make us so *late*.' He almost wailed. 'It takes an hour and a half at least to get home from here, especially with all this weekend traffic.'

'They can sleep in the car. And if you get away by six-thirty or so, you won't be so terribly late anyway. Just sling them into bed as soon as you're home.'

'They'll be grubby for school. There's never time for a bath in the morning.'

'Drew!' Exasperation overwhelmed her. 'Don't *fuss*. It's a gorgeous summer evening in a beautiful part of the country. The kids are happy. Wipe their faces and wash their hands and they'll be perfectly presentable.'

His laugh was so loud it shocked her. It seemed to explode out of him, making his children and three passers-by all stare. 'You're right!' he shouted. 'You're *so* right. Thank you, Thea Osborne. Thank you very much.' He moved towards her, arms outspread and she waited for a hug that never happened. Instead he stopped six inches away and dropped his arms.

'Get your car and I'll follow you,' he said. 'It's not far, is it?'

'About two miles. Maybe less. Give me three minutes. Come on, Heps.' She jogged along the line of parked cars, which had several gaps in it as people went home for their tea. Hers was further than she remembered – so much further that she began to think it had been stolen. When she finally found it, she had to turn it round on a narrow sandy track. *What's the rush?* she asked herself, aware of an obligation to hurry. She'd convinced Drew that he could calm down and stop worrying, and now she was doing the same thing.

They drove back to the Manor, with Drew sticking closely to her bumper. The confusing layout of Cranham gave her pause for a moment, approaching it from the south-west for the first time. The landmarks that normally came up on the left were now on the right, and she had to struggle to visualise where the common and Manor must be. After more than a week this seemed pathetic and she rebuked herself for it. The little road alongside the village hall beckoned welcomingly, as did the church tower further along, and the small village school. Donny's Lodge was where she expected it to be, and she sped up the driveway to the Manor with a sense of returning home.

The house seemed to glow proudly as she ushered Drew and his offspring into the hall. The lowering sun was dazzlingly lighting up the big main room, through the high windows.

'Isn't it lovely?' she boasted. 'A perfect piece of architecture.'

'We'd better stay in the kitchen,' said Drew cautiously. 'They might break something.'

'I'll get cracking on the meal right away. Except I should feed the dog first.'

Her visitors sat around the table, with drinks, happy to chat inconsequentially while Thea cooked.

'I'll phone Karen,' Drew announced, fishing for his mobile. 'Is there a signal here?'

'Should be,' Thea nodded. 'I haven't had any problems.'

He stood up and went to the window, his back to the room, waiting for the rhythmic sound that told him the phone was ringing at home. He shifted from foot to foot as he waited, knowing Karen could be slow to react. Thea turned sausages and the children kicked their feet against the central pedestal of the table, and a silence descended.

'No reply,' he said, finally.

'Are you on call for the funeral business?' Thea asked, wondering why that had not occurred to her sooner.

'No, it's Maggs this weekend. We try to alternate. Maybe Karen's gone round to talk to one of the neighbours. Or she could be asleep.' The worry in his tone was muted but real. He glanced from Stephanie to Thea to the sausages, his lips tight.

'Or out in the garden,' offered the little girl. 'In the sun.'

'That's possible,' said Drew with a frown. 'Although—'

'She'll be fine,' said Thea, a shade too heartily. 'You can be on your way in twenty minutes. This will be ready in a flash.'

'It's OK. I know I'm being paranoid. But not answering the phone . . . well, that never happens. We live by the phone, in a way. That's how we get our business. For all she knows, it's Maggs needing her to do something.'

'Try again in ten minutes. She might have been in the loo.'

'Yes. I'll do that.'

Thea could tell that he was entertaining awful visions of his wife unconscious at the foot of the stairs, a cerebral haemorrhage draining her life away. He chafed as the food was placed before him and his children eagerly began to eat. He looked at the clock on the wall every few seconds. 'It's possible that Maggs had a call and Karen went to help her. She hardly ever does that, but if it was something quick and easy, she might.'

'Could Maggs collect a body all on her own?'

'Not really, no. She's done it once or twice, but it means getting somebody to lend a hand,

and that's not very professional. Den – her husband – would go with her, but we try not to need him. He's not very comfortable with it, to be honest.'

'She'd tell you if there was anything, wouldn't she?'

'She might. You can never be sure with Maggs. She's not very predictable.'

'How close to your house does she live?'

'Six miles.'

'So, if there's no answer when you try again, you could ask her to go and see if everything's all right. She could be there in ten minutes.'

He sighed. 'Stop encouraging me. You're supposed to assure me that there's nothing at all the matter.'

'Sorry. Obviously, you've got nothing whatsoever to worry about. Eat.'

He eyed the clock again, before starting his own food. Stephanie and Timmy were halfway through theirs. 'Nice to see children with healthy appetites,' she observed.

'Mm. Yes. We've never let them be silly about food.'

Drew ate quickly, and again retreated to the window with his phone. 'Sorry,' he muttered first.

Before he could begin the gadget warbled in his hand. 'That'll be her,' said Stephanie knowingly.

'No. It's Maggs,' Drew corrected her, reading

the screen. 'Hello?' he answered. 'What? Where are you?'

His side of the conversation was largely monosyllabic questions, with the occasional 'Slow down' and 'Say that again'. It took several minutes, during which Thea dished up ice cream and made a pot of tea.

When he finished, he sat down heavily at the table. 'She's been investigating,' he said. 'And she says she's found a connection between Donny and Harriet that proves our theory.'

The presence of two very attentive children made it impossible to speak openly about murder and suicide. 'What about Mummy?' demanded Tim. 'Is she all right?'

'I'm sure she is. Let me talk to Thea for a minute and then I'll phone again.' He appealed to Thea. 'Can they go outside or something for ten minutes?'

'There's not much to do out there. Maybe a bit of telly would be an idea. I think there's a wildlife programme on about now. I saw it last week.'

She led the children into the main room, and returned quickly. 'What on earth did she say to distract you from panicking about Karen?'

'She found a long review of the book posted on a website by Toby Brent. She read me some of it. All about Harriet being irresponsible when it comes to people's feelings. And some stuff about

389

his wife dying young of heart problems.'

'So how does that prove Donny was murdered?'

'According to Maggs, Toby quoted his father-in-law as being a classic case in point. He might talk about wanting to die, but it was perfectly obvious to anybody who knew him that he wanted nothing of the sort. He just thought he *might* want to in the future.'

Thea's eyebrows went up. 'That isn't proof, is it? Not by a million miles. It's not even new, really. We've said most of that already.'

Drew danced restlessly on the spot, tension visibly mounting. 'We should speak to him. Ask him about it.'

Thea put up her hands. 'Oh, no. I already tried that yesterday and got my head bitten off. I'm hopeless at that sort of thing, I've finally realised. I'm not going anywhere near any of them if I can help it. Let's just drop the whole thing. You go home and see if your wife's all right and get those kids to bed. I'll play with geckoes for a week and then fix up another job, if anybody will employ me.' She thought of the unsettling comments made by Philippe in the pub. 'Apparently I'm a minor celebrity around here now, and everybody wants me. I can't believe it's true. More the opposite, if anything.'

He wasn't listening to her. 'If I'm going to start a burial ground up here I need to have everything straight from the outset. I can't just forget what happened here – after all, I was hoping to get my first Broad Campden prepaid funeral, thanks to you.'

She stared at him. 'But you didn't get it. You never even *met* him. It can't possibly matter to you now.'

'But it does. I've been here three times now, talking to you about it. I've told Maggs and she's grabbed onto it, the way she does. Even if you don't want any more to do with it, she's not going to give up. She hates it when we lose a funeral.'

'Losing a funeral,' Thea repeated slowly. 'Is that what this is, really? Frustration? A sense of being cheated?'

'Well, yes, in a way. The business is important, you know. I came into it from nursing, which I never really took to. I made mistakes and lost a lot of confidence. What I do now perfectly suits my nature. Maggs is the same. She says she wanted to be an undertaker from the age of seven. She's amazingly focused. We both want to provide a service that matters enormously to people. So it's important to us – all of it. After all, the man is dead.'

She sat down at the table, trying to think. Being dead meant something extra to Drew and Maggs – more than it meant to ordinary people. They concentrated on the body lying in a mortuary somewhere, awaiting disposal. They imagined the various forms the funeral might take, the priorities of the family in the matter of the coffin and final resting place. To them, the matter was unfinished until after the funeral.

'But I don't understand why you should care about *how* he died,' she said out loud. 'What difference can that make to your side of things?'

He blinked, as if rousing himself from some complicated thinking of his own. 'Because it goes against the grain to arrange a funeral under the instructions of somebody who might have murdered the deceased. It leaves you feeling soiled and implicated. So I need to be sure of the full story.'

'OK, I can understand that. But you're not going to be doing this funeral, are you?'

'Aren't I?' he said with a twinkle. 'What makes you think that?'

Everything changed from that moment on. There was a purpose and a feeling of certainty. But still the logistics presented difficulties. Thea reminded Drew about the council meeting the following day. 'Surely you're planning to be there?' she said. 'Does that mean you'll drive home now and back tomorrow morning? Isn't that rather silly?'

'It was the idea, yes. Lots of people drive a hundred miles a day. The more you do it, the shorter it seems.'

'Won't Maggs disapprove? I thought she was all for reducing carbon emissions and avoiding global warming.'

'She's having rather a crisis of conscience over all that. She thinks it might be slightly hysterical, given the fact that most parts of the world have cooled in the past ten years.'

This came as news to Thea. 'Have they? Surely not.' She realised she had not given climate change a single thought for months. It had slipped out of the headlines some time ago.

'So she believes. But she would probably disapprove anyway of me driving back and forth. She likes me where she can see me.'

Thea giggled.

But Drew made no move to gather his offspring and leave. They were contentedly settled in front of the television, showing no desire to head for home. 'I suppose . . .' he began tentatively, 'we could try and find a B&B. There must be dozens within a few miles of here.'

'Don't be stupid. If you're staying, then I can find space for you here. After all, it wouldn't be the first time.'

'It would with the kids. There can't be enough beds for all of us.'

'Oh, there are plenty of beds. And it's a warm night. You won't need much in the way of blankets.'

'But they'll miss school. They'll be blacklisted for unauthorised absence. It stays in their files for life.'

'So?'

'So it's probably just what they'll need on their CVs. Shows a spirit of adventure or something. I can't help hoping that that will be viewed positively in the future, unlike nowadays.'

'Indeed,' she agreed heartily. 'But it might be tricky tomorrow, having them in tow. I'm telling you now I'm not going to mind them for you while you have all the fun.'

'Maybe we could infiltrate them into the local school for a morning and hope nobody notices.'

'Right. Brilliant idea. We can't leave them in the car because it'll get too hot, although I think we'd get into worse trouble if we left Hepzie to die of heatstroke.'

'We'll just lock them in the attic here with some colouring books and a cup of water.'

'Let's sleep on it. Something might turn up.'

They arranged the beds with a sense of mischief at making free with the Hollywell rooms. Drawing the line at using Harriet's own bed, that left a spare room with twin beds for the children, and a massive four-poster in another spare room for Drew. 'Why does she have so many rooms all ready for visitors?' Drew wondered. 'Clean sheets, no dust or fluff, everything a guest could wish for. Does she run the place as a B&B, do you think?'

'Maybe she has a huge American family who come over twice a year.'

It was almost eight when they had everything settled. The children were distressed at the absence of their toothbrushes, and Timmy's bedtime teddy bear was a major omission. Nor were there any children's storybooks. Drew explained patiently that they were being travellers, and that meant being adaptable and managing without their usual routines and possessions. Stephanie eventually embraced the idea with enthusiasm, but Timmy was severely unsettled. 'I can't get to sleep without Mr George,' he whined. 'I know I can't.'

'And I know you can,' said Drew, his patience thinning. 'After all that running about you've done today, you must be exhausted. Everything's perfectly all right, Tim. I'll be in the next room, and in the morning we'll have a great big breakfast. And you know where the bathroom is – I'll leave the light on for you so you can find it if you need the loo.'

'But what about *Mummy*?' This question was the one Drew had least wanted to hear.

'I'm going to phone her now and tell her we're having a lovely adventure, and we'll see her tomorrow.'

'And Miss Bagshot? What will she say? You're only allowed to miss school if you're poorly.'

'I'll explain it to her. It's all right, I tell you. Stop making it difficult, OK?'

The child subsided sulkily, but apparently slightly mollified by the tone in Drew's voice. Being shouted at by his father was more familiar than all this business of sleeping in a strange bed in a strange house without Mr George.

'Night, night, Daddy,' murmured Stephanie, the undisguised favourite. 'See you in the morning.'

'Night, night, Steph.' He kissed her soft cheek, and left the room.

The problem of what to do with the children was no less troublesome next morning. 'We'll just have to take them with us,' said Thea. 'I expect it'll be all right.'

'This is turning out just like last time, isn't it?' he said, his eyes sparkling. 'It's amazing how powerful it is when you do something unexpected.'

'What? I'm not following your logic.'

'It isn't exactly logical. I'm just feeling as if it'll all work out right, because of us taking the initiative. Most people don't. They wait for things to happen.'

'Mm.' She had not slept well, listening for wakeful children blundering around the gallery in search of the lavatory. The dog had been restless, too, no doubt taking a lead from her mistress. The promised big breakfast had not materialised, either. There was no bacon or sausages left, so she prepared scrambled eggs for the visitors and ate nothing herself. When she tried to recall all that she and Drew had concluded the previous evening, it made very much less sense than before.

'We don't have much of a plan,' she pointed out. 'Just drive there and ask if you can do the funeral – is that it? Before you even know whether you've got the permission for the burial ground to start operating. What time is the meeting, anyway?'

'Two o'clock. I can't wait until after it's over.'

'What did Mummy say?' asked Stephanie, as soon as she woke up. Drew had been surprised that it wasn't Timmy who wanted to know, but his son seemed to have abandoned all resistance and was happily jumping on the springy bed, tangling himself comically in the big T-shirt Thea had found for him to wear.

'Nothing much,' Drew said. 'Everything's fine.'

This was only partly true. Karen had finally answered the phone at nine the previous evening, sounding oddly groggy. 'Yeah, all right,' was all she said when Drew told her she would have a night without her family. 'No problem.'

'Are *you* all right?' he demanded. 'You sound funny.'

'I fell asleep in front of the telly. I'm all out of sync now. When are you coming home? What about school?'

The questions reassured him. He admitted that he was behaving very irresponsibly, but that it seemed daft to drive home and back again. 'It's exciting news about the burial ground, Kaz. We might have a whole new branch opening sooner than we thought.'

'Good,' she said vaguely. 'So long as we don't have to move house.'

'I'll see you tomorrow. Probably about six, all being well.'

'But Timmy hasn't got Mr George,' Karen remembered. 'You'll never get him off to sleep.'

'He's off already. I wore them out climbing up hill forts. It's great here, you know. Beautiful scenery.'

'Good,' she said again. 'Very good.'

Her voice somehow faded away before he finally rang off, and he was left with a nagging worry that pervaded his dreams, mixing with the dead man Donny Davis and the meeting of the Council Planning Committee. In one dream he was standing on the edge of a high cliff, a child in each hand, and a long row of open graves waiting for them at the bottom. The powerful sense of dread remained with him when he woke, until he managed to suppress it by going into his children's room and waking them with kisses, as was their home routine.

'So – we drive to the Hobsons' farm and take it from there, right?' Thea said, unsure about deferring to him when it came to making their plans. 'Is that what we decided?'

'It is. Jemima Hobson is the only person who can arrange his funeral.'

'I can't quite envisage how it's going to go, that's all. Wouldn't it be better to phone first and say we're coming? Less confrontational, for a start.'

'No, because she might tell us not to come. Then we'd be back where we began. Better to just drop in.'

She grimaced ruefully. 'The trouble is, I was more or less thrown out of there on Saturday. They're not going to be very pleased to see me again.'

'So you stay in the car with the kids. Or take them for a walk. Leave it all to me.'

'I hate to miss the excitement, though.'

'You can't have it both ways,' he said reasonably.

'Oh, I'm sure I can, if I think hard enough.'

They had to use his car, because of the child booster seats that were a legal requirement for anybody up to the age of twelve. Thea made a few caustic remarks about the impossibility of spontaneity in the present world, adding that she well remembered her own mother piling four children haphazardly onto the back seat, threatening them with all kinds of punishments if they didn't stop sticking their feet out of the windows as she tried to drive.

'OK, you navigate,' he ordered.

'Ah. Yes. That could be tricky. I got a bit lost last time. It's near Sheepscombe, which is off to the right, and then left at the little crossroads. I think. It's one of those situations where it's almost quicker to walk, because there aren't any direct roads.'

'Hardly,' he said.

'Look for yourself,' she invited, awkwardly opening out the large map. 'Needless to say it's on a fold.'

He peered at the maze of small yellow roads, forced to admit that there was no simple direct way from one village to the other by car, whereas the footpaths did follow a more obvious route. 'Except you'd be sure to get lost in those woods,' he pointed out. 'The path veers all over the place once you get there.'

'All designed to fox the unwary traveller,' she said. 'But we can probably manage it between us.'

He tried to conduct an organised plan of action

for when they arrived. Various strategies were considered and rejected, until Thea pointed out that they were within half a minute of arriving. 'I'll go and pick strawberries,' she said quickly. 'Me and the kids. While you go and talk to Mimm.'

'Sounds OK,' he said. 'I can phone you if I need you.'

She was still very doubtful as to the wisdom of the plan. Drew's idea that by broaching the subject of Donny's funeral he might somehow force a revelation as to just how he died seemed feeble in the light of day. The scraps of suspicion, the inconsistencies and sheer lack of credibility in the story thus far were nothing like enough to build a proper case. And, as often seemed to happen, the parallel investigations conducted by the police were hopelessly obscure. Thea had learnt not to obstruct the police in their workings, but simply to find the gaps and subtly poke away at areas they failed to notice. More often than not, she could cause a small avalanche of revelation or panic which led to the truth being exposed. As far as she could understand it, Drew possessed something of the same knack.

But when they drove through the gates of Hobsons' farm, at least one of their ideas fell to dust. 'Closed for Fruit Picking Today' said a large sign.

'Drat!' said Thea. 'Now what shall we do?'

On the seat behind her, the children had been strangely quiet. 'What's the matter, Daddy?' came Stephanie's voice, picking up on the uncertainty in Thea's tone. 'Where are we going?'

'We're going to this farm,' said Drew determinedly. 'I need to speak to the lady.'

'They're probably always closed on a Monday, after the rigours of the weekend,' Thea realised. 'We should have thought. I expect they've all gone out.'

'I don't think so,' he said. 'Look over there.'

She followed his gaze to an area beside the house, where a big open-sided barn was surrounded by a sea of white animals. 'Sheep,' she said. 'They're shearing them.'

Two associations struck her almost simultaneously. The first was an experience she had two years earlier, when terrible things had happened during sheep shearing in Duntisbourne Abbots. The second was more recent, and more oblique.

'Let's go and watch,' she said, trying to keep the excitement out of her voice. 'I don't expect they'll mind.'

'But . . .' Drew's protestations were half-hearted, or so she told herself.

'Come on. What do we have to lose?' she demanded dramatically. 'We can't go back now.'

'But . . .' he tried again. 'I can't talk to people

402

about funerals when they're shearing sheep.'

'Forget about the funeral for a bit, will you? Just let's go and see who's here.'

He parked the car close to a wooden fence and they all got out, Thea urging them impatiently. 'It'll be interesting, you'll see,' she told the children, who were obviously bewildered.

'But I want strawberries,' insisted Timmy. 'I don't like sheep.'

Thea was trotting ahead of them, scanning the scene, trying to see the faces of the few people milling about amongst the animals. 'There!' she cried. 'Come on.'

The shearing was taking place inside the barn, two clattering machines operating the clippers. Along with the cries of the sheep, it was all too noisy for normal conversation. It was evidently early in the proceedings, only a dozen or so finished ewes walking confusedly into a field, wondering why everything felt so light and cool. It was not a particularly warm day.

Thea approached a man on the other side of the temporary barrier that had been erected. 'Toby,' she said. 'Hello. Remember me?'

He glanced distractedly at her, most of his attention on another man who was trying to direct the flow of sheep, to maintain a constant supply for the shearers. 'What?' he said. 'Why are you here?'

'I thought of something I wanted to say to you.'

'What – now?' She was moving gradually away from the noise, hoping he would follow. 'I can hardly hear you,' he complained. 'And I'm busy.'

'Funny work for a college lecturer,' she said.

'They need as many hands as they can get. They want it all finished by lunchtime. Three hundred and twenty ewes. It was meant to be done last week, but it rained.'

He had automatically followed as she drifted along the line of hurdles. She glanced around for Drew, who was ushering his children closer to the action, showing little interest in what she was doing. Of course, he still thought it was Jemima they were aiming for, Jemima who had suffocated her own father because she couldn't face the long years of caring for him and arguing with him and dreading whatever might come next.

Right motive, wrong person, Thea thought in a moment of total clarity.

'I think they're managing all right without you,' she said to Toby. 'That man seems to have things under control.'

'No, they need me,' he said, still not fully attending to her.

'Can you shear sheep, Toby?' she asked.

'Never tried.'

'But you can shave people, can't you? You

404

shaved Donny, didn't you? On Monday night. I expect he preferred you to do it, out of all his friends and relations.'

He was slow to grasp the import. He might even have missed one or two words in the general clatter. 'What?' he said, with only the smallest dawning of alarm.

'When I saw him on Monday afternoon, he had about five days' worth of stubble. But when I saw him again, dead on his bed, he was clean-shaven. I thought Edwina did it, but she said not. And he wouldn't let Jemima do it. I should have realised days ago, but it only just struck me that it must have been you. There just isn't anybody else,' she added simply.

He looked around, apparently to ensure that nobody could hear them. 'Shut up!' he said fiercely. 'Mind your own business.'

'Sorry, but it *is* my business now. I *know* it was you, Toby. It all fits. Why don't you just face it?'

He looked at her, the sun glinting on his ginger hair. He seemed an unbearably sad figure to Thea. She wished for a debilitating moment that she'd left well alone, days ago.

'You think you know, but you don't really.' He glanced over his shoulder, ensuring that nobody was paying attention. Sheep milled and pushed, the machines continued to rattle.

'So tell me,' she invited. 'Please. I don't think

you can go on pretending for much longer.'

He sagged and closed his eyes for a few seconds. 'He *wanted* to die,' he said quietly. 'He'd wanted it for a year or more. What did he have to live for?'

Despite her feelings of sympathy, she could not deny the surge of anger elicited by his words. 'Quite a lot, I think. Didn't he struggle at *all*? Or argue? Or plead with you? Did he drink that muck you gave him willingly? Didn't he notice how vile it tasted?'

'Only after it was too late. And then he was too zonked to struggle.'

'How quick was it? How long did he take to die?'

'Stop it!' His jaw clenched tightly, his face hardened. 'He took a few minutes, instead of the *years* it would otherwise have been. Who did he think was going to take care of him? Who had he already handed his wife over to, who had all the right skills, all the time in the world, all the debts of gratitude? Right! So I was supposed to devote the best years of my life to the same stinking routine I'd got out of when Cissie died. I want a *life*!' he shouted. 'What's wrong with that?'

'You murdered him,' said Thea, with quiet clarity. 'Because you didn't want the burden of looking after him.'

'I helped him to kill himself because he had

nothing to look forward to. And that's the way the law's going to see it. I shaved him, and settled him into bed, and brought him the drink he asked for. I was gentle and kind and caring. He and I came through a lot together, with never a cross word between us. And nobody is ever going to prove otherwise.'

Thea felt breathless under this onslaught. Could he be right? Had things reached such a point where he just might be? She forced herself to think. 'So why did you tell the police that Edwina killed him?'

His jaw, hitherto clamped tightly closed, fell open. 'What do you mean? I never did that.'

'Somebody did. A man called Gloucester police on Tuesday afternoon, only a few hours after we found Donny.'

He closed his eyes, and uttered a deep sigh. 'Silas. It would have been Silas. He's always had a down on Weena, because of his mum.'

'But he's in Africa.'

'So? They have phones in Africa, don't they?'

'Toby!' a man's voice shouted. 'Watch that ewe, will you?' A sheep was baulking at being funnelled into the noisy barn, making a bid for freedom in a perceived gap between two hurdles. Toby turned and grabbed it by the long wool around its neck. 'Go away,' he told Thea, over his shoulder. 'Go away and leave us alone.'

She could see no option but to do as bidden, with a heavy sense of anticlimax hanging over her. Drew and the children were still reaching through the fencing to touch the sheep, and generally behaving as if at another farm park.

'Come on,' she called to them. 'We're finished here.'

They joined her with questioning expressions. 'What happened?' Drew asked her.

'We can go, we're done here,' she repeated. 'Is it too early for lunch?'

'Ten forty-five,' he said with a kink of an eyebrow. 'You've got to tell me, Thea. Stop messing about.'

History repeated itself. Slowly, inexorably, she stepped towards him, rested her face on his chest and burst into tears. Once again he rubbed her shoulders and made no effort to push her away. As before, she pulled away with stammered words of apology.

'Is she hurt?' asked Timmy.

'She's sad,' concluded Stephanie. 'Big people cry when they're sad, not when they're hurt.'

Thea smiled weakly. 'You're right, Steph. Absolutely right.'

CHAPTER TWENTY

That afternoon, Thea was engaged in three telephone conversations, two long and one very short. The first she initiated, taking several minutes to catch up with DI Jeremy Higgins.

'Toby Brent murdered Donny Davis,' she said, without preamble. 'But you'll never be able to prove it.'

'Explain.'

'He admitted it to me this morning. He gave him the sedatives and then taped the bag over his head. Against Donny's will. It was planned in advance and carried out without mercy.'

'Why?'

'Because he expected to have to care for the old man for the rest of his life, and he'd had enough of caring.'

'He was probably wrong there.'

'Pardon?'

'There was almost nothing physically wrong with Mr Davis. He was in pretty good shape for his age. He could have lived independently for several more years.'

'But the tremor! The constipation! The general feebleness.'

'He'd had the tremor for ages, and there was never any pathological reason for it. Some people do it for psychological reasons. It seems he was one of them. And his bowels were fine, just a bit bunged up in recent days. Nothing at all to worry about.'

'The deceitful old bugger! And everybody believed him.'

'He believed himself, probably.'

'Had a doctor ever suggested he might have hysterical symptoms?'

'Years ago, yes. It's in his notes. Could be that's what set him against the whole medical profession – they told him stuff he didn't want to hear.'

She digested this new light, and found her sympathies tending in a surprising direction. 'Poor Toby, then. He need never have done it.'

'Nobody heard him confess to you?'

'Not really. Even if they did, it's still hearsay, isn't it?'

'Probably. What else did he tell you?'

'He shaved Donny before he killed him. That

was the final clue. I think he really did love him, you know. Maybe he even convinced himself that Donny was better off dead. That's what he told me.'

'But you don't believe that. The old man wasn't ready to die. I can't just let it go, Thea.'

'Of course not. No. But—'

A renewed surge of sadness was welling up, preventing any further talk.

The second call was from Harriet Young on Lindisfarne.

'I'm coming back tomorrow evening,' she said. 'For Donny's funeral.'

'How did they get hold of you?'

'Jemima knew where I was. She's been keeping me updated on what's happening.'

'Oh. So I can go, can I? You won't be wanting me any more.'

'I'll pay you the full amount, of course. You've probably had a much less peaceful time than you expected.'

'You told me you couldn't be contacted.'

'I lied,' said Harriet with a forced laugh. 'Sorry.'

'Oh well,' said Thea weakly. 'I suppose it doesn't matter. Incidentally, I've been reading your book. Do you mind my asking whether Donny ever saw it?'

The reply was forceful. 'Of course he didn't. I was extremely careful to keep it out of his sight. He was already quite morbid enough without that.'

'But wasn't he exactly the sort of person it's intended for?'

A sound like a stifled moan came down the line. 'That's very acute of you, I must say. And it's precisely what a lot of people would think. Which meant I could have found myself in real trouble if anybody thought I'd been influencing him.'

'But you *want* to influence people. Why else would you write a book like that?'

The moan came again, louder this time. 'Good question,' Harriet choked. 'Which is why I've decided to withdraw it from sale. I've changed my mind, while I've been here. I've been terribly, *terribly* wrong.'

Thea heard an echo of her own inner conflicts of the past few days. 'It's not easy, is it – trying to estimate your effect on people?'

'Right. And I don't think I can carry the responsibility for what they might do to themselves. I mean – poor old Donny. I feel so *dreadful*.'

'I know I shouldn't tell you this. The police would be furious with me, but never mind. Harriet – Donny didn't kill himself. He was murdered. I'm not sure whether it'll ever come to court, but honestly, you don't have to feel responsible.'

'What?'

'I can't say any more. And please don't talk about it when you get home. Just thank your stars you didn't have anything to do with it.' She let Harriet absorb this, before adding, 'Oh, and just one more thing,' she added, 'while I've got you.'

'Yes?'

'Those paintings in the gallery. The De Morgans. Are they authentic?'

Harriet snorted. 'Of course not, you idiot. I got them for five hundred quid the lot in a flea market. Who did you think they were by?'

'Evelyn De Morgan. I suggest you have them looked at. You might be surprised.'

Harriet said nothing for a moment. Then, '*You* surprise me, Thea Osborne. Indeed you do.'

Thirdly, at seven o'clock, Drew phoned. She had taken his children for a drive and a little walk while he sat in the public gallery and listened to Gloucester County Council give outline approval for a four-acre natural burial ground just to the south of Broad Camden. He emerged at three-thirty, thanked her profusely and hurried home, where his real responsibilities lay.

'Is everything all right?' she asked him now.

'Not really,' he said. 'I can only stay a minute. Karen's been taken into hospital.'

'Good God! When?'

'Lunchtime. Maggs thought she was out, but began to worry about it when she didn't appear all morning, and went to look. It's some sort of cerebral bleed, they think. She's unconscious.'

'Oh, Drew. How ghastly. Are the children OK?'

'I haven't told them properly yet. I'm hoping there'll be some news this evening, after they've done the tests. Maggs is furious with me.'

'Bother Maggs. It's not your fault.'

'If I'd been here, I would have seen something was wrong. We would have got her to hospital sooner.'

'And then what?'

'I don't know. They think it's too deep for surgery. It might have been there since she was shot, a bit of damage they never spotted.'

'So it wouldn't have made any difference if you'd been there, would it?'

'Maybe not, but—'

'Listen. I'm leaving here tomorrow. Harriet's coming back for Donny's funeral—'

'Funeral?'

'Right. It seems they organised it last week, without telling me. Anyway, if you like I can come and help out there. I can transport the children and answer the phone, and take some pressure off.'

He was silent for some seconds. 'No,' he said. 'I can't let you do that.'

'Can't you?'

'You must see how it would look.'

'I suppose so. But you shouldn't waste a good friendship because of how it might look. Call me if there's anything I can do. I can be your agent here, or something. There's an idea! Don't you think?' She hoped she didn't sound as if she was pleading. 'I haven't got any work until the end of July, in Snowshill. I'll just be going mad with nothing to do. And I hope that's far enough off the beaten track for nobody to have heard of me.'

'Don't rely on it. It's hardly any distance from Broad Campden, if my geography serves me.'

'I'll change my name,' she threatened.

He laughed briefly, and then said, 'I must go, Thea. But thanks. I'll call again sometime.'

'Use the mobile. I don't know where I'll be. And Drew . . .'

'Yes?'

'It *will* all be all right. I promise you. You know that, don't you?'

She could hear the sigh down the line. 'It'll have to be, won't it?' he said.

Down in the cellar of Hollywell Manor, a little egg began to rock, and a small crack appeared. But by the time the new gecko emerged wide-eyed into the light, Thea Osborne had left Cranham for good.

If you enjoyed *Deception in the Cotswolds*, you'll
love our other books by Rebecca Tope . . .